Cinderella's Millionaire
by Katherine Garbera

He'd unfastened the top button of his shirt.

Tufts of hair were visible through the opened collar. She reached out towards him before realising what she was doing, then dropped her hand and looked up.

Joe stared at her with that me‍̶̶̶̶̶̶̶̶̶ gaze that made her f‍̶̶̶̶̶̶̶̶̶

'What?' she as‍̶̶̶̶̶

'Why did you st‍̶̶̶̶̶

'I'm not sure whe‍̶̶̶̶̶

'I am. You told me about your dreams. Now let me tell you mine.'

'Yours?'

He nodded. The lambent desire in his eyes made her pulse run heavier. 'I envisage the two of us—'

She put her fingers over his lips. She didn't want to hear what he had to say. She wanted him but she wanted—no, needed—to pretend that he was her dream man for this one night. She knew he wasn't. She knew this could never last. But for this one night she wanted to believe it.

The Librarian's Passionate Knight
by Cindy Gerard

ꙅ ᴥ ꙅ

He'd always thought of Phoebe as honest.
But she'd been lying to him all week.

With her eyes. With her tight little smiles. She'd been telling him that all the togetherness, all the touching that resulted from working through the self-defence moves hadn't affected her. That she wasn't as hot for him as he was for her.

The little liar.

He splashed cold water over his face then braced both hands on the edge of the sink. He hung his head and finally admitted that he'd been lying, too. To himself and to her.

This could not continue. He could not continue to mosey over to her house, pretend he wanted to be her friend and then fabricate reasons to touch her, excuses to kiss her. Not when she felt like liquid fire in his arms. Not when her mouth opened so sweetly, so greedily beneath his. Not when she looked at him with those baby-owl eyes that begged him to take her to bed.

Which was exactly where he wanted her.

Available in July 2004 from Silhouette Desire

Cinderella's Millionaire
by Katherine Garbera
(Dynasties: The Barones)

and

The Librarian's Passionate Knight
by Cindy Gerard
(Dynasties: The Barones)

Sleeping with the Boss
by Maureen Child

and

The Cowboy's Baby Surprise
by Linda Conrad

Having the Tycoon's Baby
by Anna DePalo
(The Baby Bank)

and

A Little Dare
by Brenda Jackson

Cinderella's Millionaire
KATHERINE GARBERA

The Librarian's Passionate Knight
CINDY GERARD

SILHOUETTE®
DESIRE™

*Silhouette, Silhouette Desire and Colophon
are registered trademarks of Harlequin Books S.A.,
used under licence.*

*First published in Great Britain 2004
Silhouette Books, Eton House, 18-24 Paradise Road,
Richmond, Surrey TW9 1SR*

The publisher acknowledges the copyright holders of the
individual works as follows:

Cinderella's Millionaire © Harlequin Books S.A. 2003
The Librarian's Passionate Knight © Harlequin Books S.A. 2003

*Special thanks and acknowledgement are given to
Katherine Garbera and Cindy Gerard for their contribution to the
Dynasties: The Barones series.*

ISBN 0 373 04989 7

51-0704

*Printed and bound in Spain
by Litografia Rosés S.A., Barcelona*

SILHOUETTE®
DESIRE™

are proud to introduce

DYNASTIES:
THE BARONES

*Meet the wealthy Barones—caught in a
web of danger, deceit and...desire!*

Twelve exciting stories in six 2-in-1 volumes:

CINDERELLA'S MILLIONAIRE
by
Katherine Garbera

KATHERINE GARBERA

comes from a large Italian family. Being part of the
Barones gave her a chance to once again visit
characters who share her background. She lives in the
suburbs of Chicago with her husband and their two
children. Writing romance is a dream come true for
the author who says that happy endings should be a
part of everyone's life.

To my Italian family, for making me proud of where we came from and challenging me to go in new directions. Especially my uncle, Pat Nappi, for showing me the beauty inside, and my mum, Charlotte Smith, for showing me how to carry on our traditions.

Acknowledgements:

Thanks to Eve Gaddy for taking time from her busy schedule to help critique. I'm so glad fate put us in each other's paths and made us friends!

One

There were times when it didn't pay to be a part of a big Italian family, Joseph Barone thought as he listened to his sister Gina give him last-minute instructions on how to handle the press today. She was the VP of PR, and in his opinion the one who should be escorting the contest winner—Holly Fitzgerald—around. But Gina and her husband, Flint, a noted spin doctor, thought it would be better if a top executive did the honors. And somehow he—the CFO—was the only one who could get up at five in the morning to handle this latest volley in Baronessa's PR plan.

"If anyone brings up the passion fruit gelato debacle, acknowledge that it was a mistake and one that Baronessa won't make again. Then use the fact sheet I gave you on the new flavor."

"Got it," he said.

Gina smiled at him. "Thanks for doing this."

"As if I had any choice." Joe had tried arguing but it was hard to win with his mother or sisters. Italian women never fought fair, and in the end, guilt and familial duty had won out.

"Mom thought you'd be the best one."

"Yeah, once you convinced her of it. You owe me, Gina."

She ignored his remark and consulted the schedule in her hand. "I'm going to check and see if the contest winner is here yet."

Joe watched his sister walk away. Gina was tall compared to other women, but she'd always be his little sister. She had changed in the last few months since her marriage to Flint Kingman. She now wore her curly light brown hair down instead of pinning it up. But then, finding the love of your life could do that to a person. She radiated a glow that only a woman in love had, and he was a little scared to see her so much in love with her new husband.

He'd changed after he'd met Mary. And then changed again after she'd died. But some things were better left in the past—and Mary was one of them.

Though it was only a little after seven, he knew his entire day was shot. He resigned himself to working half the night to make sure the forecasts they'd done for this new gelato flavor were correct. Baronessa needed a shot in the arm, and this contest, as harebrained as he'd thought it was at first, might be the answer.

He sat in one of the first-floor conference rooms in the five-story building that housed the executive offices, patiently having makeup put on for the television interviews he was doing this morning. He had an inkling of why neither his dad, the CEO, or brother Nicholas, the COO, had been unable to free their schedule today.

But Baronessa was worth a few sacrifices and certainly worth the ribbing he'd have to endure if any of his siblings wandered in while he was in the makeup chair.

To distract himself, he glanced around the room. A sense of well-being assailed him as it always did when he realized he was a part of something that had grown from a small family business into an international company. There was something about knowing exactly where you came from.

And there was something about being surrounded by his family history every day that soothed his wounded heart. Most of the time.

The gelateria had grown into more than an ice-cream shop founded in the forties by his grandparents Marco and Angelica and was now a Fortune 500 company. One Joe was proud to work for. He loved his job as CFO and had cut his teeth working for a large entertainment company in California before coming back to Boston and taking his place in the family business.

"Here she is," Gina said, entering the conference room with another woman.

Joe's breath caught in his chest. The woman walking toward him bore an uncanny resemblance to his deceased wife. Slim and petite, she had auburn hair that fell in waves around her shoulders. Mary's hair had been shorter, he thought. But her features were similar. Heart-shaped face, full lips and a nose that curved the slightest bit to the right at the end.

Joe prided himself on his resilience. He'd survived things that would have destroyed a lesser man. But he didn't want to tour the company's headquarters with the doppelgänger of his deceased wife. Gina would just have to do it.

"Holly Fitzgerald, this is my brother and Baronessa's chief financial officer, Joseph Barone."

"Pleased to meet you, Ms. Fitzgerald," Joe said, shaking her hand. Her hand in his felt soft, small, fragile. Damn. It had been a long time—five years to be exact—since he'd held a hand that delicate.

"Please call me Holly."

He nodded. He'd survived by keeping himself aloof from women, by letting no one but family close to him, and he didn't intend to let this contest winner rock the secure moorings of his world. "Gina, can I speak to you privately for a minute?"

"Of course. Holly, why don't you see our makeup artist. There's coffee, tea and juice on the sideboard. We'll be right back."

Joe didn't wait for his sister but walked out of the

conference room. His brother-in-law was tall with chocolate brown hair and, according to his sisters, drop-dead gorgeous.

"Where's Holly?" Flint asked as soon as Joe stepped into the hallway.

"In makeup."

"Damn. How long do you think it'll take?" Flint asked.

"I don't know. Go check on her."

"I will. Joe, don't go anywhere. The satellite uplink is ready and we have about ten minutes before the first interview."

Gina came out of the room and the look on her face let him know she wasn't pleased with him. "What's up?"

"I can't do this," Joe said.

"Joe, we've been over this. There is no one else," Gina said.

When Gina talked to him like that, he felt like a four-year-old who wasn't getting his way. But there was not a chance he was going to spend the day with a woman who reminded him of things he didn't want to remember.

"Okay, she's almost ready," Flint said, coming back out.

"He isn't," Gina said, pointing at her brother.

"We don't have time for this," Flint said. "You both have to be out in the garden now so that we can get on the morning-news segments on the East Coast."

Gina tried reassuring him again. "Joe, you'll do fine. Stick with the script I gave you."

"I'm not nervous about the interview. I just don't want to spend the day with her."

"Joe—"

"I don't want to spend the day with him, either," Holly said from the doorway. "In fact, I just want my check and then I'll be happy to go."

Of course, he didn't want to spend the day with her, Holly thought. She probably looked as if she spent too much time in the kitchen, which of course she did. In fact, this morning she'd gotten to the bakery at 3:00 a.m. because of her obligation to Mrs. Kirkpatrick, the owner of the small downtown bakery where Holly worked.

She felt out of place in this old-money office building and wanted nothing more than to get back into her chef's uniform and back into her pastry kitchen.

She hated the spotlight. She wouldn't have entered the Baronessa contest except for the thousand-dollar prize. She needed that money to pay her father's hospital bills. HMOs had pretty much alienated small businessmen from affordable health care, and her mechanic father was no exception.

But that didn't explain why Joseph Barone wanted nothing to do with her. He was attractive in a way that made her uncomfortable. She'd grown up around men, having helped to raise her three brothers, but something about this Barone made everything feminine in her spring to life.

He watched her the way a panther watches prey. Not afraid of her, exactly, but ready to pounce if she did anything threatening. Was he afraid she'd embarrass Baronessa?

Damn. She should have checked her appearance in the mirror before she'd come in. Maybe she still had flour on her face or in her hair.

Gina Barone-Kingman took her arm. "Holly, we can't do that. Baronessa needs the publicity your gelato will bring."

"I'm willing to do my part," Holly said. And she was. She'd never shrunk from her responsibilities and didn't intend to now. Even if there was something she couldn't identify in Joseph's eyes....

"Listen, Gina, we need to talk," Joseph said, stepping forward.

Flint Kingman took control. "Not now."

Holly had met the man earlier. She could tell he worked in public relations by the way he moved and talked. He had a quick smile and a confident, take-charge attitude. She liked him, but had the feeling he could charm just about anyone.

"Outside, both of you," Flint ordered.

Flint took Joe's arm and herded them all out the front doors into a beautiful garden awash with colorful flowers. A camera crew stood ready, while the makeup team put some finishing touches on Holly.

Suddenly she didn't know if she was going to be

able to talk intelligently with a camera on her. She'd never really been proficient at public speaking. She'd made it her practice to blend into the background, and she was very good at it.

"Until I arrived this morning, I didn't know we were doing television interviews," she said softly.

"Relax, you'll do just fine," Flint said, patting her shoulder. His touch and tone made her believe his words.

Although he was kind, he was steely in his determination. She made a note to read the fine print before entering another contest. In fact, the only thing she hated more than speaking in public was seeing herself speaking in public. She only hoped none of the Boston stations would pick up this satellite feed and use it.

Flint gestured for her and Joe to sit in some director's chairs that were set up in front of a screen with the Baronessa logo on it. Holly's hands shook so badly that she had to clench them together.

Joseph reached over and covered her hands with his. His touch surprised her. She glanced up to see if his expression had changed, but his eyes were still guarded. His hand on hers was big and warm, his nails neatly manicured. Not at all like the masculine hands she was used to seeing. Hands with dirt under the nails and calluses on their palms.

"Don't worry. I might not like this but I know what I'm doing," Joseph said.

"That's reassuring." She meant it. She needed his

experience to navigate this. She'd have to make sure to someday return the favor.

He removed his hand. "I thought it might be."

Around them stage techs bustled, making adjustments to mikes and cameras. Flint and Gina both gave them last-minute tips, and then everyone backed away. Through it all, Holly wondered why Joseph didn't want to spend the day with her. If it were the press, she could understand. She too, was reluctant to be interviewed all day long.

But it couldn't be, because he said he knew how to handle them. It must be her. This was a new record for Holly. She'd never had a man detest her on sight before.

"Can I ask you something, Joseph?"

"Sure, and call me Joe."

"Why don't you want to spend the day with me?" she asked. She knew she shouldn't voice the question, but couldn't help herself.

Maybe she hadn't gotten enough sleep the night before. Maybe the closer you got to thirty the less control you had over your mouth. Maybe...maybe she just needed to feel as if she was sitting by a friend in the glare of the spotlight, instead of next to a man who didn't want her near him.

"It isn't anything personal."

Let it go, Hol. Just smile at the camera, talk about cooking, collect your check and get out of here.

"It kind of sounded like it," she said. What was

her deal today? Definitely not enough sleep, she decided.

Joe shrugged. "You remind me of someone."

Though he didn't say it was a woman, she sensed it was. She knew men. Knew the way they thought and acted.

So she should have known better than to ask the question that was on the tip of her tongue. Her dad and brothers would never admit a woman had broken their hearts. "Did she break your heart?"

Joe stared at her in a way that made her feel like she had a spotlight shining on her.

"Sorry, that was way too personal," Holly said quickly. But she knew by his reaction that she'd struck a chord, and she wanted to know more.

"Yes, it was." The look he gave her made her squirm in her chair. Not in embarrassment, though. It was a male look that made her blood flow a little faster. This man had a presence of sophistication that made her feel like an inexperienced prep-chef in the kitchen of a world-renowned master.

She looked around but couldn't stand the suspense. "Well, are you going to answer?"

He laughed and the sound surprised her. It was a warm sound from a very cold-looking man. A man she sensed didn't find much humor in life.

"No."

Fair enough, she thought. The stage director came over and gave them some directions, and when he left, Holly glanced over at Joe. He didn't look nervous, but she was.

"Is it my hair?" she asked after a few minutes. Men had some strange illusions about redheads.

"Is what your hair?" he asked.

"The thing that reminds you of the other person."

"Yes."

"She's not Orphan Annie, is she? Because I thought all the makeup I'm wearing covered my freckles."

He didn't smile but she sensed his amusement. "No."

"No to freckles or to Annie?"

"Annie. I can still see your freckles."

"I knew it. I'm covered with them."

"Everywhere?" he asked in an intimate voice.

"Yes," she said, meeting his clear brown eyes. There was something sensual in his gaze and she couldn't look away.

Joe Barone was more than she'd expected him to be and that unnerved her. She felt safe flirting with him, for some reason. Well, safe wasn't really how she felt, but it was fun. It was weird to realize she didn't understand him—he didn't fit with what she'd come to expect from men—and even stranger to realize that she wanted to.

Her freckles weren't the only things about Holly Fitzgerald that lingered in his mind. Her sweet scent lingered on the air—something homey that reminded him of his mom's kitchen at the holidays and something else more elusive. An aroma distinct to Holly and no other woman.

She's in your life for a day, he told himself. He'd best ignore it.

But he couldn't. His groin was tight and his blood ran heavy whenever he thought about those damn freckles on her creamy skin. He wanted to strip that professional-looking suit from her body and find each and every freckle. To caress it first with his fingers, then with his tongue.

Whoa, boy. Obviously it was past time to start dating again. But he'd never been into casual sex. Even before Mary, he'd slept with only two other women and no one since her death five years ago. He'd completely shut off that part of his nature—until today when it roared back to life, demanding his attention.

The stage techs broke down the equipment, and the garden was slowly returning to its beauty. This place had long been one of Joe's favorites. He'd found solace here more than once, but not today.

The July sun beat down on him, but that wasn't the source of the heat running through his veins. No, a certain redhead was responsible. ''No redheads'' had been more of a safety precaution than a rule. Still, he knew better.

Why wasn't his body getting the message?

Holly laughed at something his sister said, and his groin tingled to life. He needed to get away, but for once his pager was silent. Giving in to the pull he felt from her, he joined her and Gina at the coffee and pastry table.

"So, are you over your fit?" his sister asked.

Only family treated him as if he was a defanged tiger. Everyone else in his world trod lightly around him, treating him like a loose cannon. He wished he understood why because then maybe he could wield that cannon against his sister. "Gina, I'm trying to remember why I tolerate you."

"Familial duty." Gina smiled up at him.

"Right now I wouldn't mind being disinherited."

Gina laughed. "Joe, you know we're Italian. There's no escaping the family."

He smiled at his sister. He knew she always had Baronessa's success at heart and that she'd worked hard to prove herself to the family. "Sorry I tried to back out."

"Hey, it's okay. Flint's ideas are always bigger than he makes them out to be."

Gina left to join her husband, and an awkward silence fell between him and Holly. Joe wasn't an open and gregarious man. Never really had been. But the past few years he'd fallen deeper and deeper into a silence he found comforting.

Holly lifted her hair off the back of her neck as the sun rose in the sky. She had to be hot in that suit she wore. A few tendrils of curling red hair clung to her nape. The skin there was covered with those freckles she seemed worried about. He took a sip

from the Evian bottle in his hand to keep from leaning down and blowing on her overheated skin.

"So…" she said.

He raised one eyebrow at her. If she had an inkling
of the direction his thoughts had been heading, he
was in deep water.

"Are you ready to confess all?" she asked with a
gamine grin.

"No. But I am curious about you." Joe decided
to go on the offensive and drive her back into hiding.
He'd been called brooding more than once by the
women he'd dated. Why was it so hard to keep Holly
at arm's length?

"I'm an open book," she said.

Her blue eyes said otherwise. *Interesting.* He'd really like to delve beneath her depths and uncover her
secrets. But he didn't think he could do that and still
keep her at arm's length.

"Yes. I already know you're a pastry chef," he
said.

She took a bottle of water from the refreshment
table. "In fact, I was at work this morning before I
came down here."

"You must really love baking," he said. Though
his family had made its name in the gelato business,
Joe had never taken to baking or cooking. He could
heat frozen dinners and reheat the casseroles that his
mom sometimes sent to her kids' houses. But beyond
that he wasn't even interested in trying.

She put the water down and stepped closer to him.

Again her scent assailed him. It was time to end this conversation and get on with the rest of the day's activities. As soon as she answered, he'd say something vague and move away from her.

"I do. The kitchen is the only place where I'm totally in control. Totally alone. There's a...peace to it."

"Why aren't you ever alone?" he asked.

"Family," she said. That one word summed up the way he sometimes felt about his.

He patted her shoulder trying for a brotherly touch, but knew he failed. Her arm under his hand was soft and he couldn't help sliding his hand down to her tiny wrist. She wore a charm bracelet there with a tiny gold rolling pin on it. "I know what you mean."

Who had given her the bracelet? A lover? Jealousy took him by surprise and he ran his finger under the fine gold chain, resting his finger on her pulse. It threaded steadily.

"Joe?"

Ah, hell, he thought. He knew better. Why was he even looking at her this way? "Did a man give you this?"

"Yes," she said huskily.

"A lover?"

Her pulse doubled. "No."

Her pupils had dilated and he saw more than awareness in them. He saw the same hunger that was coursing through his veins. Her lips parted and the air around them seemed to stop moving.

He leaned forward. "Would anyone object if I kissed you?"

"Are you going to kiss me?" she asked.

"Yes."

"There's no man in my life," she said. Holly watched him with feminine speculation in her eyes, and Joe knew he'd never be the same.

Two

Joe lifted her wrist slowly. Her heart beat so hard she thought it would jump out of her chest. Sensation trembled through her body, but she was helpless to stop it.

His breath brushed against her wrist, warming the gold chain her dad had given to her for her twenty-first birthday. Though Joe's mouth didn't touch her, she felt the humid warmth, and a sensual beating started deep in her center.

Holly's experience with men outside her family had been limited. She'd worked during high school, which had left her little time to date. Then she'd skipped college and went instead to the Culinary Institute.

But that didn't explain why she hadn't dated in the past six months. The truth was, few guys wanted to wait for her to finish working two shifts at the bakery, and drive to her dad's house to fix dinner for him and her brothers before getting to her place to get ready for a date. The men she had dated tended to be career-minded as she was, and ultimately more interested in their jobs than in her. None of them had had a tenth of the raw sexuality she sensed in Joe Barone.

His dark eyes blazed with a passion she'd read about but never experienced. His mouth on her inner wrist started a chain reaction that ended deep inside her. His hand on her arm forced her to remember she was more than a sister and chef.

Joe reminded her that she was a woman in every sense of the word. He called to her femininity and made her want to reach under the civilized facade and bring the elemental man to the surface. A man she sensed needed more than the solace he could find in her body.

Instincts she'd spent years ignoring forced her to take notice. Damn, she wasn't sure she wanted him to wake her up now. There wasn't time in her life for a man. Sure, this could be a little harmless flirting, but it felt like more.

She curled her fingers around his jaw. He was clean-shaven but she felt the fine stubble under her fingers. He turned his head in her palm and dropped one kiss in the center of it.

He nipped the fleshy part of her hand before lifting his head. He looked up into her eyes and she felt the world drop away. She wasn't aware of where she was or what she was doing. She only knew that she wanted to bask in the intensity of his gaze for a long time.

Standing on tiptoe, she brought her face closer to his. His scent was spicy and outdoorsy. She shut her eyes and inhaled deeply, then leaned just the tiniest bit toward him.

His suit and hers should have provided a better barrier but didn't. His heat and strength still surrounded her. His grip on her wrist changed and his hand slid around her waist, resting on the small of her back.

"Holly?" His voice was husky and deep.

She opened her eyes.

"I want more."

She shivered, afraid to ask for what she wanted. But she'd always lived by the rule that honesty was the best policy. "Me too."

"This could be complicated," he said.

"It doesn't have to be," she said. She'd learned enough about life to know that you took what you wanted when it was offered because it seldom was presented to you again.

"I thought you were going to kiss me," she said.

"I was."

"Changed your mind?"

He shook his head.

"Then what?"

"We need privacy for the kind of kiss I want to give you."

Holly forgot all about everything at his words. He'd shocked her. Not what he'd said but that she'd inspired it. She wasn't really a lust-at-first-sight kind of girl. But he made her feel like one.

"Mr. Barone?" a woman called from the open doorway.

"Yes, Stella," Joe said, turning toward the woman but not letting go of Holly.

Holly stood there watching him. The sound of his deep voice rushed over her. She didn't listen to his words, just wondered what it would be like to curl up next to him in bed, her head resting on his shoulder while he murmured words in that baritone voice of his.

"I'll meet you in the foyer for your building tour in ten minutes," he said to Holly.

"What?" she asked.

"Stella needs me to sign a few papers upstairs," he said.

"Oh. I wasn't listening," she said.

"What were you doing?" he asked, that teasing note back in his voice.

"Dreaming," she said, which was the truth. Reality was that this man would probably never be in her bed letting her rest on his shoulder no matter how much passion was between them. Because that dream was one she'd sought for a long time and had never found. No matter whose shoulder she'd lain on, it had never made her feel safe the way she'd imagined it would.

"Dreaming about what?"

"Being someplace more private," she said, then stepped away from him.

"Damn, if it wasn't for my family, I'd sweep you off to my place."

Ditto, she thought. Family obligations kept them both here when they'd rather be elsewhere. But Holly knew deep in her soul that family obligations would also keep them apart.

"Go do your business, Joe."

"This conversation isn't over."

"It would be better if it was," she said.

"Do you always do what's best?" he asked.

"Don't you?"

"You'll have to try me and see," he said, then pivoted and walked away.

Joe Barone was too sexy by half. A long time ago she'd promised herself that she'd live each moment to the fullest. For the first time she trod lightly on that vow because something in Joe made her doubt she could protect herself and remember her own rule. The rule that was more a vow she'd made to protect her heart from loss: Men were off-limits because she had her family to take care of.

Joe couldn't believe how fast the day had gone. The day that had promised to be endless was flying by. Already they'd toured the warehouse, done a lunchtime give-away of Holly's winning gelato at Faneuil Hall and granted interviews to the print media. The YMCA kids' summer day camp was their second-to-last stop.

Holly looked cute with her apron and chef's hat on. Too cute. He'd tried to retreat behind his wall of silence, but she'd seemed to sense what he was doing and hadn't let him. She'd kept the conversation going all day and he'd realized he liked the person Holly was. She was a hard worker, which didn't surprise him. Her days were as long as his, and her family loyalty couldn't be questioned. She'd taken three calls from her brothers on her cell phone at various points during the day.

He thought more about what he had to offer a woman and realized that he didn't want to hurt Holly. At best he could give her one night. That was all he had in him. All he'd allow himself to indulge in. And she deserved more.

He forced his thoughts back to the present. The kids at the day camp all got a kick out of asking her questions about baking. She was better with the kids than she'd been with the media.

"How did you come up with the winning flavor?" one of the teachers asked.

The reporters had asked Holly many times over, but still he was interested in hearing about how she'd devised Heavenly Berry.

"I just experimented with different combinations

of fruit and chocolate until I found one I liked. Then I gave it to my harshest critics,'' she said.

"What's a critic?'' asked a little girl in ponytails. He didn't know many kids, so he wasn't sure of her age, but she looked to be maybe five. Holly put her ice-cream scoop down and knelt in front of the child.

"Someone who gives you his opinion on something you've done.''

"Like a teacher?'' the little girl asked.

"Kind of. In this case it was my brothers.''

"My brothers never like anything I do,'' the girl said.

Holly brushed her hand over the child's head. She wasn't shy about touching others, except for him. She hadn't touched him at all since their morning encounter. He wondered why.

"Brothers are like that. But mine are very honest about my cooking. So I welcome their comments,'' Holly said.

"What'd your brothers say?'' Joe asked. What would he have to do to get her to touch him again?

He wanted to know more about her family. Wanted to know details of her life so he could stop looking at her and seeing a feminine mystery and instead see someone whom he knew and understood. He doubted the questions would bring him that knowledge but at least they took his mind off the way her skirt pulled tight around her hips when she'd bent to talk to the child.

Holly glanced up at him. "That I'd found the right combination."

"Really?" the girl asked.

"Yes," Holly said, standing. She handed the child a cone Joe had scooped.

The line moved quickly and soon the children were gone. The empty gym felt strange with only him and Holly. Joe's mind wasn't on the sticky ice cream on his fingers but on the smudge of gelato on Holly's cheek.

Ignore it, he advised himself, but he knew he wasn't listening. He reached over and rubbed his thumb lightly over her cheek. She shivered.

Damn, it wasn't fair that life should put in front of him this woman who reacted so quickly to his touch. Because though he'd lived a solitary life for a long time, he'd never been any good at denying himself. And it had been a long time since he'd seen a woman he'd wanted as much as he wanted Holly.

"Why are you staring at me like that?" she asked as they cleaned up the gelato containers.

"Like what?" he asked, removing his apron and folding it with exaggerated precision. Somehow he couldn't look into those clear blue eyes of hers for another minute without taking the kiss he'd wanted all day.

"Like you're wondering if I'll taste as good as the gelato," she said.

"Because that's what I'm thinking," he said, taking a step toward her. He should be backing away but he was tired of living his life in solitary confinement. Even if he'd placed himself there. Holly reminded him what he was missing, and for this one day he wanted to wallow in it.

"Dangerous thoughts, Barone," she said, knitting her fingers together.

"I know, Fitzgerald." He wished he could banter with Holly the way he did with Gina, but he'd never once had the white-hot burning desire to kiss his sister.

A long minute passed and he knew he should just grab his suit jacket and walk out the door. Gina and Flint had already left to go ahead and get the press ready for the check presentation.

But he also knew Holly awakened something deep inside him that he couldn't silence. "You're a very touchy person."

"Easily offended?" she asked.

"No, demonstrative. You've touched Flint's arm every time you talk to him and Gina's, as well," he said.

"It's part of how I communicate."

"Why haven't you touched me?"

Stark silence followed his question. He heard a car horn outside and the kids laughing on the playground. Even the sound of Holly's breathing seemed loud.

"I hadn't noticed I wasn't."

He knew the fine art of evasion when he saw it, and Holly Fitzgerald was doing her best to tap-dance out of his reach. He should let her go. Would if he had a lick of sense. But for some reason sense had deserted him. His body said he wouldn't miss it. But experience promised he would. "I did."

She shrugged. She tilted her head to one side and nibbled at that full lower lip of hers. "I'm not myself around you."

"How's that?" he asked.

She shook her head and looked away. "I can't explain it."

"Can't or won't?"

She glanced back and shrugged again. Why was she running scared? What had he done that had made her put up her shields and hide?

"All right, won't," she admitted.

She removed her chef's hat and apron and picked up her purse. "If memory serves, our last stop is at the gelateria."

"Yes," he said.

"I'll meet you there," she said, pivoting on her heel.

"Holly?"

She glanced back at him, her red hair reflecting the late-afternoon sun that streamed in through the high windows.

"I don't want you to be uncomfortable," he said.

"I know. It's not a bad thing. It's just that…" She walked back to him. "You make me feel too much, and I'm not sure how to handle it." She reached up and brushed her fingers against his jaw. "Does this make you feel better?"

"In a hundred ways," he said.

"But we have someplace to be," she said.

He nodded. She turned again and this time he let her go. He watched the sway of her hips with each step she took. He watched her leaving and knew deep in his soul that he should remember this picture of her. That he shouldn't let himself get involved because she wasn't going to stay in his life.

Holly had never been in the flagship Baronessa Gelateria. She had a pint of Baronessa's Rocky Guava in her freezer at home. It was the one constant in her kitchen aside from cooking and baking staples.

Gina and Flint had the press stationed in one area and a few customers at the tables. Off to the side was a group of people clustered together. There had to be at least twenty-five of them looking on.

In came Joe. He had his suit jacket on and looked polished and professional. Holly wondered if that was the barrier he used to keep people at a distance.

She was relieved the day was over but she wished she'd had more time with Joe. Alone time.

But that was something she'd be better off without. He made her feel that human spontaneous combustion might be possible. He made her want things that she was used to living without. He made her ache with the knowledge that who she was and who she wanted to be still weren't the same person.

She sighed.

"Hang in there. We're almost through," Joe said.

She smiled up at him. The drive to the gelateria had been in rush-hour traffic, which had been good. It had forced her mind off of this disturbing man.

But here he was filling the crowded room and making her want things she knew better than to ask for. The press had been trying, but his company had made it a nice day. Tonight when she went home she'd dream of him and what might have been.

"It has been a long day," she said. Great, she'd gone from flirting to inane. He'd knocked her off balance and she was having a hard time finding her footing.

He reached for her and then dropped his hand, cursing under his breath.

"What's the matter?" she asked.

She didn't understand why but she needed to know more about him. To probe those depths that he kept hidden. Though he'd been flirtatious and teasing with her most of the day, he'd protected himself carefully from her. She knew there was more to him than his civilized exterior showed her.

He was a tall, dark and brooding man who watched her with that keen sexual desire that made her ultra-aware of him. Yet he didn't want to give her anything but the sexual awareness. She didn't have to be a genius to figure that out. The part she didn't understand was if it was only her or all women that he reacted to in that way.

He rubbed his jaw where a faint five o'clock shadow could be seen making him look rougher than he had earlier. It was as if the real man under the facade was starting to come to the surface. Her palms tingled and she wanted to cup his face in her hands and feel the roughness of his skin against hers.

"My family is here," he said at last, nodding toward the large group she'd noticed earlier.

"How many siblings do you have?"

"Three brothers and four sisters, plus four cousins. It looks like most of them decided to put in an appearance."

"And that's bad?" she asked. She'd be flattered if her father and brothers ever showed up at something she did.

"Hell, yes," he said.

"I think it's sweet."

"Really?"

"Yes."

"Why?"

She should have kept her mouth shut because there was no way to tell him why without revealing her vulnerability. She could only hope he wouldn't notice. "Because it shows how much they care about you."

He flushed at little. "Well, it might not mean that. This is a big Baronessa deal, and my dad is the CEO and Nick is the COO. So technically they have to be here."

Holly glanced again at the group of Joe's family.

They were a city unto themselves, talking and laughing. And he had sisters. And maybe sisters-in-law. She'd always wanted a sister. And she envied him not only the support of his family but also his sisters.

"Why is it so hard to believe they'd want to be here for you?" she asked.

"It's not. Except the last few years I haven't been the easiest person to get along with."

"You?" she asked, surprised.

"You don't think so."

"You've been… I'm afraid to say it in case you take it the wrong way."

"You'll have to take your chances," he said, moving closer to her. Barely an inch of space separated them.

"I'm not a risk taker," she admitted, taking a half step back.

"I am," he said, and the words seemed to surprise him.

She didn't want to be the only one revealing a weakness. Why didn't she just make something up? She didn't have to tell him that he reminded her of a fairy-tale prince. A white knight on a charger who'd ride to her rescue. She didn't have to say the words out loud. Wouldn't have to hear them and cringe. Wouldn't have to acknowledge that he awakened dreams she'd buried deep and hoped to forget about for the rest of her life.

"If I tell you, you owe me an explanation about who I remind you of."

"Stop stalling," he said.

She glanced up at him and found him waiting patiently.

"You have been my white knight today," she said softly.

Before he could speak, Gina came over. "Okay, you two, this is it. Joe, you'll present the check. Holly, you'll accept it. Then you're free to go."

Holly followed Gina to the front of the store, while Joe stood there. She knew he wanted to say something to her. Maybe it was for the best that he hadn't. That way she could keep him hidden in her memory as a dream of what could have been.

Three

Holly placed the check from Baronessa carefully in her wallet. Joe's family had been a little intimidating, almost more than the press, but now everything was over. She could return to being regular old Holly.

Tomorrow morning she'd be back in the bakery and Joe would be back to his life. She'd miss the feminine excitement that Joe had sparked, but apparently fate had given them only this one day.

She hadn't even had a chance to try her winning flavor, which the Barones had decided to call Heavenly Berry. Holly was impressed with Baronessa's savvy marketing and PR team. It was easy to see why they were the number one gelato company in the U.S.

She adjusted the strap on her purse and headed toward the door. Leaving without saying goodbye to Joe seemed weird to her, but, then, saying goodbye would be awkward.

She wondered if she could get to the bank before the drive-up teller closed. She glanced at her watch. Not unless traffic was light.

"Got a date?" Joe asked from behind her.

She turned and noticed the crowd had dispersed.

"No. Nothing that exciting. I was trying to decide if I could make it to the bank before it closed."

His gaze met hers. She'd always thought brown eyes were kind of average, not very exciting, but something about Joe's eyes made her react. Made her think of deep pools of rich warm chocolate. She licked her lips, sure he'd be just as yummy as the decadent dessert.

"What did you decide?" he asked.

"That the chances are slim."

"Good."

"Good?" she asked. Damn, he liked to tease her and she enjoyed it. Too much, she thought, because he made her want to be reckless.

He arched one eyebrow at her. "That's what I said."

"Why?" She smiled at him.

"I hoped you'd join me for dinner."

She swallowed. "You move fast."

"I wish we could move even faster."

She didn't know why, but that line of questioning seemed even more dangerous than his touch. A couple brushed by them to be seated. "We should get out of the way."

Joe took her arm and led her outside. The late-summer evening was warm and the street traffic in the North End wasn't too bad considering the hour. The sun lay low on the horizon.

His touch made her remember all the reasons she'd enjoyed his company. And all the reasons she'd been careful not to touch him all day. She didn't want to have to feel alive in the way only he made her feel.

She took a tiny step away from him, to give herself some breathing room, but he just stepped closer. Damn, he smelled good.

"About dinner," he said.

"What about it?" she asked, not trusting the excitement building inside her.

"Are you available?"

She had to choose whether she was going to take the chance of getting to know him better or return to her normal life without knowing what those lips of his felt like on hers. "Yes."

"Great. We can go to the best Italian kitchen in Boston."

"Antonio's?"

"No. My place."

"Your place? Do I look naive?"

"No, you look tempting."

"Tempting? Not bad. But I'm still not going to your place on our first date."

"Which number does it have to be?"

"I don't know. Let me check my *Dating in the New Millennium* book."

Pretending to withdraw a book from her purse, she studied the imaginary pages for a minute. "There's no firm answer. It depends on the guy."

Joe scooted even closer to her and she closed her eyes, afraid he'd see that she wasn't the sophisticated, witty woman she'd been pretending to be.

"What are you looking for, Holly?"

"Tonight?"

He nodded.

"A nice dinner with a good-looking Italian."

"I can get you the nice dinner. Would a surly Italian do?"

"I have yet to see surly but if he shows up, we'll renegotiate."

"Deal."

"There's a nice quiet little deli around the corner. Does that sound good?"

"Yes," she said. They walked next to each other. His heat enveloped her and she wished she'd worn a blouse under her suit jacket so she could take it off and feel his touch on her skin.

"Do you have big plans for your money?" he asked.

"Yes."

"What are you buying?"

She just shook her head. She didn't want to talk about her father and his health problems.

"My sisters would spend it on clothes or shoes."

"I'd love to spend it on shoes," Holly said. In fact, she'd had her eye on a pair of strappy sandals since spring, but she didn't really need them since she spent most of her time at the bakery or home.

"What is it with women and shoes?" he asked, but there was a teasing note in his voice.

His gaze skimmed down her legs, stopping at the Enzo pumps she'd bought on sale last summer. "Those look nice, by the way."

"My legs or shoes?"

"Your legs," he said.

"Thanks. I'd return the compliment but I haven't seen yours yet."

He laughed and it made her feel good deep inside. She wanted this day to never end. She thought maybe she'd been too hasty in telling him she couldn't go to his place tonight, because suddenly she wanted to—very badly.

Marino's reminded him of being a kid again. Until he walked in the front door he'd forgotten that it had been five years since he'd been in there. He'd suggested the Italian deli because it made sense and he was a logical guy most of the time.

But suddenly logic had flown out the door. He remembered why he'd avoided the place. He'd met Mary here. It had been the summer before he started college. They'd met near the end-cap with the homemade Italian cookies. Mary had been from New Jersey and missing home. Joe had brought her to his family, and the rest had been history.

The smell overwhelmed him—spicy oregano, pepperoni and garlic. They were the scents of his boyhood and brought with them dreams he'd done his best to forget. He paused in the doorway, doubts penetrating the desire that had been motivating him since he'd met Holly. What the hell was he doing?

Holly bumped into him. ''Is it too crowded?'' she asked.

Joe shook his head. Only in his mind was it crowded—with two women who looked the same. Actually, there was only a couple of teenage boys at one of the tables in the front and Robert behind the deli counter.

''Joseph, it's been a long time since we've seen you. Mama, come out here and see who is in the shop,'' Robert said in his heavily accented English.

Joe embraced the shorter older man with true fondness. Robert and Lena were a part of his past. For the first time he was cognizant that he'd quit living when Mary died. His mom had tried to tell him but he hadn't wanted to believe her.

''Robert, how's it going?''

''Today, it's good, Joseph. For you too, eh?'' Robert looked right at Holly and then winked at Joe.

''Today is good,'' Joe said. Though he wasn't sure. Days that passed with numbing quickness were what he usually wanted. Today had gone quickly but he'd started to feel again and it was painful. Frostbite wearing off was painful.

He turned to the source of his reawakening. "Robert Marino, this is Holly Fitzgerald. Holly, this is Robert, the proprietor of the finest Italian deli in Boston."

"Nice to meet you, Miss Fitzgerald."

"Likewise," Holly said.

Lena came out of the back and let out a little shriek of joy, ran over to Joe and embraced him. Holly was watching him with a smile in her eyes, and he realized she knew he was uncomfortable and was amused because of it. He arched his eyebrows to let her know he'd get her back later.

After they ordered their sandwiches, they made their way to one of the tables in the front. Joe felt awkward. Sexual awareness he was comfortable with, but sitting at this small table in the crowded market felt too intimate to him.

He hated being irrational and exploring his emotions, so he forced his attention to the sandwich put in front of him. He'd eat dinner with Holly and then say good-night. It had been a day out of time, but he wasn't interested in getting involved with a woman again for the long term. Sex was fine but Holly made him want more, so he wasn't going to pursue her.

"This is a really nice place. It reminds me of the bakery where I work," Holly said, shifting on her seat. Her legs rubbed against his under the table. An image of them swam in his brain, and he knew he was going down.

"You work in a bakery?" he asked. Right now he couldn't remember anything except that she had incredibly long legs for a petite woman. And all those tempting freckles on her skin.

"I told you, remember?"

"Yes, you did." If his groin would stop trying to control things, maybe he'd have a chance of sounding halfway intelligent.

"The bakery is owned by a couple like the Marinos. It's really nice. We do some Italian pastries but not too many."

"You said you started baking to get away from your family?" he asked. As long as he kept her talking, he could distract himself from those long, slim legs resting in between his.

"Did it sound like that? I didn't mean it that way. I bake because it's what I know how to do and I'm good at it. My family doesn't enter the kitchen."

"Why not?" he asked.

She shrugged. "Because my brothers don't like to cook."

"Really?" She always hedged when the subject of family was brought up. He didn't know why that bothered him. Maybe because she made him feel unsteady and he wanted to rock her boat as well.

"Do you like to?" she asked.

He could grill but that didn't seem like real cooking to him. Not the way his mom or some of his sisters cooked. Not the way Mary had. "Not really. But I can get by if I have to."

"I know. That's how they are."

Holly's cell phone rang, and she glanced at the caller ID and then smiled an apology at him. "I have to answer this."

He tried to ignore her conversation but couldn't. When she disconnected her call, she stood up. Her face was pale and her hands were shaking.

"I've got to go," she said, then glanced around for her purse.

"Is everything okay?" Joe asked, standing as well.

She found her bag on the floor and slung it over her shoulder. "I don't know. My dad is having an episode. I need to go home."

"Do you want me to drive you?" he asked. He hated illness and how it made the healthy feel impotent. He sensed that Holly shouldn't be alone. He barely knew her, really, but he'd sat alone in a darkened hospital room watching his wife's life slip away and he didn't want her to have to do that for her father. Though the situation with her dad sounded different, Holly's reactions were similar to his.

"No. Thanks, but I better go alone. He might have to go to the hospital." She couldn't stop shaking, and he did the only thing he could do even though his gut shouted for him to let her walk away. He pulled her into his arms and hugged her close.

"Does your dad have a chronic condition?" Joe asked after a minute.

She pushed away from him. "Yes. I don't want to talk about it."

He understood how acting normal in an emergency was sometimes the only way to keep from breaking down. "Fine. Let me walk you back to your car."

The Holly he'd first met was back. The one who had told them all she wanted was her check. The vibrancy he'd come to expect from her was hidden away, and in its place was a mask of cool indifference that seemed wrong to him.

"That's not necessary," she said.

He'd been raised better than that. "It is to me."

They gathered the remains of their aborted dinner, and Joe shouted a goodbye to the Marinos. He knew that for his own sanity he should be glad for the premature end to the night, but he wasn't. He caught up with Holly, who walked so quickly she was almost running.

"It won't do your dad any good if you hurt yourself trying to get to him," he said quietly.

She slowed her pace a little, then stopped altogether. She wrapped her arms around her waist and stood there, comforting herself when he would have gladly offered her his shoulder. But he knew she wouldn't take it. She'd proven that minutes ago in the deli when she'd pushed him away.

"I know," she said. "It's just that I won't be able to calm down until I've seen him."

They reached Baronessa's and Holly was still agitated. She shifted her keys from one hand to the other, then dropped them. She stooped to retrieve them. He worried that if she got behind the wheel in this kind of condition, she'd have an accident.

"I really think I should drive you," Joe said.

"No." She closed her eyes and took a couple of deep breaths, and when she opened her eyes, the upset woman of only a few seconds ago was gone. "I can handle this on my own. Thanks for dinner," she said. She walked away from him, and he had no choice but to watch her go.

She'd started a fire inside him that wouldn't die, but there was more to Holly Fitzgerald than awesome legs, curvy hips and sex appeal. And that was something that he wasn't sure he wanted to get involved with.

At nine o'clock in the evening Holly left her father and youngest brother, Brian, at their father's house. Brian was in college and the only one who didn't have to be at work early in the morning, so it made sense for him to stay with their dad tonight. Holly would have done it, but her brothers had insisted she go home.

They'd teased her about her television interview from that morning. Her dad had even managed a gruff compliment about the way she'd looked and sounded.

She was wiped out. He'd taken his nitroglycerin tablets, and finally the pain had subsided. But he had a heart condition and any pain was cause for alarm by her and her brothers. Sometimes she felt her dad was living on borrowed time, even though Dr. James had assured her that her father would live to give his grandkids a hard time.

A weird melancholy settled over her as she walked to her car. The 1979 MGB had seen better days but it ran like a dream, thanks to her brothers and their weekly tune-ups. She was grateful because money had been tight for as long as she could remember and a new car was way down on her list of priorities.

She drove home noticing things she hadn't thought about in a long time. Like the summer was halfway over and this morning was the first time she'd been outside in the sun. She needed to make some decisions about her life. She knew her responsibilities to her family would always be there, but she really wanted to start enjoying herself. She was almost thirty, which was scary to think about, and the most exciting day of her life had come from winning a gelato-flavor contest.

What did that say about her?

She turned onto Hanover Street and drove slowly past Baronessa's. She still hadn't sampled the new version of her flavor. She'd bet the taste wasn't exactly the same as when she made it. When you multiplied a recipe some of the nuance of the flavor changed. She'd seen it happen once or twice with a pastry filling.

She pulled into a parking space. She'd get a sample of the new flavor and take it home. She had plans with her VCR and her favorite pajamas.

Baronessa Gelateria was doing a steady business. She scanned the tables, which were a little lighter at this time of night than the take-out line. Joe was still here. She started to glance away before he looked up but then decided not to. She wanted to see him again. Especially if the crazy beating of her pulse was any indication.

When he saw her, she waved. He waved back reluctantly. She had the feeling she was seeing the surly man he'd warned her about.

The couple he was dining with glanced around at her, and she recognized them from earlier—his parents. For what seemed an eternity they chatted with Joe, and Holly waited in line. Finally the couple in front of her left and Holly ordered. She was almost to the door when Joe's hand on her shoulder stopped her.

She'd didn't question how she knew it was him. She just accepted that her body knew his touch by instinct.

"I guess your dad must be okay," Joe said from behind her.

"Yeah, he's fine," she said.

"Do you have time to join me?" he asked.

She did but wasn't sure she wanted to. Today she'd realized she wanted to be the one to give her dad grandkids, and that meant she had to start dating guys who were looking for commitment. "I…"

"Why are you suddenly shy?" he asked.

"I'm not shy," she said. And she wasn't. It was just that he brought to life so many contradictory emotions that she didn't know how to react around him.

"Then what's the problem?"

"Driving home, I realized I'm in a different place than I was before I'd gone to see my dad," she said.

"So?" he asked. She had the feeling that he really wanted to know. Even though they'd known each other only a few short hours, there was a history between them. She thought it might be the same thing that linked victims of tragedy together. Once you'd been in an intense situation with someone, you formed a bond with him. But she wanted more than a passing bond with this man.

"I want more than a brief fling with you, Joe."

"I didn't know that's what I'd offered you."

She couldn't read him but she sensed he wasn't angry, only curious. He took her arm and led her outside the restaurant. He didn't stop until they were by an empty storefront a few doors away.

"Now, tell me what you're talking about," he said.

She wasn't sure she could, now that they were so close to each other in the dark with only the moon and faint glow of a streetlight to illuminate them. His features were stark and his eyes glowed with an intensity that told her to be careful what she said.

"I only meant that this morning I would have settled for one."

"But not now?" he asked.

"I don't know. I just feel like something is changing inside me. I think you made me realize I wanted more."

He sighed and rubbed the bridge of his nose. "Well, I'm not looking for more than a fling, Holly."

"I'm not sure what I'm looking for anymore," she said. She only knew that flirting and teasing weren't enough.

"Then I guess this is goodbye," he said.

She thought about it. The old Holly would have walked away without another word, but she was a new Holly. One who wasn't afraid to ask for what she wanted—well, kind of.

She took his hand in hers and stood on tiptoe, leaning toward him. "This is goodbye."

She brushed her mouth against his. His hands came up and cupped her face, tilting her head and taking control of the kiss. His lips on hers were warm and tempting. Time and place dropped away. She'd never been so totally under a man's possession before.

His lips, teeth, tongue all bade her to delve deeper. To learn every bit of this man who wouldn't be in her life after this day. His tongue traced the outline of her lips, and heat shot through her body. She shook with the force of the desire awakening in her.

She lifted her hand from his wrist, touched the edge of his jaw. His skin was warm and she rubbed her fingers over his cheek as his mouth consumed hers.

She canted her body into his, letting him support her—and wishing he was a different man but knowing that if he were she wouldn't want him with the same fire that was burning her soul.

Four

Joe's rational mind tried to warn him that he was making a foolish mistake, but he didn't care. He'd been asleep too long and Holly felt too good in his arms. He wanted her. He'd been too long without a woman to stem the desire for Holly.

She shifted, not grasping but clinging to him as her body succumbed to the web of desire he wove around them. A hot, humid breeze blew, fanning the flames that her tongue and mouth had ignited in him. He altered his grip on her, adjusting his hips to ease his hardness against her softness. When she melted into him, he'd have given ten years of his life to have nothing between them but her freckles instead of the frustrating layers of clothing.

He slid his hands down her back, cupping her buttocks in his hands, and held her still while he ground his hips against her. She moaned deep in her throat, a more sensuous sound than he'd expected from her.

He was so damn hard he could feel his pulse between his legs. He needed release—now. He needed her naked underneath him—now. He needed to stop—now, before he went too far.

He pulled back not out of any manly restraint, though that trait would be admirable. He pulled back because he'd crumble the carefully cultivated wall he'd built to protect himself from emotions.

She moaned a little, her hands still in his hair, holding him close.

"Why'd you stop?" she asked, her husky voice brushing over him like a velvet glove.

He wasn't about to reveal himself to her. To let her know or see that he wasn't the aloof man he pretended to be. "You said you didn't want to see my place tonight."

"Maybe I've changed my mind," she said.

Could he handle an affair with her? He wasn't sure he'd let it end after one night. The way he felt, once he had her in bed they weren't leaving for a long time. And could he walk away from that—from her?

He didn't want to know.

"You're tired and you had a scare with your dad. Tonight's not the right time," he said, leading her to her car.

She was stiff and tense under his guiding touch,

and he regretted that. Regretted that he'd had to stop the only thing that had made him feel good in a long time. For years he'd watched his siblings fall in love, watched Baronessa's go through numerous changes, watched life pass him by. Watched it, not lived it.

When had he turned into such a man?

"What is it?" she asked.

There was caring in her voice and he knew he shouldn't say anything else to her. Just get her to her car and get the hell away from her. But he couldn't walk away—not yet. She'd given him something he wasn't sure he wanted. But all the same she'd changed him and he owed her.

"Nothing," he said, leading her the rest of the way to her car. She'd left the top down and he wanted to warn her about criminals and safety but knew it wasn't his place. At best he was a man who'd kissed her, at worst nothing more than a stranger.

For the first time he wanted to be more. But how much more? He'd known for a long time that he'd never love again. And having lived with love, he knew he couldn't ask a woman to enter a relationship that had less than love to offer.

"I think I'm glimpsing the surly Joe," she said, leaning against the side of her car. She reached over and deposited her purse and carton of gelato on the front passenger seat. There was something different about her now. She seemed lighter almost and he wanted to know why.

He gave her a half grin. "Yeah, you are."

She tucked one of her long red curls behind her ear. "You still owe me an explanation of who I reminded you of."

"Now?" he asked.

She shrugged, the movement shifting her breasts against her jacket. "I doubt we'll have many other chances to talk," she said.

"Ah, hell, Holly."

She just waited. She wanted to know about Mary. The one woman he didn't want to discuss with Holly was Mary.

He'd been to a psychologist. Knew all about survivor guilt. But he didn't feel guilty he survived. He felt angry that Mary was gone. She'd made living more intense. And though he was a big guy and could stare down any danger, that emotional vulnerability was the scariest thing he'd ever experienced. And he never wanted to be in that place again.

Say it out loud, he told himself. A deceased spouse would provide an effective barrier between him and Holly. It would give him an escape hatch.

"You remind me of my wife," he said quietly.

She blanched. "You're married?"

Joe shook his head. "I was. She died a few years ago from cancer."

"I'm sorry," Holly said.

"Yeah." In his mind Joe clearly remembered the night five years ago when Mary had slipped away from him. Remembered clearly how a light inside him had extinguished. Remembered clearly how he'd vowed to never let another person affect him the way Mary had.

And staring down at the redhead in front of him, he knew he'd failed. Because even if he never saw her again, Holly Fitzgerald would live on in his dreams.

She felt inane. She couldn't think of a single thing to say to ease the pain that still lingered in his eyes. She knew what it was like to watch someone you loved waste away from something you couldn't control or make better. Sometimes the only solution was to escape. To get away from it all. And she didn't know if Joe should get away from her or from his memories.

Joe seemed so strong that it was hard to imagine him having the same weaknesses as she did. But his words and his eyes told her he did.

At six foot two he stood next to her and made her feel small and delicate. That was a strange feeling for her, because she'd always been the strong one others relied on. Maybe she could do that for Joe. Help him find his way and get back on his feet.

She ached for him. Ached to wrap him in her arms and comfort him in the age-old way of men and women. Ached to give him the most basic of human comfort.

The old Holly would have lingered on the North End street. But the new Holly was a woman on the cusp of change, and Joe Barone was a man not ready to make a commitment. She needed a man who was ready. Or at least able to acknowledge she was more to him than a good time.

She wasn't sure she could walk away, but common sense said to. This was a man who'd been badly hurt and wasn't going to risk injury again.

"I guess I'd better go," she said.

"Yeah, you should."

She opened the door to the MG and slid into the car. Looking up at him in the dim light, she noticed he looked alone, aloof. Much like the man she'd first met this morning. She knew she should drive away.

For her own best interest, leaving was the right choice. But she'd been alone too long. She knew exactly what it was like to always be on the outside.

He needed to get away, she thought again. Take time to do something that made no sense. Something that would take him outside his shell and into another world.

Her world? a voice inside her asked.

She wasn't sure that she wanted him in her world. But she had an idea. She told herself it was only because she needed to forget how frail her dad had looked, but the truth was, Joe had started a burning deep inside her that wasn't going away.

She needed to do something physical. Something to assuage that restlessness, even if only for a short while.

"Want to go for a ride?" she asked.

He seemed surprised but hesitated only a second. "Sure."

He walked around the car, moved the gelato and her purse and got inside. "What about your parents?"

"What about them?"

"Don't you need to say goodbye?"

"No."

He didn't say anything for a few miles as she drove through the darkened city. The wind in her hair made her feel free. Made her forget that the man next to her wasn't just a good-looking guy that she found attractive. Made her forget that she had to be at the bakery at five the next morning. Made her forget all the reasons she shouldn't bring Joe home with her tonight.

Why couldn't she? Not to stay the night but to play a little basketball.

He raised an eyebrow when she turned into her residential neighborhood.

"Where are you taking me?"

"To my house."

"I'm not objecting but why?"

"To burn off some energy."

"In your bed?"

"Maybe," she said.

"Maybe?"

"That's what I said."

"What's it going to take to make that a yes?"

"Beat me at a game of basketball."

His eyes skimmed her figure. He reached over, placing his hand on her thigh.

"What are you doing?" she asked.

"Trying to see if I'm being conned."

"Conned how?"

"Are you sandbagging me with this feminine suit and girly nails?"

She looked at him. "I'd never do that."

"I don't know. This thigh feels like it's seen its share of exercise."

"Would you believe I own a stationary bike?"

"I bet you don't use it."

"How'd you guess?"

"Because you enjoy being outside. The sun on your skin, the breeze in your hair. You, Holly Fitzgerald, are a very sensual woman."

She glanced over at him again. She wasn't sure what the teasing note in his voice meant. But his touch on her leg had changed. Now it was more caressing than probing. His fingers slid under the hem of her skirt, and with only the thin barrier of nylon to keep him from her flesh, his touch was more than enchanting. It was a fire that consumed her. Her foot jerked off the gas pedal and the MG stalled.

She removed his hand from her leg, ducked her head to avoid Mrs. Jeffers's nosey glance and restarted the car. Don't look at him, she told herself. Not until you have to.

She pulled into her driveway. Though silence filled the car, the night sounds surrounded them, and for a minute Holly lingered there. She wanted to let the sultry July air sink into her skin. Let the starry sky weave its promises. And let the man sitting next to her make his move.

"Am I still invited in?" he asked.

How the hell had she gotten herself into this? She needed to start thinking before acting. "For basketball."

"And later?"

"I'm still waiting to see if you can be the man your touch promised you were."

"That's asking a lot out of a little caress."

"I was afraid that'd be your answer."

Joe turned sideways in the passenger seat. "What do you want from me, Holly?"

"More than you can give," she said, knowing that she'd once again been shortchanged. Once again she'd settled for less than she deserved. She jerked her keys from the ignition and fumbled for the door. His hand on her arm stopped her from exiting.

"How do you know that?"

"Because your kiss was more profound than anything I've ever experienced," she said as she left the car then turned to look at him. "And it didn't mean a thing to you."

Joe wasn't used to hurting women's feelings. Hell, he didn't really interact with all that many women. Stella, his secretary, was efficient and always anticipated his needs. His mom and his sisters wouldn't let him wound them with words or deeds. Mary had been sickly for most of the time they'd been married.

Seeing Holly's deep-blue eyes shutter as she looked away made him feel like a bastard. The kind of bastard who had no business being alone with this kind of woman.

She was still shaky, and a real gentleman would have declined her offer of a ride. But then he'd proven time and again he wasn't a real gentleman. Why was it taking him so long to learn this lesson?

Despite money and breeding, Joe Barone had always been rough around the edges. And now Holly knew it too. She presented a sophisticated and professional facade, but there was something very soft about Holly Fitzgerald. He remembered her bending down to talk to the little girl at the YMCA and knew that she was lifetimes too soft for the man he'd become. The only man he knew how to be.

He climbed out of the little car and caught her arm before she could disappear. He didn't know what to say. He'd never been one of those suave guys who always sounded clever, like his older brother Nicholas. He'd give any amount of money right now for Nick's panache. Or Alex's charm.

But he didn't have it and never would. Life had proven that it took more than style and a smile for Joe to navigate it. He didn't mind, really. He did, however, mind hurting this woman.

"You shouldn't read so much into every man who kisses you." His own words sounded stilted to him.

He was out of his depth with her in this setting. Why had he allowed his gut to make a decision his mind knew was wrong?

She stood a few feet away from him, arms crossed over her chest. Spending the majority of his career in the corporate world had taught him to read body language. There was nothing open in her stance. She was angry and she wasn't afraid to let him see it.

She stepped closer. "I don't let a lot of men kiss me. And trust me, I won't let you do it again."

He could see the expression in her clear blue eyes. They were deep and mysterious and though he had no right, he wanted to explore those secrets. To find out what made her tick. He knew what made her mad, knew what upset her. But what made her laugh—suddenly he needed to know.

"The hell you say."

She arched one eyebrow at him and gave him a haughty look. "Don't go there, Joe."

"I'll go wherever I want, Holly. Or haven't you figured that out?"

She didn't back away, just stood there in the deepening night as if she'd hold her ground forever. And she probably would.

She wasn't going to let him bully her or ride roughshod over her. Even now when he wanted her to just back down and let the matter drop, she wouldn't. He wanted her to let him have his way and knew he was acting like a bully. But she'd come too close to him. Pushing her away was self-preservation.

Holly reminded him of his sister Gina. She fought when backed into a corner too, same as Holly.

But fighting hadn't been his original intent.

"I was trying to apologize," he told her finally.

"Well, you need practice."

"I know," he said wryly. He'd always hated admitting he was wrong. Especially to anyone other than himself.

She studied him. "Apology accepted."

"Are we still on for basketball?"

She nodded. He realized that she was dealing with more than just him. She had to still be worried about her father. He didn't blame her.

His parents were healthy, thank God, but they were getting older and Joe knew enough of life to know he wouldn't have them around forever. That was one of the reasons he tried to have dinner with them once a week.

"I didn't mean to push you."

"Then why did you?" she asked.

He didn't want to think about it. But the truth was, he didn't know how to manage a relationship with a woman without getting in over his head. He'd survived Mary's death but by cutting off all of his emotions.

"I don't have women friends," he said.

"So?"

"It's been a long time since I've been with a woman. You make me feel like I'm fifteen again."

She smiled and reached up to brush her fingers

across his cheek. The touch shot through him like an electric wire. He wasn't sure he could stay near her and not give in to the urge to make her his.

"You make me feel young again too, in a way I never was."

Let it go, he thought. But he couldn't. "Why?"

"My mom died when I was eighteen, but she was sick before that. I've always had to take care of my family."

"Your dad?"

"Yes, and my brothers. I'm not complaining. I'm just saying that you make me feel free."

He reached up and clasped her hand in his, leading her toward the house. Holly was a special woman who needed to be given more than one night of hot sex. He knew for both of their sanity he had to back off. He only hoped the physical exertion of basketball would cool the fire burning deep inside him. But doubted it would. That flame had been dormant too long.

Five

Though her life was very busy, basketball was the one thing Holly had always made time for. The basketball court was the one place where brothers didn't need to be reminded to do their homework, fathers didn't need to be reminded to take their nitroglycerin and pastries didn't have to be made. It was the one place where she could forget the familial responsibility that drove her and just be herself. Tonight, however, Joe made her remember more of herself than she wanted to.

She lived in an older residential neighborhood. Her garage was detached and behind the house. She had a backboard hung above the garage, and the driveway served as a court. She'd purchased the house

only a year ago and was very house-proud. It wasn't
one of those showplaces you saw in *Architectural
Digest* but it was hers.

When she'd led Joe through the house to her spare
bedroom for him to change into the clothing her
brothers kept at her place, he seemed to crowd the
small bungalow with his sheer presence. She hadn't
realized how broad his shoulders were until she saw
him framed in the doorway. Clearing her throat, she
said, "Let's go outside."

"Ready to meet your match?"

"Honey, I was born ready."

She had a spotlight attached to the garage for these
late-night games. It seemed she never made it home
in time to play before sunset. She glanced at Joe
again.

He had nice strong legs, and his arms and chest
were a solid wall of muscle, his skin darkly tanned,
and she regretted that there was too much between
them now for a night of mindless sex.

They'd reached the point where going to bed
would bring more complications. And her life was
complex enough.

Joe looked younger in her brother's shorts and
T-shirt than she'd expected. It was as if she were
glimpsing the man he'd been before losing his wife.
And though many of her feelings for him were un-
resolved, she was glad she'd invited him to her home
tonight.

"Like what you see?" he asked.

She flushed a little at being caught staring at him. "Maybe."

"Maybe?" he asked, flexing his arms like a body-builder. "What about now?"

"Still only a maybe."

He took a menacing step toward her and she giggled. This playfulness was something new to her. Her life was so busy and so full of have-to's that she'd forgotten what it was like to just have fun.

She smiled. "Let's see what you got."

She passed him the ball and he dribbled toward the hoop, jumping and sinking the ball with an ease that would have done Michael Jordan proud. Now she'd have to concentrate on her game, when she wanted to loaf and ogle him. She took his pass and sank a jumper.

"Not all window dressing, huh?" she asked, remembering his comment in the car. And the hot touch of his hand on her thigh. Oh God. She was never going to be able to concentrate on anything while he was standing next to her all big and male.

"Lucky shot," he said, passing the ball back to her.

She dribbled the ball a few times, then ran to the hoop and scored again. She felt his eyes on her the entire time. Her concentration was shot but luckily the ball went into the hoop.

"Not bad," he said, patting her on the backside as she went by.

"Foul," she said when she could speak. His hand

was big and strong and she'd liked his touch. She wanted more of it, but knew better.

"Sorry," he said, but he didn't look sorry.

"You will be, buddy, if you don't watch out."

He smiled again, a slow, sensuous grin that made her blood heat and called everything feminine in her to the front. "It was an accident."

She wriggled her eyebrows at him. "I can cause accidents too."

"Bring it on," he said.

They played fast and furious and in the end he won. The glow of victory gleamed in his eyes. Holly had played her best and had more fun than she'd thought possible tonight.

"Good game," she said.

He nodded. "Next time we'll have to make a wager."

"I don't bet."

"Not the gambling type?" he asked.

"I wouldn't have pictured you for the risk-taking type," she said.

"Normally I'm not. But you bring out a different side to me, Holly."

He did the same to her, but the day had been long and her emotions had run the gamut from nerves to sexual attraction to fear for her dad and then back to sexual attraction before ending at the spot she was in now. A kind of weary curiosity.

She wanted to know more about Joe Barone. Already she knew he liked her freckles and played basketball to win. But she wanted to know what it would take to turn the desire burning in his eyes into something more. Though her mind said tonight was the only time they'd meet, her heart didn't want to believe it.

Joe was sweaty and tired from the exertion but he felt alive. All his senses were attuned to the woman in front of him. A long tendril of hair clung to her freckle-covered neck. Her breasts rose and fell with each exhalation of breath and her eyes watched him—warily, he thought.

He stunk at the mating dance. He'd always thought he'd gotten lucky that he'd married Mary so young because he didn't like to play the games that men and women played in the getting-to-know-you phase. He preferred honesty and passion.

But they'd already shared too much honesty. Passion now seemed a risky proposition, when lust should never be anything but straightforward—two bodies twisting hotly on the sheets. His body was ready, but his mind warned that this woman would want more than he could comfortably give her.

He understood suddenly why his younger brother, Alex, had dated all those women before meeting and marrying Daisy. If Joe had been doing the same thing since Mary's death, Holly probably wouldn't be affecting him now. Yeah, right.

"What side do I bring out in you, Joe?" she asked.

He regretted his earlier words. But then he'd never been smooth around women.

"A dangerous one."

She walked closer to him. His instincts told him to back away but he didn't. He knew from firsthand experience that once you gave ground it was hard to get it back. Besides, she was a rather slight woman. She didn't scare him.

"Funny, you don't frighten me," she said, tiptoeing her fingers up his chest.

She was so close now he could smell her scent. Kind of sweaty, but also sweet. He breathed deeply so that the essence of her was branded on him. Damn. He had to get her into his bed and quick. But he'd never been one to indulge in one-night stands. For him, sex was more than scratching a physical itch.

"I'm not trying to alarm you, I'm just warning you that I don't know myself right now." He'd tried earlier in the car to caution her. Though he knew she was a strong, independent woman, he didn't want to hurt her emotionally. And even the toughest person could be injured by someone whom they cared about. And when he'd touched her leg and she'd stalled her car, he realized she cared more than she wanted to admit.

"That's only fair," she replied, "since you do the same thing to me. Right now I should be concerned with a million things, but the only one I can think of is you."

"Don't say things like that," he said.

"Why not?"

He was trying to be noble. But lust rode him hard and the only thing he could think about was that thin tank top she was wearing and stripping it from her slim body. He wanted—no, needed—to feel her naked flesh under his. He longed to trace the patterned freckles that ran the length of her long neck and disappeared beneath the clinging line of her shirt.

"You might regret them later," he said, because truth was one of the tenets he lived by.

She looked up at him, her blue eyes filled with compassion and understanding. "I doubt that."

"Women always want more than I can give them."

"Even your wife?" she asked.

For a minute he was shocked. No one mentioned Mary to him. It was as if everyone had forgotten her existence. They'd let him create a dark little cave where only he remembered her. He wasn't sure how he felt about having Holly ask him about her.

"I don't talk about my wife." The ball, which he'd been holding, slipped from his hand and rolled to the edge of the driveway. She didn't drop her gaze from his.

"I didn't know that."

"Well, now you do."

The moment had changed and he supposed he should be glad, but he regretted it. Mary was a barrier between them. A very effective one. Why, then, did he feel like a coward for using it?

"I guess we should get you back to your car," Holly said. "I have to be up early in the morning for work."

She walked toward the house and all thoughts about his deceased wife left him. Holly was vibrant and alive in a way that made everything around her pale. Though a part of him was unsure of what he wanted, he knew deep down that there was no indecision. His reluctance was the unwillingness to risk his happiness again. He'd made an odd peace with fate and he didn't want to rock the boat.

"Yes," he said, his voice sounding rusty to him.

She glanced over her shoulder. "Yes, what?"

"Mary wanted more than I could give her."

She didn't move, just watched him with her cat-shaped eyes. "In what way?"

He closed the distance between them and took her slender shoulders in his hands. Her skin was soft and smooth under his. He flexed his fingers, wishing this moment were different. Wishing he could slip his hand under the thin fabric of her T-shirt and feel her skin under his touch. "I'm not exactly sure."

"Then how do you know?"

"There was something in her eyes…. I'm not sure it wasn't disappointment."

"Maybe it was your own feelings projected on her."

He let go. He didn't want to be having this conversation. "What makes you an expert?"

"I didn't say I was."

"Listen, Holly. I've given up on dreams of lifelong love and happiness. But you haven't."

"Maybe right now I'm just looking for a physically satisfying relationship."

"Is that all you look for in a relationship?" he asked, not believing for a second that was the only thing Holly wanted from him.

"Yes," she said, her voice trembling.

"Liar."

She shrugged out of his grasp. "You're right. All around me are women who date casually, but I've never been able to. I don't know if it's because of my family or what...."

Something in her told him that was an excuse she used to protect herself. He wanted to tell her to trust him, but deep inside he wasn't sure he was trustworthy.

"Self-examination is never easy," he said.

"How do you know?"

"Despite the way talk shows and sitcoms make us sound, we guys think about things other than getting laid, sports and beer."

"I know," she said seriously.

"You do?"

"I have brothers."

"Yes, you do. So, where does that leave us?"

"I'm not sure. I feel like if I don't get to know you I'll be missing out on something wonderful."

"Why?"

"Joe, as much as you try to project otherwise, you do have a heart."

He felt as if she'd seen behind his shield to the soft underbelly he'd tried to hide. He'd become an expert at keeping his family at arm's length, trying to protect the part of him that had ached so badly after he'd learned he wasn't a superhero when Mary had died.

"Holly, I don't think I can live up to any mythical expectations."

"I'm not asking you to. I just would like to get to know you."

He was used to analyzing all the angles before making a sound decision, but right now his mind wasn't working. His body ached for hers, and his soul, the part of himself he always tried to ignore, whispered that maybe this woman was worth the risk.

"Will you have dinner with me tomorrow night?" he asked.

She shivered visibly, watching him with her intense gaze. "Okay."

Holly downshifted as she pulled her car up to Baronessa Gelateria. The shop was empty. Empty and dark. She knew from experience the building would be cold too. It seemed whenever a room was vacant it froze from the lack of human warmth.

She'd been lacking that for a long time. She had closeness from her father and brothers but it wasn't the same. What they shared was a deep bond, but she craved something else. Something she'd almost come close to with Joe tonight. Instead, she'd decided to settle for an affair.

"This is it," Joe said, pointing to a BMW sedan. For some reason his choice in cars surprised her. "This is yours?"

"Yes," he said.

"If I'd spent that much money on a car, I'd have gotten a Jag or a Ferrari."

He gave her a half smile that made her blood run heavy and her pulse quicken. Riding in the small car with Joe had been intimate. And they'd shared too much intimacy today.

"I'm not big on flash. This is more practical," he said.

Joe hadn't struck her as a practical guy. She knew that he was CFO of Baronessa, so she figured he had to be pretty serious some of the time. But the Joe she'd met today shouldn't be driving *this* expensive automobile.

"I disagree," she said. Dammit, what was with her tonight?

"You don't know me, Holly."

She glanced away from the car to look at him. "Maybe that's why I can see the real you."

He spread his hands. "I'm the practical one in my family."

That sounded so familiar. Those words had come from her mouth more than once until she'd let a friend talk her into trying something that was just for her. Rock climbing and skydiving. They were daredevil sports that left her feeling alive in a way she hadn't realized another person could make her feel until she'd met Joe.

"You need to define yourself away from your family," she advised him.

"I know who I am," he said firmly.

"I've seen your family in the paper and met Gina today. Your family is bigger than life."

"Not all of us."

"My family is overwhelming too."

"I'm *not* overwhelmed by my family. You make me sound like some kind of wimp."

"I didn't mean it that way."

"Then how did you mean it?"

"It's just… Earlier when your sister was bossing you around, it reminded me of how I treat my brothers sometimes."

"How's that?"

"It doesn't sound nice but I kind of try to shape each of them into a better person than he'd be otherwise."

"You think my family does that to me?"

"I don't know, do they?"

He stared at her in the moonlight and she knew

she'd gone too far. She'd been pushing him all day and now it seemed that nighttime had freed her normally cautious nature.

"Forget I said anything." Who was she to shake the moorings of his world? If he wanted to pretend that his life was peachy-keen, she'd go along with it. She wasn't going to be more significant to him than a few nights of passion.

Still, he just watched her with a quiet intensity. His eyes were so deep and rich that they reminded her of a pot of boiling dark chocolate. The kind she used sparingly to flavor her most exotic pastries at the bakery.

"Be careful, Holly," he said at last.

But caution wasn't in the cards for her tonight. "Why?"

"Because you might get more than you bargained for if you keep pushing me."

"I think I can handle it," she said.

"You think so," he said, leaning closer.

Dammit, he smelled good. A man who'd just won a one-on-one basketball game should smell like a locker room, not like Joe did. Like elemental man. Maybe that was why her self-mastery was lacking.

"I know so," she said, leaning forward herself. He had a nice jaw, square, firm, confident. She wanted to rub her hand across it, but curled her fingers against the urge.

"What makes you so confident?" he asked her.

"Because of your eyes," she said at last.

He didn't say anything, only waited for her to continue. But she couldn't. If she told him what she saw, she'd reveal how much she already liked him. And she wasn't going to do that. The new Holly was a woman who owned her destiny. She didn't wait for fate to shape it.

"Forget it," she said.

He opened the car door, grabbed his clothes and got out. She watched him walk away. He tossed his suit and shoes in the back seat and then turned to her.

"Your eyes tell me something too," he said, unlocking his car and opening the door.

"What?" she asked.

"That I'm not the only one letting other people's expectations shape me."

"You're wrong."

"Prove it. Tell me why I don't frighten you."

She swallowed. She'd felt safe and powerful in her car, but the balance had shifted. Still, she was a woman of her word. She shifted the car into first gear and looked directly at Joe.

Then she told him. "Your appearance is one of suave sophistication but in your eyes I can see your soul. Reflected there is a European sports car barreling down the autobahn."

She stepped on the gas and drove away before he could respond, the night air blowing through her hair. In her mind were all the words she'd wished she'd never said. But caution hadn't been her forte. Tonight that lack may have been her fatal weakness.

Six

Joe's day couldn't have been any slower. For the first time something other than Baronessa Gelati was at the forefront of his mind. He'd spent the day going through the motions but not really being there. Even going so far as begging off lunch with his dad and bagging work on the company's new five-year plan. Instead, he surfed the Internet.

"Got a minute, Joe?" Gina asked from the doorway.

He closed his Internet connection and glanced up at his sister. His brother-in-law Flint was there, as well. "I'm not doing any more press. I don't care what you've convinced Mom of."

Flint laughed and Gina rolled her eyes. "Nothing

like that. I'm taking an informal family poll. Flint wants to do some promo around the annual family reunion.''

''Unless I have to be the family spokesman, I'm all for it. By the way, I think Nick should be the family spokesman. He is the eldest and the COO of Baronessa.''

''Stop using my name in vain, Joe,'' Nick said from the hallway.

Joe lifted his hands innocently. ''Who, me?''

''Great. I'll put the plan in motion,'' Flint said, heading toward the door.

''Coming, Gina?'' Flint asked.

''In a minute.'' Gina watched him with her wide violet gaze, and Joe had the uncomfortable feeling he should have left work early.

''Uh-oh, I'm outta here,'' Nick said, disappearing down the hall.

His sister paced over to the windows and looked down on the street. Joe knew whatever she was going to say he wasn't going to like. He put on his toughest face. The one that made everyone leave him alone.

''What's with that look?'' Gina could always read him.

He shrugged. Sure, he knew he had feelings, but admitting them to the family was something he hated.

''Mom said you disappeared from the gelateria last night with Holly.''

"Why were you talking to Mom about me, Gina?"

"I like my brothers to be happy, Joe. You know that."

"Sure you do. Why the concern?"

"You were acting weird yesterday, even for you."

"Geez, was that a compliment?"

She smiled. Despite her annoying tendencies, he liked his sister. "I just wanted to let you know I'm here. If you need to talk about Holly or anything."

"There's nothing to talk about. Everything's fine."

"Joe, everything hasn't been fine for you since Mary died."

Joe shuddered. That was the first time anyone in his family had said Mary's name to him. Why now? Was he changing, or was the world around him different? Gina watched him with an intensity that made him uncomfortable. Italian women were witchy and superstitious. She'd brought up Mary to see how he'd react.

But he remained expressionless.

"Still stone-faced, I see," she said. "Well, be careful because I know there's a man behind the stone." She walked toward the door.

"Gina, did I try to tell you what to do with Flint?"

"No."

"Then let me do this on my own. I know I'm not Alex but I can handle a woman."

"Okay, big brother," she said, walking out of his office and closing the door behind her.

For once Joe didn't care about his family. Tonight was something between him and Holly—though he knew the evening wouldn't remain a secret.

Especially since he'd chosen Atlantic Fish Co. for dinner. It was one of Boston's most favorite restaurants. It had opened in 1978. He liked the place because of the detailed woodwork and murals of the spirit of the sea. Plus they had intimate, cozy booths.

His mother would find out about the date and then the inquisition would start.

The intercom buzzed.

"Yes, Stella?"

"A Ms. Fitzgerald for you on line one."

Hell, he prayed she wasn't calling to cancel. If he hoped to get anything done at work the rest of the week, he needed to see her tonight and get her out of his mind. His work had been his solace and suddenly thanks to Holly it wasn't.

He picked up line one. "Barone."

"I'm running a little late at the bakery. Where are we going for dinner? Maybe I can meet you there."

Joe wondered if she was really that busy at work or just looking to direct tonight's action. Hell, he didn't blame her. Holly might look fragile but she wasn't. There was a pure fighting spirit in her that would demand she make the most of their time together.

"We're going to Atlantic Fish Co."

"Oh."

"Is something wrong?" he asked.

"I've never been there, but always wanted to try it."

"Why haven't you gone?" he asked.

"It's a couple place not a family place."

"You've never been part of a couple?" he asked.

"Not long enough to get to the stage where you go to a place like that."

Her words sliced through the barrier he'd thought he'd built around his heart, making it beat again. He leaned back in the chair and mentally started making plans.

Tonight was going to be the ultimate in romantic fantasy for Holly Fitzgerald.

Holly changed clothes five times before settling on a slim-fitting dress with little cap sleeves. It was a designer knockoff she'd purchased in an outlet mall. But for tonight she'd splurged on the Enzo sandals she'd had her eye on all season.

She spritzed her body with perfume and checked her appearance one last time before heading for the door. The doorbell rang just as she opened it.

"Ms. Fitzgerald?" the deliveryman asked.

"Yes," she said.

"These are for you." He handed her a lovely bouquet of orchids, calla lilies and a pink flower, which she didn't know the name of. The scents assailed her and she closed her eyes for a minute to enjoy the fresh-cut flowers.

The deliveryman started to leave. "Wait a minute," she said, reaching for her handbag.

"It's all been taken care of," he said and, whistling, walked away.

She closed the door and sank to the deacon's bench along the wall. There was a card. She tugged it free of the pick and turned the paper carefully over in her hands.

She was shaking a little, she realized, and tears burned the back of her eyes. No one had ever sent her flowers. Not her dad when she'd graduated high school. Not her brothers when she'd won the contest. No one had ever thought to send her flowers except Joe Barone. The man who'd told her that he wanted her for only one night.

The note was in his bold, brash handwriting.

Cinderella had until midnight to enjoy her prince, but the magic doesn't have to end for us.

The Joe she'd come to know wasn't the kind of guy who'd feed a woman a line like that, but in her heart she knew she wasn't the kind of woman who could have a red-hot affair.

She had commitments. Commitments to her family and the bakery. Commitments to herself, she realized. But there was nothing that would stop her from enjoying this night with Joe.

The phone rang. She debated answering it, not wanting reality to intrude. But in the end the chance that it could be her dad decided her, and she picked up the phone. "Hello?"

"It's not too late for me to pick you up," Joe said.

"Where are you?"

"About a block from your place."

"I feel like I'm being manipulated. The Atlantic Fish Co. is across town."

"You aren't being manipulated. I'm just being gentlemanly."

"Are you sure?" she asked. Around men she'd never been as confident as she'd like to be.

"Hey, would I lie to you?"

Would he? "I don't know."

Silence buzzed on the line, and she wondered if she'd offended him. It was just that he was a guy who'd learned not to risk his heart, while she might not be looking for happily-ever-after but still believed it existed.

"I guess I'll just have to prove to you that you can trust me."

She shivered at the sincerity in his voice. Oh, God. She was in over her head. "Thanks for the flowers."

"You're welcome."

"I didn't get you anything," she said.

"Your company is gift enough."

"Don't say things like that."

"Why?"

"I might think you mean them. And we decided to go slowly."

"I am going slowly."

"Nothing seems real since the moment we met," she said more to herself than to him.

"I disagree," he said.

She waited.

"Everything finally seems real to me."

Hearing that was sweeter than the flowers he'd sent her. Sweeter than the dinner at Boston's most romantic restaurant. Sweeter than the fire he'd started in her last night. "Oh, Joe."

"Oh, what?"

"I just don't want to disappoint you," she said at last.

"Are you riding with me?" he asked, changing the subject.

She thought maybe Joe didn't really know what to do with her. It made her feel better to think he was as unsure as she was. "Okay."

She disconnected the phone before he could say anything else. She went into the kitchen and got a vase for the flowers, then put them on the counter. The setting summer sun streaming through the window was hot and she closed her eyes for a minute, enjoying its warmth for the first time that day.

The doorbell rang again and this time she hesitated. She'd spent the entire day trying to convince herself he was nothing more than a date, but her heart beat quicker as she walked toward the front of her house. Her pulse raced as she saw his silhouette through the front window.

Everything feminine in her awakened and she realized that these reactions were what she was afraid of. Not Joe or the date, but the way her sentimental heart would react to flowers and a romantic dinner. He'd already told her he wasn't her forever man and she needed to remember that.

She opened the door. Joe was backlit by the setting sun, so the expression on his face was unreadable. But he took a quick breath and reached for her. His fingers trailed down her arm, stopping at her hand. He rubbed his thumb over her knuckles before lifting her hand to his mouth and dropping a warm kiss on the back of it.

"You are beautiful tonight."

Sensation spread up her arm, making her insides puddle. She was uncomfortable not only with the sensuality he wove around her so effortlessly but also with the sophisticated man standing in front of her. His suit was not a knockoff but a hand-sewn Italian one.

"You are making me feel like Cinderella tonight," she said.

"That was my intent." He closed her front door and led her down the walk to his car.

She didn't say a word as he seated her and walked around to the driver's side. For this one night she'd forget that in the real world a man like Joe wouldn't really be interested in her. For this one night she'd simply enjoy the fantasy.

"Want to stop by Baronessa's for dessert?" Joe asked as they exited the restaurant.

It was nights like this that made living in Boston worthwhile. The breeze was warm and blew over his skin. Being with Holly sensitized him, making everything seem magnified a hundred times. It was unnerving.

The Atlantic Fish Co. had added to the charm of the evening. Somehow, dining there had created just the romantic atmosphere he'd been hoping for.

She stopped him on the sidewalk, reaching out to grab his hand. Hers was so small in his, he was reminded once again that it was the man's job to protect his woman. But Holly wasn't his...at least not yet.

"I have gelato at my place if you'd rather just go there," she said softly.

Her husky voice brushed over his senses like a match to kindling. The warm breeze around him stirred up his senses. He tugged her closer, so that her body was pressed neatly to his side. Her dress was a fantasy and a nightmare at the same time. Light and frothy, it moved around her as she moved. And he wasn't the only guy who noticed.

Telling himself he had no claim on her didn't work. No matter how much he tried to fool himself into believing that this attraction between them meant nothing, he knew better.

"Let's go," he said.

He seated her in his car and drove quickly through town. Frank Sinatra played quietly in the background. Normally, he favored hard rock but he'd decided tonight called for something else. So he'd broken down and called Alex, figuring even though his brother had settled down with Daisy, the old ladies' man would know what to play on a date.

But in the end it had been their father's advice that Alex had passed on. "The old man swears by Sinatra."

Joe had been reminded again today how much his family really cared for him. Alex had given Joe a list of recommendations for CDs and told him how glad he was that Joe was finally dating again. It was scary to realize that he hadn't been fooling anyone with his stoic mask.

Every damn song on the CD had to do with love— the very last thing he wanted to confront while Holly was in the car with him. From now on he was listening to hard rock.

"Is this Sinatra?" she asked.

"Yes, one of his early recordings."

"I've never listened to his stuff much."

Joe took his gaze from the road for just a minute. "You can't grow up Italian and not listen to Old Blue Eyes."

"I can imagine. So what was it like being one of eight children?"

"Craziness most of the time."

"For me too. But the boys were younger so I could distance myself a little from them."

"Did it work?" Growing up, he'd felt protected being surrounded by his siblings and parents. Everything in his life had seemed charmed until Mary's sickness.

"Probably not as well as I've always thought it did."

"What do you mean?" he asked. Holly was an enigma. Frail and ethereal on the outside, tough as nails on the inside. Except there was a part of her that was very soft. That part was clear in her eyes tonight.

"Just that even when I was the older sister pretending to be bothered by the boys, I still spent the majority of my time at home with them. I've always liked taking care of my brothers."

"Do you take care of your family?" he asked. She'd carefully kept the conversation away from her dad tonight and he knew it had been deliberate. But because there had been subjects he too hadn't wanted to discuss, he'd let her.

"Most of the time."

"Who takes care of you?" he asked. She looked like someone who needed pampering and had never been indulged.

She was silent for a minute, her serious face illuminated in the flashing lights of the street lamp. "I do."

"Have you ever thought about letting someone else do it?"

"Have you?"

He braked to a stop for a traffic light and glanced over at her. He didn't like how easily she saw into his soul. "I'm a man."

"Oh, so it's different for you," she said. Her words sounded solemn, but he sensed the laughter beneath them.

"Of course it's different. Men are expected to suck it up and shoulder on."

"Women are too."

"But no one thinks less of you if you lean on a man."

"I think if two people really love each other then leaning on each other is the best thing in the world."

"I thought you didn't believe in love."

"Of course I believe it exists…for some people."

"Not you?"

"I don't know. I can't fall in love now."

"Why not?"

"Dad's health insurance is still iffy and I've got obligations to fulfill. Love takes time and effort. Two things I don't have."

Joe concentrated on driving, pulling into her neighborhood and finally her driveway. "Maybe you haven't met the right man."

"There's no maybe about it."

"Really?" he asked. "Then what about me?"

Seven

Holly took a deep breath, fumbling in her purse for her keys. She wasn't about to think of Joe Barone and Mr. Right in the same breath. Illusion, she reminded herself. That was all he had to offer her. Her fancy dress and the nice dinner they'd just shared made her feel like Cinderella. Midnight was only a few strokes away and then the magic would end.

Her first instinct was to hedge and duck, but she'd never really been able to follow through on it. She liked dealing honestly with those around her. "You think you could be my Mr. Right?"

"I don't want to be ruled out of the running," he said. His voice was deep and husky, brushing over her senses and making her remember how long it had been since she'd shared whispers with a man.

And she brought a lot of baggage with her. One-night stands and red-hot affairs were one thing; Mr. Right was forever, and forever was scary. "I'm not sure you'd really want to be."

"Why not?"

"Because there's a part of you that you keep locked inside."

"The surly part?" he asked almost teasingly.

"I wish I could joke about this but you asked me about my dreams."

His face was stark in the shadowed light provided by the street lamp. She felt as if she'd crossed a line that neither of them even wanted to admit existed but she knew it did. Life had taught her that nothing lasted, that nothing was ever really secure and that the unexpected was closer than it seemed.

"Your dreams aren't a joke," he said.

"I know. They're all I have."

He put his hand on her thigh, and a flash of sexual desire flooded her body. She was ultrasensitized to his touch, and each caress—even the most innocent one—sent shock waves through her system. "I want to make your dreams come true."

She knew he could. His eyes promised dark dreams of carnal delight—but she wanted more.

"Let's talk about this inside," she said.

She got out of the car before he could open her door. His footsteps were heavy as he followed her up the walk to her small house. She unlocked the door and led him inside.

The kitchen was the biggest room in the house, and her favorite. She had a professional-grade oven and a large island in the middle. "Have a seat and I'll get the gelato."

"Thanks."

He slid out of his jacket and loosened his tie.

"I made some butter cookies last night. I'll get those out too," she said. From the first they'd been able to banter, but now they were reduced to inane small talk that made her wish she'd never brought up the subject of Mr. Right.

"Why don't you go wait in the living room," she said. She needed a few minutes to compose herself.

His sharp gaze told her he wasn't fooled. "Sure."

She prepared dishes of gelato and a plate of cookies as well as snifters of cognac. She picked up the tray and entered the living room, setting it on the coffee table. Joe wasn't seated as she'd hoped but studying the pictures on the wall.

Holly wasn't sure she liked him seeing her family. This man whom she wanted to have a passionate affair with shouldn't know the personal details of her life. Not if he only intended for them to be together for the short term.

"Here's dessert," she said.

"Your family looks close," he said, walking toward her.

"We are."

She cleared her throat, not sure what to say next. She smiled at him. Maybe he'd forgotten about the whole Mr. Right thing. She certainly wished she could. She realized that this man was really her ideal man. The one she'd secretly dreamed about since her mother had died and she'd been left with the boys to raise. The one she'd been hoping to meet since she'd started dating and realized that real men weren't the same as dream men. The one she'd come to know as a man of honor.

Joe handed her a snifter and took a seat next to her. She could feel his warmth, he sat so close to her. She shivered a little and resisted the urge to slide closer to him on the couch. It would be so easy to do. The leather was slippery against her silk dress, and if she shifted her weight, she'd coast right up against him.

He'd unfastened the top button of his shirt. Tufts of hair were visible through the opened collar. She reached out toward him before realizing what she was doing, then dropped her hand and looked up.

Joe stared at her with that mesmerizing dark gaze that made her feel exposed…vulnerable.

"What?" she asked.

"Why did you stop?" he asked.

"I'm not sure where we stand."

"I am. You told me about your dreams. Now let me tell you mine."

"Yours?"

He nodded. The lambent desire in his eyes made her pulse run heavier. "I envision the two of us—"

She put her fingers over his lips. She didn't want

to hear what he had to say. She wanted him, but she wanted—no, needed—to pretend that he was her dream man for this one night. She knew he wasn't. She knew this could never last. But for this one night she wanted to believe it.

She searched to find her voice. "I don't want to be too forward."

"Honey, I don't think you could be."

She wasn't sure she wanted to be given free license to his body. But she did want to touch him. She reached for him again, this time brushing her fingertips along the edge of his jaw and down his throat. His Adam's apple bobbed as she moved her hand over it.

His gaze held hers and she felt she was drowning in Joe. His heat, his soul, his body all called to her, making her forget everything about herself except that she had this one night as a magical princess. This one night that her fairy godmother had given her and she didn't want to waste it.

He took her snifter from her and placed it on the table. Taking her face in his hands, he caressed it, touching her cheeks, tracing the line of her nose and then finally rubbing gently against her lower lip. Her mouth tingled. She licked her lips and tasted the edge of his thumb.

Bending, he tilted her head back and brushed his lips against hers. They'd kissed before, so this should be no big deal, but Holly felt as if this time something deeper was happening.

Magic, she realized.

His mouth moved on hers with a quiet strength. There was passion, of course, but also something more like affection. And that caring made the difference to her. A well opened deep inside. She framed his face with her hands and took control of the kiss.

Joe pulled away slowly, his lips and tongue leaving her mouth.

"Are you sure about this, Holly?"

It had been a long time since Joe had felt this rush of physical desire. The gentlemanly behavior he'd carefully cultivated over the years was stripped away, leaving in its place a primal man.

This was just one more awakening that she'd brought about in him. He'd been frozen, locked away from life for so long.

He watched her, staring at him. Her eyes were luminous and wide, dominating her entire face. Her freckled skin was flushed. He trailed an unsteady hand down her bare arm, tracing one of the many patterns on her skin.

As his blood pounded an ancient rhythm in his head, his noble ideas of slow, romantic seduction slipped away. He didn't miss them, and watching Holly through narrowed eyes, he didn't think she would either.

Her breath rushed in and out, forcing her breasts to strain against the silk bodice of her dress. Her hardened nipples were prominent through the thin fabric. She still hadn't spoken but he couldn't resist touching her.

He rubbed his thumb over one distended nipple. When she moved more fully into his touch, he cupped her breast. Between his thumb and forefinger he lightly rubbed her nipple. Holly moaned deep in her throat.

The sound made his flimsy control disappear. It had been so long since he'd had the solace of a woman's body, so long since he'd given in to the physical side of his nature that he didn't know if he could restrain himself. Didn't know if he could bring her along with him.

"It's been a long time for me," he said at last.

Her crystalline-blue gaze met his. "Me too."

"I mean it, honey. I locked this part of myself away."

She sat up. "Are you telling me you haven't had sex since your wife died?"

He rubbed his forehead and looked away. "Yes."

She didn't say anything and he was afraid he may have finally found the way to slow the pace. Damn, he didn't want to leave now. But she cupped his face in her hands and brought his mouth to hers. The kiss she gave him was full of passion and caring. More caring than a man who felt as shaky as Joe did deserved.

"I promise it won't be painful," she said.

He laughed. "It could be quick."

"That's okay with me."

"I want to take my time with you."

"There's always next time," she whispered.

Next time. The words were the balm he needed to indulge himself in Holly's sweet body. To take what they both needed. This wasn't a romantic fairy tale that demanded perfection. They were both human and understood that need sometimes was just that. Need. And control wasn't something that could be counted on.

Her hands on his head urged him closer to her bosom. He lowered his mouth to her turgid nipple and blew lightly on it. It tightened even further and Joe could wait no longer to take her in his mouth. The barrier of her dress served to heighten the sensation and at the same time to frustrate him. He sucked harder, pulling her deep into his mouth. He used his hand to cup her other breast, rubbing his forefinger over her nipple.

Her hands left his head and massaged his back. "Joe, I want to feel you."

"How do you get out of this damn dress?" He too wanted flesh upon flesh. He needed it. He needed to feel this moment in blinding Technicolor and not the dull gray his world had become.

Holly shimmied out of her dress, leaving her clad in only those damned gorgeous freckles of hers and a pair of panties so scanty that he couldn't think of anything but getting back to her body, removing that last barrier and joining them so deeply, so tightly that neither of them would ever be free.

He sat up, pulled off his tie and unbuttoned his shirt in quick, hurried movements, then tossed it away. He kicked off his shoes and removed the condom he'd put in his wallet earlier. Holly just lay there watching him.

He unfastened his pants and pushed them and his briefs off his legs. Standing naked in front of her, he felt everything in him swell. His groin was so hard, his muscles were flooded with strength and he felt like a warrior who'd been away too long and finally had come home.

Only home wasn't a place. It was one fragile woman who watched him with radiant eyes and opened arms and legs. He knelt next to her and caressed her skin. Her flesh tightened under his touch, shivers of sensation visible in the way she quaked.

He felt powerful and masculine. The need to savor her battled with the need to bury himself in her humid warmth. He spread his fingers and ran his hand down the length of her midriff and stomach. Her muscles tightened as he slid past her tiny waist and neared the waistband of her panties.

He slipped one finger under the elastic, searching for the center of her desire. He found it and teased it with a soft touch.

She moaned again. "I thought you were in a hurry."

He had been. Until he realized that exploring Holly was more important than giving in to the maddening need to climax inside her. Right now he needed to know all her secrets.

"I changed my mind."

He pushed her panties down her legs and she kicked them aside. She grabbed the condom from his fingers, tore it open and sheathed his aching flesh. "I can't wait, Joe."

He nodded. She tugged him up and over her. Propping himself on one elbow, he used his other hand to test her readiness. Though he knew she was eager, he wanted to make sure her body was ready for him. She was warm and wet when he slid his finger into her. She lifted her hips, beckoning him closer. He adjusted himself, braced himself on his forearms and slid inside her.

He stopped when he was hilt deep inside her and looked down at her. She watched him, eyes wide open. Her hands clasped his buttocks and urged him to move, but he waited, teasing the both of them for a long minute.

When her hips shifted beneath him, he started to thrust. Watching her carefully, he brought her along with him. Everything in his body tightened, and he felt his climax building at the base of his spine. He reached between their bodies and touched her once and then twice. She dug her nails into his back and then let out a moan of completion, her body tightening around his.

He shifted, held her hips and thrust quickly into her three times before he climaxed as well. His body was drained of everything. Slowly reality came back to him and he realized he'd just lowered a barrier he'd never meant to lower.

Holly hadn't felt this free since the first time she'd skydived. She held Joe tightly to her, aware that she never wanted to let go. She pressed her face into his shoulder so he couldn't see how deeply she'd been affected by his lovemaking.

She'd experienced good sex before but this went beyond good. She felt completely exposed to Joe, and that caused a chill of apprehension in the pit of her stomach. She'd been too used to taking care of herself and now she'd let someone inside the wall of caring that she generally reserved for her family.

But maybe luck was on her side and Joe would snuggle with her. This was her magical night, after all, she reminded herself. Her night of illusion with a genuine Prince Charming.

But instinct told her that the illusion was over and that reality was waiting in the wings.

Joe shifted on her, pulling his body from hers. A cold chill shook her even before he levered himself up off her. She crossed her arms over her chest and pressed her legs together. Joe watched her through half-lidded eyes, as if each move she made was being recorded in his mind.

"Where are you going?" she asked.

"To get rid of the condom," he said without meeting her gaze.

He padded silently out of the room. He was a solid, muscular man and she was amazed that she hadn't taken more time to explore him. She'd been overwhelmed by the lust in each of his touches. He'd carried her along in a wake of desire and passion until she'd forgotten everything.

But it seemed the time to remember was upon

them. She sat up and tugged the chenille throw off the back of the couch, wrapping it around her body. What should she do? For the first time she was uncomfortable in her own home.

He reentered the room and started to dress. She couldn't believe it. He was going to abandon her. She glanced at the melting gelato in the ice-cream cups and knew she wasn't going to just let him leave.

"Joe?"

He fastened his trousers and looked at her. She hesitated, unsure what to say. How did you ask a man to stay with you when it was obvious he wanted to leave?

"I'm sorry, but I've got to get out of here," he said.

His face was shuttered, showing her no emotions at all, and she felt the way she had the day they met, when she'd heard him say he didn't want to spend the day with her.

She wished she had something other than her dress to put on, feeling distinctly defenseless wrapped in the blanket. She didn't want to leave the living room because she knew he'd leave without saying goodbye. And she needed to talk to him.

"Why?" she asked.

"I just do. Listen, I'll call you," he said, picking up his shirt and shrugging into it.

"Will you sit down with me for a minute?" she asked.

He froze. In his eyes she saw that he didn't want to do anything but get away. Find someplace private and restore himself.

She held her hand out to him and slowly he took it. She drew him down to her side. He sat as stiffly as she had earlier this evening. The irony of the moment wasn't lost on her.

"Don't think about it," she said, trying to figure out what he needed from her.

He reached out toward her cheek but dropped his hand before he touched her. "I wish it were that easy."

"You said yourself we should just enjoy this thing between us and take it one moment at a time."

"That doesn't mean I was right." He stood and walked to the front door.

His leaving hurt worse than anything she'd experienced at the hands of the opposite sex. Even being stood up the night of her senior prom paled in comparison.

"What bothers you the most, Joe?" she asked. "That you had sex with me or that you enjoyed it?"

He pivoted to face her. Maybe she'd gone too far but she wasn't sure how to get through the protective layer he'd donned the minute he'd pulled out of her body. She wasn't used to letting men use her.

When he said nothing, she said, "I don't think Mary expected you to quit living."

"I haven't."

"Yes, you have. Everyone is too afraid of your scowl to tell you, but they all know it."

He stalked back to her side. He was angry but she sensed not with her.

"What do you want from me?" he asked, his voice crude.

"Perception is too much to ask, huh?" She didn't want to say that it had been a long time for her too. That no man had ever blown into her life the way Joe had and then shaken her the way his presence had. She didn't want to watch him walk away because she had the feeling she'd never see him again.

"I'm trying not to hurt you," he said.

"That's funny because leaving is what hurts me the most."

"I never wanted that."

There was something so sad in his eyes that her heart melted. She reached out for him, took his hand in hers and tugged him down the hall to her bedroom. He paused for a minute, resisting her, then sighed and gave in. Only the moon lit the room, and the shadows were comforting because she didn't have to face the fact that she'd done the one thing she'd sworn she'd never do again. She'd cheapened herself for a man who didn't want her as much as she wanted him.

Eight

Joe never thought of himself as a weak man until this moment. He knew that he shouldn't follow her. But he felt a bit as if he imagined Adam had when Eve had offered him the apple. Mind saying one thing, body saying something else entirely.

Staying would only make things worse. And as much as he longed to comfort himself in Holly's arms, he wasn't sure he could afford to pay for the pleasure.

For his own good and Holly's he should leave. But the temptation of her sweet curves was too great to resist. He admitted to himself he didn't really even try.

Once in her bedroom, she dropped the blanket

she'd used to cover her body. Gradually her long limbs and slender curves were revealed in the moonlight. Her freckled skin was barely visible but he knew the patterns from earlier on her couch when he'd made her his. The image of her creamy skin was branded in his brain, and he'd never be able to envision her again without being reminded of it.

She stood before him more vulnerable than any woman should ever be. If he'd learned one thing from his father it was that men protected the women. And he'd done a poor job of protecting Holly. Though he strongly believed everyone controlled their own happiness, he'd dealt her a strong blow and she'd snapped back, reacting with caring.

Oh, God, could it be more than caring?

Joe removed his clothing quickly. Whatever was going on in Holly's head, he needed to let her know she wasn't alone. That he too was unable to resist the web of passion that ensnared them. She seemed so fragile standing in front of him with no defenses, but he realized she'd been the stronger of the two.

She'd been the one to reach past her hurt and take him by the hand. Leading him from the brink of self-reproach and regret. Leading him to her bedroom. Leading him, it seemed to his greatest weakness. But if he was staying, he was going to enjoy every minute of it and not think. Not remember. Not call himself a bastard.

The room was hidden in shadows and though normally he preferred to make love with the lights on, he welcomed the darkness. Welcomed the chance to take Holly again without looking into those crystal-blue eyes of hers.

"I did promise the magic wouldn't end at midnight," he said, taking her hands in his.

"Is that what you call sex—magic?" she asked. Something quivered in her voice, and Joe thought maybe she was regretting leading him down the hall.

It was too late now. Too late to keep from inflicting the pain. But he could soften the blow. "With you, I do."

"Oh, Joe."

He pulled her closer in his arms, wrapping himself around her. He needed her. Needed her in a way that went beyond physical. And that scared him, because he was a logical man.

"Let me make love to you," he said.

She nodded. He lifted her in his arms and carried her to the bed. He held her with one arm and flipped the covers back with another. Setting her in the middle of the bed, he realized darkness wasn't going to work for them. He needed to see her. To memorize every reaction she had.

"Where's the light switch?" he asked.

"No lights. Come to bed, Joe," she said, grasping his wrist and holding him in place.

He could have easily escaped her hold. He worked out twice a day and could bench-press more than she weighed. More than her touch held him in place. "I want to see you."

She tightened her grip on him and spoke so softly he had to strain to hear her words.

"You've already seen too much."

Her words struck through his tough-guy exterior and he sank to the bed. He pulled her into his arms and savored the feel of her pressed full-length against him. He lowered his head and took her lips, thrusting his tongue leisurely into her mouth. Her tongue teased him with shy touches, driving him to the brink.

He slid down her body, leaving his mouth on her skin, savoring Holly. Her skin was smooth, scented and hot under his lips.

This was ridiculous. He was a grown man, not a teenager, but he was aching to bury himself deep inside her again, as if it had been days since they'd last made love instead of only minutes. What was she doing to him?

Her hands swept down his chest, stopping when she met the blunt tip of his arousal. "I see you recover quickly."

He caressed his way to her center. Humid warmth greeted him. The rest of her tasted so good that he was powerless to resist knowing all of her. Besides, he wanted this night to be enchantment for her. "This is fast even for me."

"Must be that magic you were talking about earlier."

"Or it might be something else entirely," he said.

"What?" she asked.

Her fingers tightened around his shaft in a way that was making him forget this evening wasn't all about his pleasure. What the hell had she said?

He kissed her deeply and then skimmed his tongue down her body, lingering to suckle at each of her breasts. Her nipples were hard and her breasts ripe. He cupped her, squeezing gently while he drew deeply on her flesh. Deep in his soul he felt he was getting some form of sustenance from her. Something life-sustaining.

She was moaning, her hands running up and down his back, lingering at his buttocks. He groaned, unsure how much longer he could last. He grabbed her hands, manacled her wrists in his grip above her head. Then he moved farther down her body.

He kissed her abdomen, brushed his lips against the springy curls that hid her secrets from him. Secrets he'd come close to unraveling earlier. But this time he wanted more than a fleeting glimpse at them. He wanted to explore and discover the very heart of Holly.

He freed her hands, sweeping his touch up and down her body. She raised her hips, bringing her warm center more fully into contact with his mouth. He sought the point of all her pleasure and teased it with the tip of his tongue. When her hands gripped his head tightly, he scraped his teeth along the nerve center and felt her go over for him.

She called his name. Her thighs squeezed his shoulders and her body convulsed in his hands. She was magnificent. She was beautiful. She was tugging at him. And he slid up over her and thrust into her warm body while the tremors of her climax still rocked her.

Her hands came up to hold his head, and she brought her lips to his and kissed him deeply. The magic he'd promised her seemed to fill the room. He felt it flow from her mouth to his as everything in his soul reached forward toward her. They moved in unison until they climaxed, this time together.

Joe didn't have words to speak or energy to think but he knew something mystical had happened in this bedroom and it frightened him more than anything he'd ever faced before.

The alarm went off at five o'clock the next morning. Holly jerked from sleep as she always did and reached for the off button, stopping when she encountered warm, male flesh.

Joe.

Oh, God.

She levered herself up on an elbow and reached across his body to shut off the radio. He groused in his sleep but didn't waken, which she was thankful for. She sat up and the sheets slid down his body.

She resisted the urge to rub her fingers along his biceps. Even resting, it was strong, solid. Much like the man himself. He was so big that it never occurred to her that he might have a weakness. Until last night.

He hadn't made love to a woman since his wife's

death. Until her. She felt overwhelmed by that. Overwhelmed by the fact that she'd moved something in him that other women hadn't. Overwhelmed by the fact that it might mean more to her than she should let it.

There was something about a well-built man that got to her. Only this time he'd found his way past her defenses before she'd seen his six-pack and deltoids. Dammit. She was almost thirty. When was she going to stop making decisions with her heart instead of her head? Like she had with Roger, her guitar playing ex-boyfriend who'd let her support him for three years.

Except her head didn't understand how lonely it was taking care of everyone all the time. She got out of bed before she did something really stupid like call in sick to work and stay home with Joe. Joe needed her. The way he'd turned to her the second time they'd made love had stirred a part of her soul that she'd never let anyone see.

The sex had been incredible, but sleeping with him was what had made her throat close up with suppressed emotion. Her other lovers hadn't cuddled her close. They hadn't wrapped their bodies around hers and cupped her breasts in their hands while they'd slept. Joe had. His face had nestled into her neck so that she felt each breath he took. She'd been surrounded by him, and as she stood next to the bed now, she realized how cold she felt without him.

Get used to it, she ordered herself.

Quietly, she got clean underwear from her dresser and padded into the bathroom. Maybe she could sneak out of the house before he awoke. She'd leave him a note.

Except she wasn't a coward. Never had been and didn't intend to start now. She'd made her decision to fight for Joe last night when he'd turned to walk away from her.

Entering the bathroom, she turned the water on and waited for it to get warm. She was concentrating intently on her day, trying to pretend it was almost normal to wake up with a man in her bed. Only it wasn't just any man in her bed.

It was Joe Barone. Joe, who wasn't even close to someone she'd ordinarily meet, much less date. He came from another world. Hell, she'd known that when she'd accepted his invitation. Now she understood why Cinderella had left at midnight. She hoped it had been easier for Cinderella to deal with reality in the early hours of morning, because it sure as heck wasn't easy for Holly.

The door opened and Joe stuck his tousled head around the doorjamb. "Is this a private shower?"

She shook her head. He looked like a cover model standing in the doorway. He propped his arm against the door frame and stood there unconcerned about his nudity. She hadn't taken her time last night to look her fill, but she did this morning.

His chest was covered in a smattering of dark hair that tapered down to his...very eager manhood. She smiled despite herself. One thing was distinct—whatever might be keeping them apart emotionally didn't affect them physically.

She glanced up and met his gaze. He winked at her. ''Yeah, you do that to me.''

It seemed that the passion of the night before hadn't been exorcised as she'd hoped. Instead, her entire body seemed to jump to alert. Her skin felt sensitized, her breasts full and heavy, and between her legs there was a dampness.

''Holly?''

She realized she'd been staring at him. ''Sorry. I don't know the rules for this kind of thing.''

''There aren't any. Just do what feels right.''

''Is that what you're doing?'' she asked.

''I'm certainly not thinking.''

Did he regret last night? She'd made him stay. Oh, why had she done that? She turned away and tested the water, which was steaming up the bathroom.

She stepped into the shower quickly, lathered herself and started to rinse before Joe joined her. She handed him the soap. She'd never showered with another person before. She knew the shower had the potential to be very sensual, but she couldn't do that right now. Her body ached from last night and inside she felt quivery. There was a part of herself she'd always managed to keep protected from the men she'd dated. A part that only Joe had touched.

He watched her as warily as she watched him, it

seemed. Two battered souls, she thought. Both longing for comfort but still afraid to reach out.

"Can I rinse?" he asked. The question was mundane, the actions that accompanied it were anything
but. His body rubbed against hers as they maneuvered in the small shower. Her nipples throbbed and
she wanted to press herself against him.

But she couldn't. There was work and she didn't
want to have sex with him again until she'd had time
to think. Time to figure out if the sex had been as
sacred as it had felt in the middle of the night.

She pushed the curtain back and got out of the
shower without washing her hair. She toweled dry
and pulled her underwear on in record speed, then
braided her hair. She heard the water stop.

"I'll get you a towel," she said and escaped down
the hall.

Holly tossed a towel through the door and didn't
reenter the steamy bathroom. He was hard and aching and wanted nothing more than to bury himself in
her sweet heat one more time. But it was clear she
was putting up fences that said No Trespassing.

He stared at himself in the mirror, hardly recognizing the man he saw there. Hell, he didn't blame
her. He had wanted to get away and lick his wounds
in private, but she'd stopped him. Last night hadn't
been his smartest move, yet he didn't regret it. He'd
never wanted any woman as much as he'd wanted
Holly. Maybe not even Mary.

"Joe, I've got to go," she said through the door. She sounded tired and unsure. Not at all like the Holly Fitzgerald he'd come to know. For the first time he looked objectively at their relationship. He'd been kidding himself that one night of sex with her would be enough. That one night would make the ache for her go away. That one night would enable him to get back to normal.

Normal had disappeared the first time she'd walked in the door, and he wasn't sure he missed it. He only knew that he had to figure out how to make these new feelings not so unsteady. He needed a plan. He'd approach it the same way he did an amortization. Rules and limits had to be established.

He wrapped the towel around his waist and opened the door. Just once he'd like to have a relationship with a woman in which everything went smoothly. Or at least appeared to. Even his life with Mary hadn't been smooth before her illness.

She stood in front of him in her chef's uniform—dark pants and white shirt. There was nothing sexy about a plain white unisex shirt. His mind knew that but his body said that when it was Holly's body underneath, of course there was.

"Can you give me five minutes to dress? I'll leave with you." Her hair was caught back in a braid and her long neck was visible at the top of her shirt. He saw the slight discoloration on her neck and remembered giving her that love bite in the middle of the night when they were both more asleep than awake.

"I didn't mean to disturb you," she said softly.

"Too late," he said. She'd woken the sleeping beast and Joe wasn't sure how he felt about that. Last night had shattered a part of himself that he'd always felt confident of. But in her arms he'd had no control, no boundaries, and that made him question the truths of whom he was.

"I'm sorry. Do you need a lot of sleep?" she asked. If she were in his bed, he wouldn't waste a minute sleeping—ever. He'd make each night as incredible as last night had been.

"No." He never had. Even as a child he'd been a night owl and up with the sun. Four hours were the most he'd ever needed. It had come in handy when Mary had been so sick. He'd rarely left her side.

"Then what'd you mean?" she asked.

He wasn't sure he wanted her to know how deeply she'd affected him. But those damn crystal eyes of hers looked sad and he knew she needed to hear the truth. "You disturbed my soul."

She blanched and took a step back. "I have no idea where we're going to end up. We were talking about one night."

"I know. That's why we're both dancing around each other like two prizefighters. Each knows the other's strengths and weaknesses."

"Now what?" she asked.

He didn't answer her. He'd forgotten what it was like to have to protect someone weaker than he was. What if he let her down the way he had Mary? He didn't know if he could give his soul to a woman again. To plan to be her mate and then watch her slip slowly from his grasp.

He dressed quickly, noticing that Holly kept her gaze firmly away from him but didn't leave the room. He realized then that neither of them knew what to do here or how to react. He needed a plan, but at the moment he just needed some distance.

He sat to put on his shoes and Holly looked at him again. She wrapped her arms around her waist and watched him with wide eyes that made him want to protect her from the world. He stood and opened his arms.

Holly hesitated.

"Come on, baby. I won't hurt you."

Her eyes said it was too late and the damage had already been done. But she took a step toward him. It gave him hope.

"We'll figure this out. We just need a plan."

She stopped. "A plan. What is this, a business merger?"

He hadn't considered that. A business merger. What a great idea. He added it to the variables he already had in the back of his head. The file labeled Holly and Joe.

"No, but if we treat it like one I think we'll both come out of it whole."

She shook her head sadly. Her arms dropped from her waist and her hands curled into fists. "You don't believe that, do you?"

He realized she was angry. He didn't blame her. But he was helpless to react as anything other than the man the past had taught him to be. "I have to, Holly. It's the way I've learned to live."

She closed the gap between them and stood toe-to-toe with him. She tapped his chest with her index finger. "That's not living, that's hiding."

"Are you calling me a coward?" he asked, his own anger building.

"No... Well, yes, I guess I am."

"I'd punch a man if he called me that."

"Do whatever makes you feel better. But the truth is something you can't fight your way out of."

"I'm not delusional."

"I never said you were. Just that it's easier for you to hide than to face life."

"I lead a very full life."

"I'm not saying you don't. Just that you don't *live* it."

"What do you want from me?"

She narrowed her eyes and skimmed them over his frame. "Just for you to be the man you were last night."

"What man was that?"

"One who didn't analyze with his mind what he knew in his heart."

"I don't have a heart anymore, Holly."

"Then I guess this is goodbye."

"No. Not goodbye. Not yet."

He tugged her into his arms. He held her close,

ignoring the arousal she drew from him so easily, and concentrated instead on the fresh clean scent of her. He wanted to absorb her into his skin.

"I'll call you tonight and we'll work this out," he said.

"Will we?"

"Trust me."

She didn't say anything else, just walked out of her house. He followed her car to work, watching her drive with abandon. Twice she was almost in an accident. He was sweating by the time she'd pulled into Kirkpatrick's Bakery. And he knew then that he couldn't fall for Holly. If he did, he'd never have another moment's peace.

Nine

Two days later Joe still hadn't called.

Why would he? Holly asked herself. She'd called him a coward and driven him away. No man wanted to face his own weakness, much less be with a woman who pointed it out. Hadn't she learned anything from her brothers?

Joe wasn't the only one who was hiding. She'd worked late at the bakery the first day, and then spent the night at her dad's house because the boys couldn't be there. Deep inside she knew she'd been hiding from Joe the first day.

Still, he hadn't tried to get in touch.

He had to be running scared. She'd felt the same way after she'd left him. The entire morning at the bakery she'd taken her frustration out on the rolls and bread. Instead of using the new kneading machine, she'd kneaded by hand, hoping to clear her mind by putting her hands to work.

But her mind still wasn't clear. Joe was an enigma and she wasn't going to be satisfied until she understood what made him tick. He made her feel like more than some fairy-tale princess. He made her believe that dreams were still viable and sometimes really did come true. She wasn't going to give him up that easily.

Holly had called his office twice. Once, early in the morning, he'd been in a meeting. The second time he'd been in the office but unable to take her call. Since she didn't know where he lived, she made the decision to go and wait in the lobby for Joe.

She got there just after five and watched the building empty of workers. Joe's car was still parked in his reserved spot. She left her car and walked to the doors.

She wasn't sure she'd made the right choice in coming. She told herself to stay home. To respect his silence and let go. But Joe had touched a place deep inside her where she'd never been touched before, and letting go wasn't an option.

Baronessa's executive headquarters were near the Prudential Center on Huntington Avenue. She had no reason to be in this part of town. She couldn't pretend she was in the neighborhood and decided to drop by. Besides, she didn't want to be dishonest.

Entering the building, she wasn't sure what to do. Hang out in the lobby until he left? What if one of the security guards asked her what she was doing here?

That would be too embarrassing and way too weird for her. She turned to leave but stopped when she saw all the pictures on the wall. There were plaques, as well, for all the awards Baronessa had won over the years for their gelato.

It seemed odd that after so many years in the business they'd have problems with one of their flavors as they had earlier this year. But a part of her was very grateful they had, otherwise she wouldn't have won their new-flavor contest and met Joe.

Small brass plates under each picture detailed the people in them. Joe's history was here. On this wall he passed every day was his life. She studied it, looking for clues as to why he was running from her.

"Holly?"

She turned. Joe looked every inch the business executive in his Hugo Boss suit and sedate tie. Signs of fatigue were visible around his eyes. He watched her wearily and she wondered again if she'd made the right decision.

"Hi, Joe."

"What are you doing here?" he asked. He took a step closer to her as the elevator opened and a group of people moved by them.

Taking a deep breath, she said, "I got tired of waiting for your call."

The elevator emptied again and more people streamed past them. Holly felt their curious gazes on her as they walked by. Okay, this really was a bad idea.

"I'm sorry. I shouldn't have come."

She started toward the lobby doors, but Joe's hand on her shoulder stopped her. She could feel the heat from his touch right through her thin rayon sundress. It radiated downward from her shoulder, spreading gooseflesh along her arm and tightening her nipples.

This was why she'd come. She missed his touch. She missed his eyes, so dark and guarded but burning with desire.

"Let's go someplace private where we can talk," Joe said.

"Do you have time?" Holly asked.

He cupped her elbow and led her toward the elevators. "Yes."

"I tried to call earlier."

"It's been a crazy couple of days," he said.

They entered the elevator and Joe hit the button for five.

"Is that why you didn't call?"

He glanced at her. His hand was now on her elbow, his fingers rubbing slowly back and forth, making thinking nearly impossible.

"No."

"Maybe I shouldn't have come today," she said, tugging free of his grasp.

"I'm glad you did."

"Why?"

"Because I just realized how much I've missed you."

"Really?"

He nodded.

"Then why didn't you call me?" she asked angrily.

He hit the emergency-stop button. "I know you're upset with me and you have every right to be. But dammit, woman—"

"Don't swear at me."

He pulled her into his arms and bent his head, whispering words she couldn't understand. But her soul understood the message in his embrace. He held her so closely and so tightly that she thought he didn't ever want to let go. She held him just as securely, realizing that maybe he wanted her as much as she wanted him. Maybe he needed her in his life as much as she needed him. Despite the comfort of his arms, that scared the hell out of her.

Joe held Holly tighter to him, realizing as he did so that the frozen barrier he'd used to protect his heart was melting. After being cold and alone for so long, he'd finally found the woman who could waken him. His Persephone bringing spring.

His feelings roared through him, laying waste to the excuses he'd used to keep his distance from her. The reasons he'd been using to justify taking this woman and making her his and then not calling. Laying waste to the lies he'd used to protect himself. In one minute he realized that he hadn't protected himself at all.

He bent and took her mouth in a kiss that said all the things he was afraid to say out loud. She responded reluctantly, it seemed to him. He leaned against the wall of the elevator and held her tighter, then lifted her off her feet and thrust his tongue deep in her mouth.

She moaned, tilted her head to the side and cupped his face with her hands. Those small, slender hands that had wrought magic on his frozen soul.

Arousal rushed through him—strong, powerful and unwilling to be denied. He shifted his legs, lifted her higher into the cradle of his thighs. Her legs parted and he was nestled against the center of her. Damn, she went to his head faster than ninety-proof whiskey. He set her aside before he did something really foolish like taking her in the elevator.

Ah, hell, he needed to get away from the office. To bring her to a place where they could work out the details of this relationship they were in. Because he'd realized as he'd seen her standing alone staring at pictures of his family that he wanted her by his side for the rest of his days.

He just didn't know how to keep her.

His hands were shaking and he felt like a weak man. What he felt for Holly was wildly different than anything he'd experienced before.

"What does this mean, Joe?" she asked.

Her lips were still red from his kiss, her lower lip a little swollen and her skin flushed with the first blush of sexual excitement. Concentrating on her words was hard, but he forced himself to do so, knowing that they needed to talk.

"It means so many things," he said, though he didn't feel confident to list them. He was more confident of Holly's reactions.

"That kiss felt like the beginning of something very hot and very carnal."

He gave her a wicked grin. "You do that to me. Will you come home with me, Holly?"

"For sex?" she asked, crossing her arms over her chest.

He tried to see this situation from her viewpoint but he couldn't. He was a man and he wanted her. But she was supposed to be the perceptive one. Women were supposed to understand feelings men had trouble vocalizing. Why wasn't she doing that? Why didn't she understand that it was a heck of a lot more than just sex when they were together?

"Stop saying 'sex' as if the physical act is all that's between us."

"Well, let's review the facts. Fact one—you didn't call me for two days. Fact two—as soon as we're together again you kiss me like you want a quickie in the elevator."

He clenched his hands. "I want a hell of a lot more than that. And I think you know it."

"I've given up second-guessing you, Joe. I'd have

wagered all the money I won in the Baronessa contest that you were going to call me. I don't understand anything about you.''

''Understand this. If I wanted sex I could have it with any number of women. But I've never wanted a cold act between two strangers. The other night when we *made love,* you touched my soul, woman.'' He took her face in his hands and kissed her with all the feelings in his soul and realized that if he had to let her go he'd be a shattered man.

She stared at him, her eyes wide and her mouth open the slightest bit. He knew she had to be mad because he hadn't called. But explanations would take time. And he didn't want to do that at work where his family could interrupt them at any moment.

''Please, come home with me,'' he said.

''Why?''

''I have things to say to you that I can only say there.''

She watched him, eyes questioning but burning with a hope that he felt in his soul. He wasn't sure how but he knew he'd fallen in love with her. The moment they'd met he'd known there was something special about her. Something that no other woman held. But it was two short nights ago, when she'd taken his hand and led him to her bedroom, that he'd realized she'd found the soft underbelly he'd always hidden.

Realized that this woman had the power to heal a

hurt he'd never known he'd been carrying with him. And that realization was the kind that crippled a man.

He didn't want to have to acknowledge that she'd become a part of him that he couldn't live without. Wasn't sure he was ready to let another woman past his defenses. Because if Mary's death had taught him one thing, it was that fate was fickle.

He realized he was holding his breath as he awaited Holly's answer. He looked at her beseechingly.

"Okay." It was all she said, but it was the word he was longing to hear.

He released the emergency-stop button and then pushed the lobby button. He held Holly's hand tightly in his, barely able to wait until the ride was over to get to his house.

"Do you want to leave your car here?" he asked.

"No, I'll follow you."

"I promise you won't regret it."

"Don't make promises you might not keep."

"I'm not."

He walked away and felt her gaze on him all the way to his car. His hands shook, and he realized that more than lust and love were riding him. There was also the very real fear that Holly might love him back.

Holly followed Joe to his house. His neighborhood was newer than hers and more exclusive, having a security guard at a gated entrance. The guard waved her through. Each house was beautiful, each yard neatly landscaped. From where she sat it looked like a perfect world—and one she could never fit into.

As she followed Joe's sedan she realized that their lives were worlds apart. She didn't see a way they could ever really be together.

Each of these houses probably cost five times hers. Aside from the financial aspects, her family needed her. She couldn't imagine Joe wanting to spend the night in her childhood bedroom, because her father couldn't be left alone at night.

Joe pulled into a three-car garage and Holly parked in the driveway. Joe walked toward her and opened her door. But she just sat there, staring up at him.

Whatever had happened in the elevator had freed him. It had almost paralyzed her when she realized she would have had sex with him again even though he'd avoided her for two days. Even though only an hour earlier she wasn't sure she'd ever hear from him again. It scared her to think he meant that much to her. And that her own self-esteem meant so little.

But Joe went to her head and her heart. From her past she'd learned that men like Roger would take from her whatever she was willing to give. But Joe was the first guy who cherished her. He'd sent her flowers and taken her to a romantic restaurant. He'd played basketball with her and let her see his vulnerable side.

"Holly?" His voice reached through her thoughts.

"I'm not sure why I'm here," she said.

"Because we need each other," he said.

"We do?"

He nodded. She climbed out of her car and before she could move, he picked her up and carried her toward his house.

"Why are you carrying me?" she asked. No man had ever carried her before. She clung to his shoulders and tried not to think about the fact that he was fulfilling her secret dreams.

"Because you need romance."

How did he know? It made her vulnerable to realize that he saw things she thought she'd hidden. That he didn't look at her and see a strong person who could support and shelter her family. That he might be the one man who saw straight to her soul. Because Joe wasn't the kind of man she could protect herself from. She'd become aware of that when she'd driven to his office.

"Do you need romance too?" she asked. She wanted to be his equal not the needy one.

"Oh, yeah."

She forgot about her worries as he carried her over the threshold of his house and set her on her feet. Fresh flowers sat in a vase on the table in his foyer. The marble entryway led to a grand staircase. She should be dressed to the nines instead of wearing a three-year-old sundress. "I wish I were wearing something more appropriate."

"I wish you were nude."

That surprised a chuckle out of her. "Joe."

"It's the truth, but I promised you we'd talk, so perhaps it's better you are clothed."

His place was professionally decorated, immaculately clean and, she saw as he flicked on the lights, very much like the man himself. At first glance the modern furniture with sleek lines appeared smooth and sophisticated. But the dark and disturbing realism in art showed the real man.

"Should I remove my shoes?"

"Only if you want to."

She slid out of them because, unless she was mistaken, he had Berber carpet and she loved the way it felt under her feet.

He led her into the living room. Through a wall of glass she saw a deck that overlooked a large swimming pool complete with a waterfall at one end.

"Please sit down," he said.

She seated herself on the love seat and watched Joe pace the room. Whatever he had to say he was nervous about it.

"I'm sorry I didn't call you," he began.

"Why didn't you?"

"When Mary died my life changed."

"What does that have to do with not calling me?"

"I'm not good with words. But I'll try to explain," he said.

"That's all I ask."

"I vowed to never again feel defenseless."

"In what way?"

"Emotionally. I'm not comfortable talking about

my feelings, Holly. So I'm not going to say this again.''

She went to him, put her arms around his broad shoulders. There was a part of Joe that he didn't want her to see but he showed her anyway. Despite her earlier accusation, she knew this man wasn't a coward.

''I'm afraid of love,'' he whispered against her hair.

She held him tighter. ''Why?''

''Because of the heartache it can bring.''

''Love doesn't always end that way.''

''In my experience it does.''

''I've never experienced love,'' Holly said at last.

''Why not?''

''I don't know. I think, like you, I've been afraid of it.''

''When I saw you waiting for me this afternoon...you seemed so brave and unafraid.''

''Don't let appearances fool you. I was shaking in my boots.''

''That's just it. You were scared but you'd come to find me. And I knew then I couldn't let you get away again.''

Holly's heart froze in her chest. What was he saying? Oh, God. She didn't want to hear whatever he planned to say next. He opened his mouth but she went up on tiptoe and covered his lips with hers.

Ten

Joe had always been the aggressor in all his relationships. That was what had enabled him to keep others at bay for so long. And not just in his relationships with the opposite sex. In all relationships he'd manipulated people in a way that allowed him to be comfortable.

With Holly it had been because she was as leery as he was and they both needed time to adjust.

He wanted to tell Holly how he felt about her but she'd kissed him in a way that made thinking stop and feeling begin. Two days had been too long. He wanted to take her to bed and keep her there until neither of them had any strength left.

"We'll talk more later," he said, lifting her off

her feet and carrying her upstairs to his bedroom. "It feels like it's been years since I buried myself in you."

She wrapped her arms around him and toyed with the hair at the back of his neck. "For me too."

There was something different about Holly. He couldn't put his finger on it but he'd figure it out. She whispered seductive promises in his ear as he carried her, and by the time he'd reached his bedroom he was rock hard and ready for her.

Unlike the rest of the house, his bedroom wasn't immaculate. A big-screen TV dominated one wall and his king-size bed the other.

He tossed her on the bed and followed her down, covering her body with his. But she stopped him, holding him at bay. "I'm in charge this time."

The thought brought him to his knees. He rolled onto his back and waited for her to make her move. She stood at the foot of the bed and removed her clothing with carefully measured movements. Her eyes never left his.

He reached for the buttons on his shirt but she shook her head. "Not yet, I'll get your clothes in a minute."

He propped two pillows behind his head and watched her through narrowed eyes as naked now, she removed his shoes and socks. Then she climbed up on the bed and unfastened his belt, tugging it free of his pants. She unbuttoned his shirt and pushed it down his arms. Joe flung it across the room.

She walked her fingers down his chest and then slid one under his waistband. He was so painfully hard now that he was afraid he'd come when she touched his zipper.

"Holly, no more. I need you now." He needed to bury himself in her again. He wanted to seal the two of them together so that nothing could come between them. Not fate, not family, not anything.

"Please, Joe. I want to make love to you."

He clenched his fists, reaching for the control he'd always had in the past. But everything was different with Holly. "I'll try."

"That's all I ask," she said, lowering his zipper and pushing his pants down his legs. He kicked his feet free of them and lay tensely waiting for her to make her next move. She took him in her slender hands, holding him carefully.

He had to touch her. He caressed the curve of her buttocks, the long line of her legs, the weight of her breasts. "I can't hold out much longer."

She gave him a seductive smile. "Waiting makes everything better."

"You've got thirty seconds, then I'm in charge."

"We'll see about that," she said, lowering her head and taking him in her mouth.

Everything inside him clenched. Just the sight of Holly with her red hair brushing his thighs and her mouth moving so passionately on him was enough to bring him to the edge. But he wasn't going over without her.

He tugged her up and over him, brought her mouth to his and tasted himself on her. She rocked against him, her humid warmth making him realize that he didn't have a condom. He almost didn't care.

He wanted to feel her naked flesh on his. Wanted to experience only Holly without any barriers. Not the ones in his heart or the ones on his body.

But he knew they weren't ready for the consequences that making love without a condom could bring. He stretched for the nightstand and opened the drawer.

"Let me," she said.

He didn't know if he'd be able to bear her hands on him again. He was so close to the edge. Only the look on her face as she tore open the packet and covered him in one long caress made it possible for him to wait. "Come here, Holly."

He pulled her over him, held her hips firmly and thrust up into her. She threw her head back and gripped his shoulders. Her nails bit into his flesh in a way that made him feel good. Something more than a physical act was taking place between them.

He lifted his head and took her nipple in his mouth, teasing her with his tongue and then suckling deeply. She moaned and started rocking faster against him. Using his grip on her hips, he slowed the pace. Now that he was inside her he wanted to take his time. He needed to drive them both crazy with wanting before they reached the ultimate satisfaction.

''Joe, hurry,'' she said.

''Uh-uh, now I'm in charge,'' he said with a wicked grin.

Leaning forward, she found the pulse beating at the base of his neck with her mouth. She suckled strongly and he felt his control snap. His grip on her hips changed. He thrust heavily into her. Once and then twice. She called his name and he felt her body tightening rhythmically around his. He thrust into her one more time and let his orgasm wash over him.

Holly collapsed on his chest and he held her tightly to him, knowing he'd never let her go.

She had to go.

That was Holly's first awareness when she woke in Joe's bed the next morning. Careful not to disturb him, she dressed quickly while he slept and left. It scared her—how much he was coming to mean to her. She wasn't ready for that kind of all-consuming relationship in her life.

The bakery was busy, so Holly didn't pay any attention when Colleen, the manager, entered the kitchen. ''There's a man here to see you.''

''Who?'' she asked. It was busier than usual for a Friday, thanks to a feature in the *Boston Globe* food section this week. More people were here to sample their pastries.

''I don't know. He's tall, dark and Italian.''

Joe. ''Tell him I'm busy.''

''Too late,'' Joe said from the doorway.

"I really can't talk right now, Joe."

"Then listen."

She glanced warily at him. Colleen left the kitchen and Holly slid the tray of cream puffs into the oven and returned to the counter where she was in the process of frosting a wedding cake.

"Can I call you later?" Holly asked. She didn't like to have different areas of her world colliding. Joe belonged to her and her alone. Now that he'd been here Colleen would want to talk about him. Then, when he didn't want to see her anymore, Colleen would want to analyze it. Holly preferred to keep her relationships to herself.

He moved toward her. Darn it. He'd obviously come from the office and she wished he looked stuffy in a business suit instead of handsome and sexy. Seeing him so neat and put together made her remember what he'd looked like underneath her last night, his face flushed with desire and his body ready for hers.

Joe shook his head. "I'd say yes but I get the feeling you're avoiding me. I thought you'd forgiven me for not calling."

"I did."

"Then what's up?"

"I'm at work, Joe."

"I know. Can't you take a break for ten minutes? We can go out back and talk."

Holly checked the timer on the cream puffs and looked at the cake. "I've only got five minutes."

"I'll take it."

She led the way out the back door to the battered picnic table in the alley that she and Colleen sometimes ate lunch at. A warm afternoon breeze blew through the alleyway, stirring the hair at the back of her neck.

Joe gave her a light kiss and pulled back quickly. "There's a lot I have to say to you, Holly, but this isn't the place for it."

"I know. I'm sorry we're so crazy here today," she said. Joe looked like a man with a mission and it scared her to think she might be what he was focusing on. He had an intensity that frightened her sometimes.

"Will you have dinner with me tonight?" he asked, holding her hand lightly in his. He traced the pattern of her freckles up her arm until they disappeared under her sleeve. His touch made her shiver and everything feminine in her clenched and softened.

She wanted to. But she was afraid of the emotion she saw in his eyes. She didn't want to know how he felt or hear things that would tempt her to break her commitment to her family. "I can't. My brothers are all going out and I promised my dad I'd stay with him."

His dark-chocolate gaze met hers. "I'd love to meet your dad."

For all his money, Joe was a very basic guy, and her dad and brothers would like him. Too bad they could never meet. "I don't think that's a good idea."

"Why not? You've met my family," he said.

She didn't want to tell him the truth. That she didn't want him to meet her family because once he did then she might have to choose between them. A lover demanded a few hours of her time, but a man who'd met the family, who wanted to spend the evening with her and her dad, that was a man who'd want more than late-night hours. And she didn't have that to give.

She gave him a stock reply. "Dad can be surly and he hasn't been feeling well. Maybe another time."

He watched her and she felt as if he could see past her half truth to the heart of the matter. She was tempted to hold her breath until he said, "If you're sure."

"I am." She forced a tight smile and changed the subject. "Isn't tomorrow your family's big reunion?"

"Yes. Will you come with me? The picnic will be a lot of fun and I'm sure we can avoid the press."

"Why do you want me to come?" she asked.

"You're important to me, Holly."

"It scares me to hear you say that," she admitted. It also made her heart fill with those impossible dreams she'd been having since he'd taken her to his house and let her make love to him. She'd never touched a man the way she'd touched Joe. Never felt so close to another person and never wanted to share her burdens with another person. Until Joe.

"Why?" he asked.

"I can't talk about it now. I've got to get back to work." Besides, before she explained her feelings to him, she had to work them out for herself.

"Will you go with me tomorrow?" he asked.

She wanted to spend the day with him. To meet his family again and see Joe in the environment where he was most at ease. One last day, she thought, then she'd break it off with him. "Yes. I'd like that."

"Good. I'll pick you up in the morning. It's an all-day thing with fireworks after dark."

"Okay," she said.

She started back toward the kitchen.

"Holly?"

"Yes."

"I know you're running. And eventually I'm going to catch you."

The family picnic was held at his parents' town house in Beacon Hill. Joe always loved going to his folks' place especially when the family was all there. Last night, sitting in his empty house alone, he'd realized what Holly needed to stop running from him. She needed him to make a commitment to her. In the beginning he'd been the aloof one and Holly the outgoing one. Now, however, she kept a part of herself walled off from him. A part of her that was very soft and very vulnerable.

But after today neither of them would have to be

alone any longer. Because today he planned to ask Holly to marry him.

After leaving her at the bakery yesterday afternoon, he'd realized that he had to show Holly that he regretted not calling her and that he meant for her place in his life to be a permanent one. He'd gone to the jewelry store and purchased a marquise-cut engagement ring for her.

He glanced into the rearview mirror for a glimpse in the back seat. It contained a change of clothes, which he'd no doubt need after the annual male versus female volleyball game. More important, it contained the ring.

Holly was waiting on the porch when he pulled up in front of her house. She wore khaki shorts cut high on her thigh, a slim-fitting sleeveless white shirt and deck shoes. She took his breath away. It amazed him to think that she was his woman.

She walked toward the car and he got out to open the door for her. She smiled when she saw him but she seemed tired and tense.

"Is your dad okay?"

"Yes, he's fine."

He took her in his arms and kissed her the way he'd wanted to yesterday at the bakery. She rose on tiptoe, wrapping her slender arms around him and holding him tightly to her. "Damn, I wish we could skip this thing and spend the day here in your bed."

"We can't?"

"No. This is a command performance for the

press. All Barones must be present and accounted for.''

''Flint and Gina again?''

''Yes,'' Joe said with a wry grin.

''Well, then, let's get going. I'd hate for you to get in trouble.''

''My folks have a spa tub at their place. Why don't you bring your swimsuit and a change of clothes.''

Holly ran inside and was back out in a flash. The drive to his parents' place went quickly, but as they neared the house, traffic became heavy and Joe knew from the past that parking would be hard to find.

''Do you mind walking from here? It's about three blocks.''

''No. It's a nice day.''

''Good. It'll give us time to talk.''

''Okay,'' she said.

Joe parked the car and they both got out. Holly carried her straw beach bag and Joe his duffel. He put his free arm around her waist and kept his pace shorter to match hers. It was the first time in a long time that he felt at peace with himself and the world around him. He saw the beauty of the summer day and the beauty of life with Holly by his side.

''I've been thinking about our relationship,'' she said.

''Me too.''

''I wasn't expecting you, Joe.''

He smiled down at her. ''Me neither, but I'm glad I found you, Holly.''

"Really?"

This woman needed to realize her own importance to those around her. She was so giving and caring, he doubted she understood how deeply she affected the people she interacted with. "Really."

He dropped a kiss on her lips.

"Hey, Joe."

He turned to see Nick standing behind him, carrying two bags. His eldest brother looked happier than Joe could remember seeing him in years. But then the love of a good woman could do that to a man.

"Nick, this is Holly Fitzgerald. Holly, this is my oldest brother, Nick."

"Nice to meet you," Holly said.

"The pleasure's all mine. I'd stay and chat, but I've got to get this ice to Dad," Nick said.

"We ran out already?" Joe asked. His father was meticulous in the planning of the family reunion.

"No, there was an accident with one of the coolers, so we needed a few more bags."

"Where's Gail?" Joe asked, looking for his brother's wife.

"With the women, planning volleyball strategy."

"Oh, they think they can win this year?"

"I believe so," Nick said as he disappeared around the corner of the house. "What's this about volleyball?" Holly asked Joe.

"We have an annual grudge match, boys versus girls."

"Who's ahead?"

"We're tied but the boys won last year."

"Should be interesting," Holly said.

"It should be. Come on, let me introduce you to everybody." Joe deposited their bags on the patio and put his arm around Holly. He'd been alone so long that he'd forgotten how good it felt to have someone special by his side.

His cousin Daniel was here and brought his friend Ashraf ibn-Saalem. Holly waited until they moved away from the friends before she said, "Ash looks strong. The boys might have an unfair advantage if he plays."

"Reese and Alex are both not here this year, so Ash will even the playing field. Besides, the girls have Gail on their team."

"Listen to you. Is she their secret weapon?"

"She might be. She plays on a coed team. Besides, the women in this family are tricky."

"Watch it, Joe. Mom might hear you," Gina said from behind them. She smiled a greeting at Holly. "Hello, Holly. Want to help us teach the Barone men a lesson?"

Holly returned the smile. "I might enjoy that."

Joe groaned. "Is Flint playing?"

"I don't think so. He's got the press to wrangle with."

"Why aren't you with the press?" Joe asked.

"Who'd give you a hard time if it wasn't me?" Gina asked with a smile.

Joe turned toward Holly. "Hey, help me out here."

"I think you're doing fine," she said, laughing up at him.

Joe looked at her and felt a confidence he hadn't felt in a long time. He was in love with Holly Fitzgerald and he couldn't wait to make her his wife.

Eleven

Holly, at Gina's urging, joined the women's team for the volleyball match. Joe was sexier than any man ought to be in gym shorts and no shirt. His chest muscles rippled as he tossed the ball in the air before the game began and caught it. It was a hot late-July day and most of the women wore bikini tops and shorts, Holly included.

On the sidelines cheering the teams on was Alex Barone's new wife, Daisy, with her new baby, Angel. Everyone knew the baby's biological father wasn't Alex, but he was the only daddy Angel would know. And it was clear from what Holly had heard that Alex adored his daughter and his wife.

The baby was so cute that Holly had been tempted

to ask to hold her. But this wasn't her family so she'd watched from the sidelines, feeling a heaviness in her heart that this clan wasn't her own.

Though there was a good deal of ribbing, it was clear this year the Barone women weren't going home losers. Joe huddled close with the men's team, and as Holly watched him, she understood the missing piece of the puzzle he was to her.

Seeing him with his family, watching him move and interact with them, made one thing crystal clear: Joe wasn't meant to be a single guy. He was meant to be a family man. He played with Nicholas's toddler daughter, Molly, as if she was his own.

Did Joe want kids? Despite the closeness they shared, she knew little of his dreams for the future. Holly was amazed. For the first time she actually wanted to think about a future with a man.

Though there were eight kids and four cousins, the Barones were a tight-knit clan. She suddenly wanted to learn more about them all.

"You all are descended from two Barone brothers?" Holly asked Gina right before the game started.

"My uncle Paul is a twin. When they were two days old, Uncle Luke was abducted and never found. The family was shaken by that," Gina said.

"How horrible for your family."

"It was. But that was a long time ago." After a few minutes, Gina remarked, "Joe seems happy today."

Holly wasn't sure she wanted to have this conversation. She wasn't sure she herself knew what was going on with Joe. "Yes, he does."

Gina said nothing for a few minutes, watching her family and friends mill around the backyard. "It's about time."

Holly didn't want her to have the wrong impression. "Gina, we— Things aren't— Look, your brother and I are just friends."

Gina put her hand on Holly's arm. "I think friends is a good place to start."

Holly felt tears sting the back of her eyes. She'd always wanted sisters just to even the score in her family, but now she realized what she'd missed. Holly stood at the sidelines, watching the Barones interact, feeling a keen sense of longing that she'd never felt before.

Though her family was close, that closeness was tinged by a sense of duty and obligation. She'd promised her mother that she'd take care of the boys and keep the family together. She'd never really felt comfortable relaxing around her family the way she did here today with the Barones.

"Ready to get your butt kicked?" Joe asked, coming up and putting his arms around her. Most of the Barones were taking a last-minute break before the game started. Carlo and Moira, Joe's parents, had chairs set up on either side of the court, and those who weren't playing were on the sidelines already.

"Hardly. According to Gina, the men are better at fireworks than volleyball."

"Really?" he asked, running his finger down the side of her face. She shivered as awareness lit a fire that ended in the pit of her belly.

"Yup," she said, giving in to the urge to caress his stomach. His muscles rippled in response and his eyes narrowed. She recognized the gleam in them as a purely sexual one.

"I beg to differ. Fireworks are all flash."

Joe was different today. Lighter somehow. No longer aloof and brooding but almost happy. It scared her to think she might be responsible for the change because that meant she'd have to be responsible for keeping him happy and she didn't know if she could do it. She had enough to worry about with Dad's health and her brothers' lives.

"Are you trying to say there's more than flash to you?" she asked, still teasing him. He'd pulled her more fully against him so that only an inch of space separated their bodies. She could scarcely breathe as she stood there wishing they were in a private place so she could caress him as she longed to. Why had she decided to turn him down for dinner last night?

The reasons, which had seemed so relevant yesterday, paled as she stood trembling in his arms. Joe tilted her head back with his hand, and as she gazed up at him she felt her heart lurch. She realized in that moment that she loved him. Loved his tough-as-nails side, loved his soft side where his family was concerned and most especially loved the way he made her feel—as if she was the most beautiful woman on earth.

"I think you know there is," he said softly.

Bracing her hands on his shoulders, she stood on tiptoe so their lips were only a breath apart. "Maybe."

He brushed his lips against hers and then pulled back. "Maybe?"

She just raised one eyebrow at him.

"What do you think of this?"

He bent his head and kissed her in a way that left no doubt there was something very solid about Joe Barone. And that he wasn't just a quick burst of bright lights.

Catcalls and whistles broke through the spell Joe was effortlessly weaving around her. He pulled back and gave her a tight hug before walking toward the men's team. Holly went to join the women, feeling more dazed and confused than she ever had before. Something magical had taken shape between them. But could magic last the rigors of her everyday life?

As the sun began to set, Joe took the ring he'd purchased for Holly from his gym bag and went searching for her. His sister Maria had gotten sick during the volleyball game and was now sitting on a lounge chair with a cup of Sprite. She seemed a little pale to Joe, but his sister Rita, who was a nurse, ruled the episode as heat exhaustion.

Even without Maria's help the women had beaten

the men in the first match. The second match, the men had come back. The tie breaking game had been when Maria had gotten sick, but even without her, the women had beaten the men, making them the new Barone family volleyball champions. The women had done their victory dance and earned bragging rights for the coming year.

But there was only one woman he was interested in now. Where was Holly? Joe started toward his brother Nick to ask him if he'd seen her, but then realized Nick and his cousin Derrick were having a heated discussion. He turned instead to the cluster of women by the food table.

"Have you seen Holly?" he asked his mom.

"No, dear, I haven't. But I meant to tell you, I really like her," she said.

"Me too," said Emily, his cousin. She'd been going through a rough spot, having amnesia and witnessing the fire that had been started at the Baronessa factory. But being outside today with her fiancé, Shane, she seemed happy. Shane had been a great addition to the Barone men's team.

"She's not like Mary," his mom added.

His mother was right. Mary had always been fragile, never able to participate in any of the family activities. She was always on the sidelines, watching, while Holly was in the middle of the action, a part of the group.

"Dad's looking for you, Joe. You're needed at the fireworks bunker," said Gina.

"If you see Holly, tell her I need to talk to her."

"I will," his mom said.

Joe joined his father, uncle Paul, his brothers and male cousins at the fireworks bunker. They worked quickly to set the fuses and ready the explosives for the annual display. The new men in the family were there too, fitting easily into the group of joking men.

Joe worked at his father's side, realizing that he wanted a son to pass on this tradition to. He wanted to share his family's customs with his kids and make sure they took pride in them and passed them on to their kids.

It was a humbling moment. He hadn't thought about the future in so long that he'd been locked in the present. Asking Holly to marry him today wasn't just something he was doing for himself and Holly. It was something he was doing for his family.

When everything was set, he headed back toward the house and found Holly standing with the women. He took her hand and led her away from everyone. He found a bench nestled in the corner of his mother's garden. Carefully, he seated Holly on the bench and sat down next to her.

"Did you have fun today?" he asked. He wanted to make sure his family hadn't overwhelmed her.

"I did. Your family is wonderful," she said.

"They are. I have something important to say to you, Holly."

She tilted her head to look at him. Her eyes were dreamy. "What?"

Wrapping his arms around her, he took a deep breath. Now that she was in his arms, all the vulnerabilities he had came rushing back. Love was a risk he'd fought taking for a long time.

But this was Holly. The woman who'd freed him from the deep, frozen place his life had become. The woman who'd lit a fire in his blood and sent those flames through his soul. The woman who'd made him realize he wanted to dream again.

"I love you," he whispered against the top of her head.

He felt her shudder. She pulled back and looked up at him, her eyes wide with fear and something else. A knot formed in the pit of his stomach.

She was probably worried that he wasn't ready to make a commitment to her. He eased off the bench and went down on one knee, fumbling in his pocket for the ring.

She started to speak, but he covered her lips with his hand. "Part of me died with Mary, Holly. And I thought I'd never find a reason to love again. But you showed me what I'd been missing. You made me realize how lonely life was."

She reached out and cupped his jaw. "You weren't lonely. You had your family."

"You're right, I did. But I needed more."

"What did you need?" she asked.

"I needed you. Holly, will you marry me?"

Holly gulped and fought back tears. He *loved* her. No one had said those words to her since her mother died. And never had she needed to hear them as much as she did now.

She couldn't control the thrill that speared through her or the sudden tightness in her throat. These twin responses made it impossible for her to speak for a few minutes.

This was the one thing she wanted and dreaded. She couldn't marry Joe. Couldn't possibly become Mrs. Joe Barone because he didn't know the real Holly. He'd never even met her family. And her family was her first duty. A long time ago she'd made promises at her mother's deathbed that she'd make sure the Fitzgeralds were always together. They needed her 24/7, and if she lived up to that commitment to them, she couldn't take another vow with Joe.

She didn't realize she was crying until she felt the moisture on her face. She pulled her hands from his and wiped her cheeks. She didn't face the other truth that lay beneath her obligation to her family. Joe made her feel emotions that were uncomfortable. They were the extremes of her soul. He made her want to be daring in ways she'd never anticipated.

"Joe, I..."

Suddenly she couldn't do it. She couldn't sit here and tell him no in front of his family. But marrying him would be a mistake, for both of them, she wasn't going to make.

"I'm sorry," she said. She stood and ran from him as if demons were chasing her.

She reached the street and realized she had no way of getting home. She'd ridden to the picnic with Joe. She took her cell phone from her pocket and called her eldest brother, Clint. He promised to come and get her. But she had to hang out for fifteen minutes.

Joe didn't follow her and she didn't blame him. What kind of woman had soul-sex with a man then turned him down when he asked her to marry him? She didn't like the answers she found deep inside. She sat on the stoop waiting for Clint, wondering if she'd ever really be able to share her life with anyone.

More important, she wondered if she'd ever come to terms with her hang-ups. Because the real reason she'd run away from Joe wasn't her family. The real reason was that she knew life was fragile. She knew how quickly and how unfairly fate could change. One minute you were the cherished daughter of a happily married couple, the next minute you were the only woman in your family and had enormous responsibilities.

"Holly?"

She glanced over her shoulder at Joe, standing in the front doorway of his parents' house. He was backlit by the wall sconces in the foyer, making it impossible to see his expression. Life had dealt Joe enough heartache, she thought. He shouldn't have fallen in love with her.

"I'm sorry," she said again. She didn't know what else to say. She hadn't expected love. It seemed this relationship of theirs had started out as a one-night stand but then turned into something she still couldn't define.

"Is this anything we can work out?" he asked.

She wished. But asking him to wait a few years for her didn't seem like much of a solution. "I don't think so."

"Is it me?" he asked at last.

"Oh, Joe. No, it's not you." She laced her fingers together to keep from reaching out for him.

"Holly, I'm trying to be patient and understanding—two things I'm not known for."

"I appreciate it." She wished her brother would show up. She didn't like the direction this conversation was going.

"Then give me some explanations," he said.

"Listen, my family needs me. I'm the glue that holds them together. I can't walk away from that."

He sighed and rubbed his jaw. "Believe it or not, I wasn't asking you to cut off your relationship with them."

"I know. Only it's a full-time job. I have to spend the night at my dad's house occasionally. I have to finish paying for Brian's last year of college. I have to—"

"You don't have to do that stuff."

"If I don't, who will?"

"Those brothers of yours aren't children anymore. They can take care of themselves."

"I know they aren't babies."

"Then why do you insist on treating them like they are?" he asked.

"I don't."

"You do and I think I know why."

"What makes you such an expert on my life?"

He narrowed his gaze on her and she shivered under the intensity there. "I know you intimately, Holly. I think that counts for something."

"Physical knowledge doesn't give you any insight."

"The hell it doesn't. You don't share yourself easily and you're crazy if you think I don't know it."

She hugged herself to keep from exploding into a million pieces. But didn't say anything, only waited to hear what else he thought he knew about her.

"You accused me once of being a coward. I just realized that I wasn't the only one who was running away."

"I'm not."

"You are. You're afraid to let yourself be happy."

"What makes you so confident you make me happy?"

"I'm not—at least not anymore."

Clint pulled to a stop at the curb and honked the horn. "That's my brother."

"Go ahead, run, I'm not stopping you. But if you decide you're tired of playing the martyr, give me a call."

Joe walked inside without another word. The sound of the door closing echoed in her heart and she knew she'd just thrown away her chance at happily-ever-after.

Twelve

Holly hadn't been able to sleep in her bed last night or on the couch. The memories of Joe were still too strong. So she'd grabbed the quilt she and her mother had made when Holly was thirteen, wrapped herself in that and slept in the Kennedy rocker on the back porch.

Sleep, she decided, was highly overrated.

Holly had always wanted to think of herself as daring, as taking risks that seemed to be exciting. But only yesterday, when she'd heard Joe ask her to marry him, did she realize that all those risks had been superficial.

When the time came for her to really put herself on the line, she'd ducked and run for cover. And she'd hurt the one man who'd made her feel like a woman. The one man who'd always treated her as if he cherished her. The one man who'd proven to be her Prince Charming.

The doorbell rang and Holly ignored it. There wasn't anyone she wanted to see this morning. Especially not one of her nosey neighbors.

"Holly, you home?" It was her father.

Darn it, he had a key. She pushed herself off the rocker and entered her house. Her dad and brothers dominated the small entryway. They all held something, her dad a carafe, which she knew would have coffee in it, Matt held the newspaper, Brian had a bag from Kirkpatrick's Bakery and Clint held a jug of orange juice.

She was touched. They'd brought her breakfast. They never had before. She blinked back tears. Hell, she was getting too emotional lately. Maybe her period was going to start soon. Or maybe she'd finally had her emotional gates battered down by a certain Italian and maybe, she thought, they weren't going back into place so easily.

"Morning, guys," she said.

She hugged her dad and brothers and they all settled at her kitchen table. In the middle of the table was the vase with the flowers Joe had sent.

The blooms were still flourishing, and seeing them made her feel like a big coward. Joe had lost way more than she ever had and yet he was willing to risk the pain of rejection again. Something she couldn't do. Even now, as much as she wanted to go to him, something kept her from doing it.

Something more than her family.

"What are you doing here this morning?" she asked, needing to forget about Joe and romantic gestures. She took the vase and moved it to the counter behind the canisters, out of her view.

"Have you seen the newspaper?" Clint asked. He took mugs from the rack on the wall and handed them around the table before filling each cup with the strong brew. Matt leaned back on his chair and opened the refrigerator and took out the milk.

Her brothers were tall and lean with auburn hair that they'd all inherited from their dad. Clint, the tallest, worked at a computer gaming company and seldom wore anything other than T-shirts with graphic designs and board shots. Matt was a bartender and wore a uniform of black T-shirts that molded to his chest and tight-fitting jeans because he said the ladies like his butt. Brian had a part-time entry-level job in an insurance company and wore button down shirts and chinos.

"No. I haven't. Is that why you all are here?"

No one said anything. Matt passed the paper to her. Holly just looked at it. The headlines hardly ever changed anymore.

"Check out page two."

She flipped it open and there was a picture of her and Joe at the picnic. She knew when it had been taken. Right before that damn volleyball game. She remembered the look on his face as he'd lowered his head to hers.

"Who is this guy, Holly?" Matt asked.

"Why haven't we met him?" Brian asked.

"Joe Barone. And because I don't have time for a serious relationship."

"These eyes might be old but that picture looks pretty serious to me," her dad, Dave, said.

She didn't realize how they'd appeared to anyone looking on. Joe was going to have to face the same questions from his family today. Did any of them know he'd proposed last night? Had any of the Barones seen them tucked away in his mom's garden?

Oh, God, she hoped not. Because after her conversation with Gina, she had a feeling the entire Barone clan might come after her when they realized how badly she'd hurt one of their own. "It's not serious anymore, Dad."

"Why not?" he asked.

Holly shrugged. The truth was hard to explain, especially since she knew she'd have to admit she was a chicken. "Because I still have commitments to you all and I can't give myself to him only halfway."

"Who asked you to?" her dad asked.

"Dad, you know I need to be available to you guys."

"Sweetheart, we're a family. That means we take care of each other."

She stared at her father and brothers stubbornly. She knew her job. They weren't the ones Mom had pulled close right before she'd died. They weren't the ones Mom had made promise to nurture and protect the family. They weren't the ones who'd ever noticed that without her the family would fall apart.

Her dad took a deep breath. "In that case, then, you're fired."

"What are you talking about?" Holly asked.

"Just what the old man said. You don't have to take care of us anymore," Matt said.

"Why not?"

Brian took her hand in his. "We grew up, Holly. Your job is done."

"What about Dad?" she asked. He was the one that she worried about. He needed someone to watch over him.

"What about me?" her dad asked.

"You're still not healthy," Holly said.

"There's no reason I can't be if I just follow the doctor's orders."

"But you never do," Holly said.

"Maybe it's time I did."

"Are you guys serious?" she asked at last.

"Yes." Clint spoke for them.

Everyone was quiet for a few minutes. Holly took a sip of her coffee, realizing that her family had given her the green light to go after Joe if she wanted to. Oh yeah, she wanted to. But would he take her back?

She'd have to take a big risk. She'd have to show him that her love for him was as deep as his was. He'd made a grand gesture—giving her the romance he thought she needed. Only, he needed the romance too.

"I hope we're going to get to meet this Joe Barone."

"Oh, Dad. I hope so too. But I hurt him pretty bad."

"How are you going to make it right?" Clint asked.

"I don't know."

She finished breakfast with her brothers and father. They talked about going fishing later. Holly tried to pay attention, but one thought kept rolling through her head. How was she going to convince Joe that she loved him and was ready to make a lifetime commitment to him?

Joe had made some bad choices in his life. Coming to dinner at his folks' the night after Holly turned down his proposal probably ranked up in the top three. But he'd felt that family guilt again, and his mom wouldn't take no for an answer.

He left their house and drove slowly back through the city. Boston at night was one of his favorite sights. It was still as busy and active as Boston during the day, only at night it seemed cleaner somehow, more mysterious. And he was the first to admit he loved a good mystery.

He also admitted to himself that Holly was still a mystery, which was probably why she'd turned him down. He'd asked only one other woman to marry him. He wasn't the type of person who gave himself easily, and it bothered him that she'd not given herself to him with the same depth.

His house was big and lonely and he didn't want to go back there without Holly. He didn't want to sleep in his king-size bed and feel that it was too big because there wasn't a tiny redhead nestled next to him on the mattress.

He'd slept in one of the guest bedrooms last night. The same one he'd used for six months after Mary had died. It was a sparsely decorated room with a narrow single bed and no memories. To be honest, he'd never thought to sleep in that room again. He'd put that part of his life behind him. Learned a hard lesson about caring. Apparently he wasn't as quick as he'd always thought, because Holly's rejection had caught him by surprise.

He'd hedged his bets by proposing to her with his family surrounding him. He'd counted on her caring for him enough to say yes while his family was close by. But he'd forgotten that Holly was a sassy woman and not one who made decisions easily.

Aside from the timing, which he thought most women would find romantic, he didn't regret asking her to marry him. His love for Holly had come unexpectedly. It seemed to him a man shouldn't have more than one shot at the brass ring. But having been given that second chance, he'd known better than to let it pass him by.

No, he didn't regret asking her to marry him. He

just wished he'd understood better why she'd turned him down. But he refused to spend any more time thinking about it. He was going home, getting drunk, and on Monday he'd worry about it again.

Maybe after he'd drunk the better part of a fifth of scotch he'd be able to sleep or at least pass out so that he wouldn't have to spend the long, lonely hours between now and dawn replaying every moment he'd spent with Holly.

He pulled into his subdivision and drove to his house. It was dark, with only the automatic landscape lights illuminating it. Sitting there, he let the car idle and he worried that his life was becoming like this house. Nice on the outside…empty on the inside.

He drove into his garage and parked the car. No more thinking. He went to his bedroom and changed into a pair of low-slung jeans. With his chest and feet bare, he entered the wet-bar area of the living room and snagged a bottle of single malt scotch that he'd picked up last summer when he'd visited Scotland with his oldest brother.

He grabbed a highball glass and tossed some ice cubes in it. Just because he was drinking didn't mean he had to go totally low-class. His mother had raised him to be a gentleman. Even when he planned to get sloshed, he hung on to that thought.

Not that his manners had impressed Holly.

He poured the liquor into his glass and walked out onto the deck. The night sky was full of stars, and the smell of jasmine filled the air. As he lowered himself to the hardwood lounger, he wondered why life would give him two women to love and not let him keep either.

He took a swallow of scotch. He wasn't a self-pitying guy, so he wasn't about to go down that road. But it pissed the hell out of him every time he remembered the last sight of Holly. Arms around her waist, tears gleaming in her eyes. Sure made a man feel like a bastard to make a woman cry.

He took another swallow from his glass. This looked like an all-night project, which was okay with him because he had the time. In fact, he had nothing but time looming in front of him.

The doorbell rang when he was about halfway through the bottle. He ignored the first summons, feeling the effects of the booze and not wanting to have to be sociable with anyone.

The doorbell rang again, this time a continuous ringing as if the person on the other side was not lifting his finger off the buzzer.

It had to be a family member—probably Nick or Gina or one of his other siblings who continued to fall in love around him. They paired up like animals on Noah's ark, making him feel like a damn unicorn, not making the trip. He walked through the house.

"Go away," he growled through the door.

"No."

It sounded like Holly but he knew it couldn't be. He'd said unforgivable things to her. Called her a coward and a martyr. And if she was on the other side of the door he wasn't sure what to do.

The liquor bottle was still in his hand. He took a quick swig and then opened the door. She stood in front of him, looking like temptation. Like the woman he'd thought he'd come to know but with something more. Her eyes were clear and met his gaze, and she seemed nervous.

"What are you doing here?"

"You told me when I was tired of running to come and find you."

"Hell, Holly, I'm not at my best tonight."

"That's okay. I am."

She pushed against his chest. Her small hand was cool on his skin. He resisted for the simple reason that he wanted to enjoy her touch a little longer.

She flexed her fingers, her sharp nails biting the slightest bit. Lust settled low in his body and he almost grabbed her, tossed her over his shoulder and carried her to his bedroom.

But he'd told her he loved her and she'd walked away.

"Can I come in?" she asked.

He shrugged and backed up, letting her enter the house. She noticed the bottle of scotch in his hand and reached out to take it.

He lifted it out of her reach.

"Give me the bottle, Joe."

"I'm not done yet."

"Yes, you are," she said firmly. He'd never noticed that bossy tendency of hers before now. He had noticed her hair all red and pretty, falling around her shoulders. He wanted to feel it in his hands again. As he reached for her, Holly snagged the bottle.

Joe didn't let go at first, not sure he wanted to get rid of his only barrier. She tugged on it until he lost his grip, and some of the scotch sloshed over the side, splattering her hand and light raincoat.

"Damn," he said.

"How much have you drunk?" she asked.

"Not nearly as much as I plan to," he said, smiling at her.

She wiped her hand on her coat, then put her hands on her waist. Why was she here?

He needed his wits. He padded silently back out to the deck. There might be some more scotch in his glass. Vaguely he was aware of Holly following him.

Had he conjured her up by thinking about her? He'd planned to not think about her. He had a nice buzz going and all this thinking was messing with it.

He sank back to his chair, resting his elbows on his knees. Holly sat next to him, perched there gingerly as if afraid to relax.

Why was she here? This proved his father's point that a man should never drink too much. He rubbed his eyes with the heels of his hands. Maybe he'd imagined the entire episode and she wasn't really here.

Except he could smell. Damn, she smelled all sweet and sexy. He turned his head to the right and there she was. Sitting quietly, looking too damn beautiful with only the pool lights and the moon illuminating her. Hell, she always looked too good for him. Maybe she'd known all along that he wasn't the man for her.

"Why are you here?" he asked, his voice gruff.

"I..." She stood up, her long legs bare under the khaki-colored raincoat she had on. Her feet were shod in a pair of impossibly high stiletto heels. He had a lurid vision of her in nothing but the heels.

He squeezed his eyes shut, then he opened them again and realized it wasn't a vision. Holly had dropped the coat and stood in front of him clad only in her gorgeous freckles and those made-for-sex heels.

He couldn't think or speak. He rose in one fluid motion and staggered a bit. He wished he could be suddenly sober. But he couldn't. The least he could do was not take advantage of her, though if she stayed naked another minute he would. He picked her coat up and wrapped it around her.

"Holly—"

"I wanted to be as vulnerable as you were, Joe, when I said what I have to say."

Until that moment he hadn't realized she'd known the extent of his vulnerabilities. Until that moment he'd felt he'd retained a modicum of dignity. Until that moment he'd never realized how much he still loved her and that the anger in his heart wasn't true anger but a disguise of heartbreak so deep that he didn't know if he'd ever recover.

"I'm sorry," she said.

"I don't want your pity," he replied, realizing the words for truth. He wanted her back in his life but definitely not because she felt sorry for him.

"No, I didn't mean it like that. I apologize that I wasn't ready to be your wife when you offered me your heart," she said.

He shook his head trying to clear it. If he had half a brain, he'd go inside and make some coffee. "Why weren't you ready?"

"I don't know. I think you pegged it, though, when you said I was playing the martyr." She toyed with the strap on her raincoat, and he knew she was nervous. Hell, this was a mess. He'd never meant to hurt her.

"I was acting out."

"You were justified."

"Holly, why are you here?" he asked again.

"Would you sit down, please?"

He lowered himself to the lounger again. She shrugged out of her raincoat, laid it on the ground in front of his feet and then knelt on it.

He couldn't think with her naked at his feet. The alcohol he'd drunk earlier seemed to leave his system, replaced by desire. His blood rushed in his ears.

She took his hand in hers and looked up at him with sincerity in her eyes, and in the back of his mind he thought this was a good sign.

"Joseph Barone, you gave me a priceless gift and I wasn't worthy of it. But I ask you to reconsider." She smiled at him tentatively. "I love you," she said, tears in her eyes.

He reached out to cup her face in his hands. "I love you too," he said at last.

"I... Will you marry me?" she asked, holding up a small jewelry box.

"Hell, yes." He scooped her off her feet and carried her into the house.

She wrapped her arms around his neck as he bounded up the steps, then laid her on the center of his bed. He pushed off his jeans and briefs in one quick moment, then moved to cover her.

"Don't you want to know what changed my mind?" she asked, wrapping her arms around his shoulders.

"Later," he said, testing her and finding her wet and ready for his possession.

He thrust into her body, slid his arms up under her legs, folding them gently back toward her body. She moaned a deep husky sound that he'd die remembering and met him thrust for thrust.

Only when they were both shuddering with completion could he begin to think about their future. He knew he wasn't going to be able to wait long for a wedding.

He rolled off of her and cuddled her against him. "I'm never letting you go."

"Me neither," she said.

"I want to get married right away." Life had taught him to grasp the things he wanted and hold them close.

She nodded. "My dad and brothers have to be there."

"I want to meet them."

"They want to meet you too. I'm sorry I kept you from knowing them. I was afraid I couldn't have you and them."

"Why?"

"Love is a huge responsibility."

"Not always. Love is sharing."

"I didn't know that until I met you."

She raised herself up on her elbow and kissed him. He knew she meant the embrace to be a soft, caring one, but he'd been denied her for too long and lust reawakened in him.

"Are we done talking?" he asked.

"Why?"

He took her hand and guided it to his erection. "As long as I know you love me, everything will be fine."

Everything was fine. He made love to her all night and called in sick to work in the morning. He'd finally found the one woman he'd been searching for.

Epilogue

Their wedding day dawned bright and sunny. It seemed crazy but only three days had passed since she'd visited Joe's house and asked him to marry her. But he didn't want to wait another minute to start their life as man and wife.

Holly watched nervously from Joe's bedroom window as his family, her family and their friends gathered around the pool.

She'd have felt a lot better if her mom were with her today. But this morning her father had given her the rose-charm necklace that her mother had worn every day. She'd been so touched to have something of her mother's on her neck.

They'd asked Gina to be maid of honor, and Nick was standing up for Joe.

"Ready, Holly?" her dad asked from the doorway.

"Yes," she said, hurrying to his side.

She walked down the stairs and out onto the deck where Joe waited. He smiled at her and she felt her heart stop. She'd never expected love to feel like this. She'd never expected Mr. Right to look like him. She'd never dreamed happily-ever-after was in the cards for her.

But now she knew it was her destiny. The fate that Joe and she would make together.

She walked to him on a cloud of feeling and exchanged vows in a haze. The only part she was truly aware of was when he lowered his head to kiss her.

"You're mine," he said.

"And you are mine."

Their families and friends clapped and cheered. Holly was aware that she'd found the one man she'd spent her life searching for.... Well, maybe he'd found her.

*   *   *   *   *

THE LIBRARIAN'S
PASSIONATE KNIGHT
by
Cindy Gerard

CINDY GERARD

Two RITA® Award nominations and a National Reader's Choice Award are among the many highlights of this No.1 bestselling writer's career. As one reviewer put it, 'Cindy Gerard provides everything romance readers want in a love story—passion, gut-wrenching emotion, intriguing characters and a captivating plot. This storyteller extraordinaire delivers all of this and more!'

Cindy and her husband, Tom, live in the Midwest on a farm with quarter horses, cats and two very spoiled dogs. When she's not writing, she enjoys reading, travelling and spending time at their cabin in northern Minnesota unwinding with family and friends. Cindy loves to hear from her readers and invites you to visit her website at www.cindygerard.com

This book is dedicated to romantics everywhere.
Enjoy and believe!

And to potter extraordinaire, Val Neuman, for her
patience, her expertise and her brilliant work.
From the clay comes the vessel; from the vessel
pour my admiration and thanks.

One

Daniel Barone wasn't sure why the woman had captured his attention. In the overall scheme of things, she was little more than a small speck of beige, lost in the vibrant colors of Faneuil Hall Marketplace in the center of downtown Boston.

On this steamy August night, the open-air market was alive with colors and scents and sounds. She, quite literally, was not. Still, she'd drawn his undivided attention as he stood directly behind her at a pushcart outside the buildings of Quincy Market.

Like a dozen or so others, they were both waiting in line for ice cream. Unlike the others, who edged forward as placidly as milling cattle, she bounced with impatience. Like a child—which she absolutely wasn't—she rose to the balls of her feet and…bounced. There wasn't another word for it. She just sort of danced in place, as

if she found irrepressible delight in the simple anticipation of getting her hands on an ice cream cone.

For some reason it made Daniel smile. Her guile-
less exuberance charmed him, he supposed. And it
made him take time for a longer look.

She was average height, maybe a little on the short
side. Her hair wasn't quite blond, wasn't quite brown,
and there was nothing remotely sexy about the short,
pixieish cut. Her drab tan shorts and top showed off
a modest length of arm and leg and more than ade-
quately covered what could possibly be a nice, tidy
little body. Who could tell? Other than the wicked red
polish splashed on her toenails, there truly wasn't a
bright spot on the woman—until she turned around
with her much-awaited prize.

Behind owlish, black-rimmed glasses, a pair of
honey-brown eyes danced with anticipation, intelligence and innate good humor. And when she took
that first long, indulgent lick, a smile of pure, decadent delight lit her ordinary face and transitioned un-
remarkable to breathtaking in a heartbeat. The wattage of that smile damn near blinded him.

"It was worth the wait," she murmured on a bliss-
ful sigh before she shouldered out of line and went
on about her business.

"And then some," Daniel agreed and, with a side-
long grin, watched the pleasant sway of her hips as
she walked away.

Wondering why a woman possessed of so much
vibrant and natural beauty would choose to hide it
behind professorial glasses, an unimaginative haircut
and brown-paper-bag-plain clothes, he tracked her
progress as she moved through the crowd. He was

still watching when the kid wielding the ice cream scoop nudged him back to the business at hand.

"Hey, bud. You want ice cream or what?"

Daniel slowly returned his attention to the counter. "Yeah. Sorry." He dug into his hip pocket for his wallet and, still grinning, hitched his chin in the general direction she'd taken. "I'll have what she had. Double dip."

It wasn't Baronessa gelato, he conceded after the first bite, but it was ice cream and he'd been craving it for almost a month now. He was pretty sure, though, that he wasn't enjoying his half as much as a certain champagne-blonde was enjoying hers.

He glanced around, searched for her briefly. Not that he expected to spot her in this crush of people, not that he knew what he'd do if he did. Didn't matter anyway. She was long gone, swallowed up by the milling crowd.

Telling himself that it was just as well, he headed in the general direction of his car. He needed sleep anyway, not a distraction. The thought of a real bed with clean sheets and a soft mattress made him groan. So did the memory of his apartment with its light-darkening shades, the cool hum of an air conditioner set on seventy degrees and about twelve solid hours of shut-eye.

Simple pleasures. Foreign pleasures, of late. A month deep in the red sands of the Kalahari could whet a man's appetite for many simple pleasures.

Like sweet, rich ice cream.

Like a bed that you didn't have to check for spiders and snakes and was softer than a patch of sun-parched earth.

Like the unaffected smile of a pretty, satisfied woman.

He grinned again—this time in self-reproach—when he couldn't stop an image from forming.

Her head resting on his pillow…

Her body soft and warm and pliant beneath his…

Her incredible smile not only satisfied, but stunned, sated and spent…

Phoebe Richards wandered the marketplace among the throng of tourists and Bostonians who were out enjoying the hot August evening. She ate her plain vanilla ice cream—her reward for six days of ice cream abstinence and one lost pound—and refused to think about the calories. She window-shopped at the trendy boutiques that she couldn't afford, applauded the lively antics of the street performers whose free acts she could afford. And she spared a thought—okay, maybe two—for the handsome stranger with the incredible blue eyes and interested smile.

She didn't get many of either in her life—handsome strangers or interested smiles—and that was fine. It was fun, though, to entertain the fantasy that something might have happened between them if she'd invited it. But that would require an adventurous spirit that she could never in a million years claim. Besides, that kind of electrifying occurrence only happened in the romance novels she devoured to the tune of two to three a week. Her life to date was as far from romance-novel material as a life could get. In fact, lately, it had leaned a little closer to horror.

Determined not to think about the ugly situation with her ex-boyfriend, she walked on, opting, instead, to dwell on a lesser evil: the fact that she was too much of a coward to even encourage the spark of interest that had danced in those amazing blue eyes.

"Like anything would have actually happened, anyway," she muttered as a statuesque blonde in designer clothes and flawless makeup accidentally bumped her shoulder.

"Sorry," Phoebe murmured, even though she'd been the bumpee, not the bumper. Her reaction was automatic and had little to do with being polite. It was knee-jerk conciliation and it was an old habit she was supposed to be trying to break, just as she was supposed to be trying to learn to hold her ground on any number of issues.

As if on cue, a stockbroker type in pricey Italian shoes and a dark scowl barreled toward her.

"Excuse me," she murmured and stepped aside before she could stop herself.

"Why do you always do that?" her friend Carol had asked her the last time they'd gone to lunch together and she'd apologized to the waiter because her soup was stone cold and the lettuce in her salad was as rusty as a junk car. "You do *not* owe the general population an apology for its screwups. You have rights, too."

Yes. She had rights. She had the right to remain timid. She couldn't help it. She was innately apologetic. Or pathetic. Or something equally as hopeless. It was simply easier to bend than to buck. Easier to yield than to stand. She'd learned that life lesson early on.

"Look," she'd told Carol once in an uncharacteristic revelation about her childhood. "When you're an ugly duckling twelve-year-old, twenty pounds overweight and constantly belittled by an alcoholic mother to whom you are an eternal disappointment, you learn to bend with the best of them.

"And I also learned to fade into the background until I got so good at it that no one hardly ever noticed me. Life was just easier that way."

Life was still easier that way, she thought defensively. And old habits were hard to break. At the ripe old age of thirty-three she wasn't really hopeful of changing them at this late date.

"Besides," she'd further explained to Carol, sorry she'd opened her mouth when her friend's expression had changed from disgusted to sympathetic. "Confrontation gives me heartburn. And sweaty palms. And a sinking sensation in the pit of my stomach that rarely makes it worth the effort."

Suddenly aware of a trickle of perspiration trailing down her temple, she dabbed it with a tissue. The lingering heat from the one-hundred-degree day rose from the sidewalk in arid waves and burned right through the bottom of her sandals.

"August," she said aloud as she bit into the last of her ice cream. "Gotta love it."

It was close to eleven o'clock and the city was still as steamy as a jungle. Since she had to get up and cover another shift at the library tomorrow, she decided it was past time to get home and go to bed. Alone. As usual.

"Just another exciting Friday night on the town for Phoebe Richards," she murmured on a wistful sigh and made room for a pair of lovers to pass her on the sidewalk.

They were so engrossed in each other, so cute, and so in love, it made her smile. It also made her ache.

The longing to fill that empty place in her chest seemed to have grown larger and more hollow as the years passed…as the world turned…as all around her, love bloomed and flourished.

She pushed out a snort that passed for a self-effacing laugh. "You are a pathetic lump," she assured herself in disgust. "And you're no poet, either."

After checking the traffic, she jaywalked across the street to walk the three blocks to her car, shoring herself up along the way. One bad relationship did not make her a failure at love. Two might, though, she conceded, gnawing thoughtfully on her lower lip. Three or four took it past failure to disaster.

All right. Her love life *was* a disaster, or as Carol frequently said with a sad shake of her head, "Girl, you sure know how to pick 'em."

Yeah, she thought with a resigned sigh as Jason Collins came to mind, she sure did. On the upside—and despite the lack of love and romance in her life, she was always determined to find an upside—she *did* know how to find parking spots.

"Maybe you ought to play on that talent if you ever get another date," she told herself with a sarcastic little smile as the scene played out before her.

"Well, you're not exactly calendar material, are you, Ms. Richards?" the man of her dreams stated bluntly as he squinted at the clipboard containing his detailed list of marriage requirements. "So what, exactly, would you consider your most stellar attribute? And don't say intelligence, because frankly, I find that's a real turnoff."

"Well, I have an uncanny knack for finding fantastic parking spots," she replied, dimpling hopefully.

His eyes widened. And then he smiled. Sunlight glinted off his perfect white teeth. Tossing his clipboard over his shoulder, he opened his arms as violins played in the background. "Darling, that's perfect. Let's get married."

"That proves it. You're definitely warped," she muttered with a shake of her head. "But darn, girl, you *do* know how to find a parking spot."

The one she'd found tonight was only three blocks from the marketplace. Closer to a streetlight would have been nice though, she thought on a sudden shift of mood. A sense of unease sent a quick and clammy shiver eddying along her nape and dampened her good humor.

"Okay, Pheebs," she admonished herself and started rummaging around in her purse for her car keys. "Time to switch genres. You've been reading too much romantic suspense lately."

She was not afraid to be out at night on her own. Well, not too afraid, she conceded, pulling out her keys. She'd lived in Boston all her life and was cautious, that was all. Generally though, she didn't jump at shadows or look for bogeymen under her bed unless Carol and the gang roped her into going to a spooky movie. At least she hadn't jumped at shadows until she'd broken up with Jason two months ago and he'd started calling her in the middle of the night and hassling her at work.

Just thinking of him sent another shiver slithering down her spine. Fighting what she knew was a false but growing sense of urgency, she told herself to let it go. Jason had been a mistake. She'd corrected it— or thought she had until she heard his voice.

"Out trying to scare up a little action, are ya, Mouse?"

She jumped and spun around so fast that she fumbled with her keys and dropped them.

"Jason." His name rushed out on a high, thready breath as her coward's heart threatened to beat its way out of her chest through her throat.

"'Jason,'" he mimicked with a nasty smirk before he bent to snag her keys from the curb where they'd landed with a loud clatter. "That's it? 'Jason.' You could at least pretend you're glad to see me. After all, I spent half the night trying to catch up with you."

Phoebe forced herself to look into his bloodshot brown eyes and hated it when she couldn't hold his gaze. Hated it more when she realized she was shaking.

He needed a haircut; his shirt was dirty. He was also drunk—mean drunk. The alcohol stench of his breath fanned her face as he moved in on her, turning her stomach, triggering a hundred childhood moments and one very recent one of the first and only time he'd hit her. Her ears had rung for a day afterward. The bruise on her cheek had taken much longer to fade. The memory never would, even though she'd written him out of her life at that exact moment.

He glared at her through an ugly smile.

How had she ever thought his smile was beautiful?

More important, how was she going to get out of this?

"Give me my keys, Jason," she said, shooting for reasonable and hoping he'd comply. Unfortunately, her demand sounded more like a plea.

He gave a pitying shake of his head and held them out of her reach. "You know, your problem always was that you didn't know how to show a man proper respect. You should be thanking me, not giving me orders."

She closed her eyes, swallowed. "Thank you...for picking up my keys," she said meekly as he crowded her backward until she bumped into the driver's-side door of her car. "Could...could I have them, please?"

Triumph turned his mouth into a sneer. "Better. Not good enough, though. Just like I was never good enough for you, was I? *Was* I?"

She willed herself not to panic as he pressed his face close to hers.

"How's that happen? I wonder," he demanded with the angry slur of a big man about to teach a small woman a lesson. "How's it happen that a mousy, old-maid librarian thinks she's better than me? Where do you get off dumping me? Huh?"

He wiped spittle from the side of his mouth with the back of his hand. "You think you're some prize?" He snorted out an ugly laugh. "News flash! You're not. What you are is leftovers. Leftovers!" He dug his fingers painfully into her upper arm, making her wince. "I was good to you. I was great to you! What's your problem, anyway?"

Like an animal could sense a coming earthquake even before sensitive scientific equipment could pick it up, Phoebe anticipated the coming blow. With a hard jerk, she pulled free and whirled away before it landed.

His fist slammed into her car door with a loud crack. His vicious curse sliced through the night as she half walked, half ran, praying that he'd curl up to nurse his pain and forget about her.

The sound of heavy footsteps pounding the sidewalk behind her told her that wasn't going to happen.

Her heart sank. Nausea rolled through her stomach as she stepped up her pace and, not for the first time in her life, wished she had the backbone and the skill to strike back.

The crowd had thinned to a handful of people when Daniel spotted his ice cream lady about a half a block ahead. Pleasure, unexpected and uncontested, had him forgetting about sleep and unnecessary distractions and heading in her direction.

He was within a few yards of her when he realized she wasn't alone—whether by choice or by accident, he couldn't tell. A big man, over six feet and roughly two hundred ten, two hundred twenty pounds, was dogging her like a jet trail.

Daniel sized him up with a practiced eye. He didn't like what he saw. Bully came immediately to mind. A real bruiser with a nasty attitude. He could only hear snippets of their conversation as they stopped by an older-model gray compact car. He heard enough to grasp that the guy was obnoxious and ugly, though, and about as welcome as a wad of gum on the bottom of her shoe. He picked up on something else, too. She was afraid of him.

Daniel's stomach bunched into tight knots when the creep grabbed her arm and squeezed hard enough to make her wince. That was as far as he was willing to let this go.

Two

Daniel picked up his pace, then momentarily lost track of her when he got tangled up in a group of rowdy, laughing teenage girls. When he finally broke free of them and spotted her again, she was heading away at a fast walk. The guy was hot on her heels.

Daniel caught up with her at a fast jog.

"Hey, babe." Moving in close beside her, he physically cut off the other man with his body. "Slow down, would you? I lost you for a while there," he added, slinging an arm over her shoulders with the easy familiarity of a man claiming his woman.

She stopped so fast he had to steady her to keep her from toppling over. When she looked up at him, the eyes behind her glasses were huge and round and scared. It took a moment but eventually she recognized him from the concession line.

He smiled and reassured her with his eyes. *Play along. I'll get you out of this.*

"How was your ice cream?" he asked and nudged her back into a walk.

"F-fine," she finally managed to say, cueing in to his intentions and falling into a faltering step beside him.

"Who the hell are you?" an angry voice demanded from behind them.

"Just keep walking," he said, lowering his mouth to her ear. For her sake, he didn't want to make a scene, and he figured the best shot at avoiding one was to walk away.

A beefy hand clamped on his shoulder and stopped him.

So much for what *he'd* thought.

"I said who the hell are you?"

Daniel turned, a deceptively neutral smile in place. "I'm the guy who's taking the lady home. Now, if you'll excuse us—"

"You threw *me* over for *him?*" The stench of alcohol explained the slurred words. "For this pretty boy? I knew it! I knew you were screwin' around on me!"

"Jason." Her voice was thin and tight. Embarrassment flooded her chalk-white cheeks with color. "We are over. We've been over for two months now. What can I say to make you understand that?"

"Yeah, Jason," Daniel echoed with false congeniality. "What can she say to make you understand?"

"Stay out of this," Jason snarled and started in on her again. "We are *not* over, Mouse. Not till I say so."

Red ringed the eyes that narrowed into angry slits.

Hands the size of small anvils clenched into tight fists at his sides. He wanted to hit something. With a sickening twist in his gut, Daniel realized what—or in this case *who*—it was.

"Don't even think about it." He shoved her behind him and stepped into the line of fire. "And then do yourself a favor. Walk away. Just walk the hell away."

Jason, who easily outweighed him by twenty or thirty pounds, snorted. "You think you wanna piece of me, pretty boy?"

"Oh, I'd love a piece of you, Clyde." Daniel smiled pleasantly. "But you're just not worth my time. Now back off and leave the lady alone or this is gonna come down to you and me and the nice policeman walking toward us. You want to go down for attempted assault with a little drunk and disorderly tacked on for good measure? Make a move and you've got it."

"Problem here, folks?"

"I'm not sure." Daniel glared at Jason as the uniformed officer approached them. "Is there a problem?"

Jason glowered but finally shook his head.

"Is there a problem?" Daniel repeated, turning his attention to a pair of doe-brown eyes, relaying with his tone that all she had to do was say the word and this bozo was history.

She hesitated then shook her head. "No."

Daniel watched her face for the length of a deep breath, not knowing what to make of that. What he did know was that it wasn't his call. It was hers, and since he'd come in at the middle of this particular movie, he wasn't going to make any snap judgments.

"Guess there's no problem." He flashed the officer a tight smile. "Thanks anyway."

Daniel shot Jason a warning glare. Then he waited to make sure the other man got the hint to move on. When he stalked off, Daniel wrapped his arm around her shoulders again. "Come on. Let's get out of here."

She tried for a smile—of relief or gratitude, he couldn't tell which. Regardless, it didn't matter, because she didn't pull it off anyway. She was shaking so hard that he expected her to vibrate right out from under his arm. She surprised him, though, because when he started walking she let out a pent-up breath that seemed to drain her of her tension and fell into step beside him.

He looked down at the top of her head, comfortable with the easy way she fit against him, not so comfortable with the intensity of the protectiveness he felt for her.

True, it wasn't the first time he'd been ready to take a fall for a woman. As a rule, though, he generally liked to know a whole helluva lot more about her before he got his lights punched out. For starters, he thought with a cheeky grin, he at least tried to make it a point to know her name.

Phoebe figured she was in shock. She couldn't think of another reason why she was letting a total stranger wrap his arm around her and walk her farther and farther away from her car. She supposed there was the very real likelihood that Jason had scared her witless. And then, there was the fact that the man steering her down the sidewalk was quite possibly the most beautiful man she'd ever seen.

"You okay?" she heard him ask. The way he said it made her realize it wasn't the first time he'd asked. His voice, as smooth and low as deep water, was filled with concern.

When she couldn't find it in her to reply, he stopped and turned to her. Cupping her shoulders in his hands, he searched her face. As she, in turn, searched his, she forgave herself for lapsing into speechlessness.

Sweet Lord, he was gorgeous. He wasn't particularly tall—just under six feet—but at five-four she still had to lift her chin to look up at him. He wasn't exceptionally muscular either, not like a bodybuilder. Instead, he was sleekly muscled, like a runner or a swimmer, a study in athletic fitness that combined conditioning and finesse to a honed perfection that overshadowed brawn any day. His black T-shirt and black shorts showed off tan arms and legs and lean, sinewy strength.

She knew what it felt like to be tucked into the warmth and power emanating from his body. She'd felt sheltered and protected while visions of a different kind of embrace—intimate, needy—further scattered her already fractured thoughts.

He wasn't a workingman either, she decided, forcefully dragging her mind back to the moment. Nothing specifically told her that. It was more of a generalization of his overall presence that quietly spoke of money. That he either came from it or was made from it was as obvious as the blue of his eyes. From the artful style of his sun-streaked brown hair that he wore longer than respectable yet looked exactly right on him, to the cut of his formfitting black T-shirt, he wore wealth. It wasn't overt. It was, instead, effortless. He was as comfortable with it as he was with his utter maleness, at ease with everything that he was.

The blue eyes that searched her face were thick-lashed and kind of dreamy, strategically set for maximum impact in that stunning, poster-perfect face. His cheeks were deeply tan and slightly stubbled, his jaw molded with love by a benevolent master.

His classic male beauty, however, had enough rough edges thrown in to save him from being pretty. A tiny crescent-shaped scar marred the corner of his full upper lip, and a nick split the arch of his dark eyebrow. Still, his face was so symmetrically sculpted it was almost painful to look at it, yet impossible to look away.

He was everything—*everything*—that a hero was supposed to be. Brave, gorgeous, wealthy.

Her heart sank on a reality check. A worthy heroine she was not.

The realization of who she was, what she was and what she wasn't, melted over her like spent wax, starting at the top of her head and working its way to her fingertips.

"Are you still with me in there?" he asked with a lazy, amused grin that infiltrated her thoughts like a spelunker breaching a turn in an underground cavern.

"I...um..."

He chuckled, held his hand in front of her face and asked, deadpan, "How many fingers?"

She blinked, focused, and remarkably, the magic of speech returned. "Four and a thumb. At least that was standard issue last I knew."

On second thought, *magic* may have been too strong a word when paired up with the words she'd just uttered. Obviously, her reply had spilled out before she thought, because if she'd thought, she wouldn't be firing wisecracks. Shock, prompted by reality, made her forget to measure her words, police her reactions.

She reined herself in and clarified. "He didn't hit me."

He smiled again, gently this time, sort of a slow, concerned unfurling that dug deep grooves in his lean cheeks and crinkled the corners of his eyes. "But he wanted to. And that in itself is a violation."

He had the most sensual mouth. His lips were generous and seemed to be perpetually tipped up in some semblance of a grin.

Too aware that she was staring again, she lifted her gaze to quite possibly the most expressive eyes she'd ever seen. In that moment, she read his pity through them and was ashamed.

"Oh. Oh, no. It's…it's not what you're thinking. I'm not one of those poor women caught up in an abuse cycle." Though he was a total stranger, she didn't want him thinking that about her. "I ended our relationship months ago. He's just not— Well, he's not getting the picture."

"And he's not likely to anytime soon unless he has a reason to consider the consequences."

Consequences. So far, she, not Jason, had been the one suffering the consequences of his unwarranted obsession.

It all caught up with her then. The fear of the past few moments. The utter sense of vulnerability and violation. The embarrassment of a public scene. And her dependence on this stranger to come to her rescue.

Jason had blindsided her. She hated him for that.

She hated violence more. She'd felt as helpless against it tonight as she had as a child. And like a child, she'd frozen in the face of it.

She knew what that made her. Leslie Griffin, her sixty-years-young friend and co-worker, could argue all she wanted that Phoebe was heroic for overcoming her abusive childhood, for putting herself through school, for enduring and establishing herself as a solid, independent citizen. The truth, however, was that at heart she was a coward. For that failure alone, she hated herself almost as much as she hated Jason for putting her in this position.

"Well." She squared her shoulders and rallied what pride she had left. "It's my problem. I'll figure out how to deal with it."

"Think in terms of a two-by-four. Right between his eyes," he said darkly.

"Do you all run on pure testosterone?" She blurted out the words before she could marshal them. Again.

She closed her eyes, pressed her fingertips to her temple. *Wrong. Wrong, wrong, wrong.*

She didn't know how to act around this man. If she wasn't gaping in stupefied silence over his glaring good looks, she was bumbling out the most inappropriate things.

"I'm sorry. You saved me from a really bad ending here and I'm coming down on you for wanting to…" She paused, lifted a hand in the air.

"To add more violence to an already violent situation?" he suggested, an apology in his voice. "Unfortunately, sometimes that's the only option."

For the first time, something other than gentle amusement hardened his mouth. She saw and heard his anger but understood that it was directed at Jason.

She also understood that he hadn't judged her as harshly as she'd judged herself.

When she realized he was watching her with an absorbed intensity that relayed both concern and the same gentleness as his smiles, she drew in a deep breath and let it out.

"Well," she said, feeling compelled to assure him, "I'll be okay. He'll give up sooner or later. In the meantime, I really don't know how to thank you. Most people wouldn't have stopped, and, you know, gotten in the middle of someone else's mess."

"I'm not most people."

That much she'd already figured out. He certainly wasn't like most of the people she knew at any rate. And he wasn't anything like her. She was strictly struggling to be middle-class mundane. And he— Well, he wasn't.

"So, what happens now?"

She let out a breath through puffed cheeks. "What *does* happen now?" she mused aloud before her brain synapses clicked into place. "Well, now I guess I walk back to my car and drive home."

It seemed simple enough, except that on the heels of her statement, she realized it wasn't going to be simple at all. She would have laughed if she could have mustered the strength.

"Well, *normally* I'd walk back to my car and drive home."

"Normally?"

She worried her lower lip between her teeth then lifted a shoulder. "He got away with my car keys."

He quirked a beautifully arched eyebrow—the one with the nick in it. "Oops. That's a problem."

Phoebe tugged on the tips of her hair where it tickled her nape and tried not to fidget as he continued to watch her with that half-amused, half-interested, all-male grin.

"So it would appear that you're stranded."

Yep. She was in a tight spot. So why was she suddenly grinning back at him?

It was ludicrous. Someone who had once meant something to her, someone she had trusted and had actually considered building a life with, had just tried to physically assault her. In addition, he'd made off with her car keys. Yet the pain of the first and the anger over the second just sort of drifted off in the comfort of this man's dazzling smile.

"I'll, um, just hail a cab," she said, sobering resolutely. "I've got an extra set of keys at home. I can come back for my car tomorrow."

"Or," he said, shoving his hands into the pockets of his shorts, "I could take you."

Yes, yes, yes.

She pulled back from that idea with a steadying breath. "No, oh no. I couldn't ask you to do that. You've done enough. And you don't even know me. For that matter, I don't know you."

"That is an issue," he agreed with another one of those knee-melting smiles that didn't make fun but teased just the same. "Here's a thought. You could tell me your name, and I could tell you mine." He paused, his grin playful and expectant. "You see where this is leading, right?"

Infectious. His smile was positively infectious.

"And then we can say we know each other," he finished, looking very pleased with himself and his silliness. "Works out pretty well to my way of thinking."

She liked his way of thinking. She was baffled that a man who looked like him would even bother with a woman who looked like her, but she liked it. In fact, she was quickly discovering that she liked everything about him.

Like his lips. Supple, sensual.

"So, what do you say?" he prompted. "How about you go first?"

"Phoebe," she murmured, dragging her gaze away from his mouth. "Phoebe Richards."

"Phoebe," he repeated, mulling it over then looking immeasurably pleased. "I like it. It suits you much better than Mouse." His expression was as sober as it was sincere.

She blinked, speechless again.

"I'm Daniel." He extended his hand. "Daniel Barone."

This time when he smiled it was full out, no-holes-barred and devastating.

She drew a deep breath and tried to shore herself up as every bone in her body sort of liquefied to the consistency of pudding.

And then she smiled like a goon again because he just made it so darn easy.

Slowly, she took the hand he offered. It was a strong hand. Her own hand felt small and protected tucked inside his. Before she could stop the image from forming, she imagined the coarse, warm strength of it caressing…well, something much more intimate than her hand.

She was thankful it was shadowy and dark on the street. Maybe he couldn't see the flush spreading across her cheeks. With luck, he wouldn't notice the slight tremble of her hand either when she finally managed to extricate it from his and lift it to her nape to tug self-consciously at her hair again.

"Let me take you home, Phoebe Richards," he said, his voice and his eyes gentle. "Now just wait a sec before you say no. Think of how bad I'd feel if after all this you ended up getting mugged or something. I'd have put my life on the line for nothing."

His easy self-assurance only reminded her of all the confidence she lacked. It reaffirmed that she had no business accepting his offer because in the overall scheme of things, it meant very little to him if he took her home and way too much to her.

Daniel Barone, she'd decided, couldn't help but play the hero. She, conversely, never had and never would fit the role of a heroine. Especially not his heroine, although she couldn't help herself from wanting to cast herself in the part.

That was when it hit her.

She knew who he was.

Her eyes widened.

How could she not have recognized him?

Maybe she was wrong, she thought, stalling panic as her gaze raced across his face. Maybe she hadn't just made a fool of herself in front of a man who, a few months ago, the *Boston Globe Magazine* had billed as "Boston's Own Sexy-as-Sin Daredevil Millionaire."

Yeah, and maybe the light sheen of perspiration that had broken out on her forehead made her look delicate instead of desperate.

"Daniel Barone?" she squeaked, like the mouse she truly was. "*The* Daniel Barone?"

When he merely crossed his arms over his chest

and grinned, she pressed the flat of her palm to her forehead.

"The *Boston Globe*'s Daniel Barone? The Baronessa Gelati Barone?"

Unless you lived under a rock, you knew about the Boston Barones. The colorful Italian family's ice cream dynasty was legend, not just on the East Coast but worldwide. The original gelateria still flourished in the North End of Boston, and the delicious gelato had made Baronessa a household word and made multimillionaires out of anyone bearing the Barone name.

He shrugged, looking a little sheepish, which only added to his appeal. "I'm getting the impression that you may not consider this a *good* thing."

"Oh, no. No, it's just—"

"It's just a name," he preempted to make his point. "And I'm just a guy who wants to make sure you get home okay. Okay?"

In spite of it all, she was helpless not to return his smile. She'd given up resisting it. Just as she'd given up on the idea of doing the smart thing and begging off on his offer of a ride.

When he extended his hand, she hesitated for only a moment before taking it.

Just a name. Just a hand. And he's just being polite, she told herself. Yet she felt as if she was walking in a dream as she let him lead her to his car.

Wasn't she entitled, just this once, to have a fantasy fulfilled? One real-life fantasy involving one of the richest, sexiest men alive?

When he opened the door for her she went with it. She sank into the plush, supple leather of the bucket seat and pretended that she belonged there. She let the classical music flowing from the stereo system wrap around her, and entered another world. His world.

Phoebe Richards, welcome to the world of the rich and famous. All she needed to complete the scene was Robin Leach with his phony accent prattling away in the background.

She sighed and regained enough of her wits to remind herself that she really didn't belong in that world. Just like she didn't belong with a man like him.

Yet here she was.

She was in a car, in the dark of night, with the man of her dreams—hers and any other woman with a beating heart.

Daniel Barone was a true-life knight in shining armor who had literally saved her. Surely the shiny silver Porsche qualified as armor. Surely he was as much of a knight as Guinevere's Lancelot.

And in the name of fair play, surely, just once in her life, Phoebe Richards was entitled to a fairy-tale ending, even if, like Cinderella's coach, she'd turn into a pumpkin at the stroke of midnight.

Okay. So she was mixing her fairy tales and her metaphors. She didn't care. For this brief moment in time she indulged. She let herself forget about pumpkins and different worlds when he turned to her.

His blue eyes were thoughtful and interested as they met hers over the tanned arm that gripped the gearshift. The streetlight cast stunning shadows and shading across his incredible face. He smiled that devastating smile. "All set?"

"To the castle," she murmured and settled back as his soft, warm chuckle enveloped her.

Three

Phoebe's euphoria didn't last past the first intersection. The adrenaline rush that had kicked into full stride during the ugly scene with Jason wore off quickly. Plus, she was far too grounded to let herself drift on this little dream cloud for long. Grounded or not, though, without the adrenaline to shore her up she was a wreck by the time Daniel had deftly followed her directions and pulled onto her street.

Daniel Barone. She still couldn't quite grasp it. And he, well, if he found her neighborhood lacking compared to the pricey Beacon Hill residence where he'd grown up and the circle of wealth in which he ran, he was too polite or too polished to let it show.

He was also the picture of the perfect gentleman. Except that he drove too fast. She hadn't needed to read the *Boston Globe* article about him to know that it was part of his MO. The speed. The thrills. The daring to do what most mortals feared. His exploits were legend. She supposed it should be exciting, racing through the night in this shining bullet of a car, but her slight case of the shakes was prompted more by apprehension than any spirit of adventure.

She was hopeless. And he was so wrong about her name. Mouse suited her perfectly. She had the backbone of a snail. In fact, she was pretty sure she'd been the victim of one of those hit and run urban legends— like the one where some unsuspecting soul fell asleep in a motel room and woke up in a bathtub full of ice and missing their kidneys. Only in her case, it was her spine that had been surgically removed.

She sighed heavily. She didn't belong in this silver Porsche. She didn't belong in either dream or reality with this man, no matter how hard he tried to put her at ease. And bless him he did try. To her utter mortification, however, their conversation on the half-hour drive to her house consisted mostly of her stuttering apologies for putting him out and his teasing her about her white-knuckled grip on the console.

Out of her league.

She should have felt relief when he finally swung the car into her driveway and cut the engine. Instead, an unsettling mix of remorse and regret swamped her.

She smoothed her hand lovingly along the melting soft leather seat, heaved another resigned sigh and reached for the door handle.

And so ended her romance with romance.

"Wait," he said. "I'll get that."

Because she wasn't as resigned to the end as she'd thought, she waited while he got out of the car, walked around the hood and opened the door for her with all the gallantry of a medieval knight.

* * *

The castle, Daniel noted, turned out to be a modest ranch, white trimmed in black, circa 1960. It was set in the middle of the block in a quiet and fairly well-kept neighborhood of Boston proper. Lamplight glowed from inside the house where a huge, fat tabby lounged in the bay window and regarded them through the glass with golden eyes and a superior attitude as they approached.

He was a detail man and noticed that the parched grass was mowed and twin rows of sunburned flowers struggled to brighten the sidewalk leading to the front porch. The porch was actually little more than a concrete stoop covered by a shingled overhang that boasted a hanging basket of deep-purple petunias and peeling posts.

He wasn't sure what affected him more: the fact that she was a woman who planted flowers, that she probably mowed her own lawn, or the peeling paint that said she was either pressed for money or time.

In the end it was none of those things. It was the sight of an ugly, fist-size plaster frog squatting on the stoop. He didn't have a clue why it got to him.

"Well," she said as he watched her avoid his eyes by tucking her chin and staring at the center of his chest. She tugged on her hair, something she seemed to do a lot when she was nervous—which she obviously was around him. "Thank you. Again. Really. And you didn't have to walk me to the door."

As she'd been doing since about midway through the drive across town, he could see her gearing up for another apology for putting him out.

"Don't you dare say it," he warned her before she wound up for a good start. "We reached an agreement, remember? You aren't going to apologize any-more."

"You're right. I'm s—" she caught herself and smiled sheepishly. "I'm so *not* going to apologize again."

Looking pink and flustered and adorable, she bent to pick up the ugly frog.

Daniel stood there in suspended silence…absorb-ing the pleasant scent of vanilla ice cream and sum-mer that surrounded her…studying the endearing lit-tle cowlick that parted her hair with a swirl at her crown…considering touching the silky soft strands that looked baby fine and so touchable he had to shove his hands in his pockets to keep from reaching out and sifting it through his fingers.

He didn't get it. He didn't get why he was so fas-cinated by her. She was as far from a siren as Dame Edith and yet she called to him. He should feel relief now that he'd done his duty. He'd delivered her safely to her door. He was free to go. So he sure as hell didn't know why, when she turned that stupid frog upside down and slipped a key out of the compart-ment hidden in its belly, he felt a surge of tenderness that sent warning bells ringing in every rational part of his brain.

Aside from general concern, it shouldn't matter so much that the woman was being hounded by an ex-boyfriend with a whole lot of mean on his mind. It shouldn't matter so much that she hid her house key in a frog and probably regarded it as a security mea-sure.

It shouldn't matter so much that at first glance, he'd thought of her as ordinary.

And yet it did.

She was as far from ordinary as a dive along the outer reefs of a Micronesian atoll. As far from ordinary as the rare Lapp Orchid he'd had the pleasure of seeing in the wild in the mountains of Abisko in northern Lapland.

Far from ordinary.

Also, far from sophisticated. She wasn't glamorous, wasn't worldly. In fact, she quite possibly needed a keeper.

He should leave before he did something really stupid and volunteered for the job.

Instead of a quick goodbye, though, he shook his head and heaved out a sigh. Then he pried the key from her rigid fingers, inserted it into the lock and swung open her front door. Cool air gushed out of the house and into the heated night in welcome waves.

She was in the process of stammering out an, "Oh, um, well, thank you again," when he propped his hand above her head on the doorjamb and looked down into a face that made him think of a very cute, very sweet, very vulnerable baby owl about two wing-fluffs away from taking flight.

"Exactly how nervous do I make you, Phoebe?" he asked with a twitch of his lips that was fast threatening to turn into another grin.

The breath that escaped her was less sigh than surrender. "On a scale of one to ten?" She glanced up at him, then away, then back again before admitting, "About a fifty-five."

A dark thought had him narrowing his eyes in concern. "Because of that Jason guy? Because you think I might turn out to be like him?"

"No. Oh no. You could never be anything like Jason Collins," she said so adamantly that he smiled. "It's not that at all."

"Because you don't know me, then?"

She tried to stall a small sound that could have been a groan or a squeak. "Just the opposite. Because I *do* know you. At least I know who you are." Slender fingers rose toward her hair again.

He snagged her hand midair, held it captive in his. Her hand was soft, graceful and trembling ever so slightly. He felt that tug again and, taking pity, let go with much more reluctance than was warranted.

"I realize it's not very sophisticated to admit it," she said, clearly flustered by the contact, "but I don't know quite how to act around a man like you. I don't know what to say. I don't know what to do…with my eyes…with my hands." She stopped and lifted a hand in entreaty, her gaze landing everywhere but on him.

Most women knew how to act, he thought cynically. At least most of the women who approached him did. Maybe that was why he found *this* woman so intriguing. She was a refreshing change from the women he generally tried to avoid when he returned to Boston. The Beacon Hill Beemer set generally wanted him because he had money or because they had money and he filled the bill as their equal. Some wanted to "snag" him. Some wanted to "tame" him. He recalled the ridiculous statements in the *Boston Globe* article with a grimace. Some, he knew for a fact, simply wanted to be seen with him. And others, for some sick reason, wanted to be used by him. He, evidently, represented their personal brush with adventure.

It was all the more unsettling to realize that he appeared to be Phoebe's personal brush with intimidation—unintentional on his part, but there anyway. The longer he stood here the less he liked knowing how he affected her. He could think of other ways—many other ways—he'd like to affect her. All of them involved something much more up close and personal than holding her hand.

"When I was a little kid," he said, "I got my foot caught in the toilet bowl."

Behind her glasses, her eyes, the color of apple cider, blinked, then opened wide and disbelieving. "Get out," she said.

He grinned at her reaction. "It's true. I'd been running from my brother, teasing him with the last cookie, I think. I ran into the bathroom and jumped up on the stool to hold it out of his reach. Because he wanted it, that automatically meant I wasn't going to let him have it. Long story short, he reached, I dodged. I slipped and fell in."

She lifted her hand to cover her mouth but not before he caught the grin twitching at its corners.

"It was very serious. And I had some anxious moments, I've got to tell you."

"Oh, I would think so, yes," she said, her tongue planted deeply in her cheek.

"Yep. It was quite the ordeal. They had to dismantle the whole shebang, but once they got the toilet free from the floor, I was still stuck tighter than a wet suit on a diver.

"So there I stood," he went on, warmed by the sparkle of mirth in her eyes, "three paramedics, four firemen and a plumber all scratching their heads and trying to figure out how to get me out of the bowl. My dad was so angry at me that he threatened to make a harness and just let me carry the damn thing around on my foot for the rest of my life.''

"You're making this up,'' she accused as she leaned back against the door frame, her hands behind her back now, cushioning her hips from the molding as she visibly dropped her guard and grinned up at him.

"Scout's honor.'' He made an X over his heart with his finger. "I was ten years old and until they finally got me loose, I'd pretty much decided I'd be pitching Little League with fifty pounds of porcelain on my foot. The part I couldn't figure out was how I was going to run the bases.''

Her lips twitched again and her shoulders relaxed even more.

"I'll tell you another secret.'' He leaned in, lowering his voice as if concerned someone else might hear his whispered confession. "I used to sleep with a night-light.''

That earned him a full-fledged and gorgeous grin along with a skeptical, "Is that a fact?''

"Yeah, but it's been, oh, I don't know, weeks now since I've felt the need to turn it on.''

She laughed finally, all gentle, bubbling pleasure and silky sounds that warmed him in places a Bora-Bora sun never had. The smile that lingered was relaxed. And amused. And quite wonderful. So was the sparkle in her eyes. Suddenly the words *turned on* took a leap to another forum entirely.

"I think, Mr. Barone, that you tell a very good story.''

"Daniel. And I was just putting things into perspective. We're not so different, you and me—well, except for the male/female thing,'' he clarified with another grin. "And you're looking much more comfortable now, by the way."

"I am. Thank you."

Okay. Mission accomplished. He could go now. A smart man would.

He, evidently, was not a smart man.

Had he really done that? Daniel asked himself later. Had he really said: "How about thanking me with something cool to drink before I hit the road?"

Evidently he had, because the next thing he knew, her cheeks were pink again.

"Oh, of course. I'm sor—" she started, then caught herself. "I should have offered," she amended. "I have tea or— Let me think. Tea," she finally decided, dimpling beguilingly.

"Iced?"

She nodded.

"Works for me."

And it did, he realized when she'd invited him in with a sweep of her hand and flicked on another light. It worked just fine, although he still didn't have a scrap of insight as to why.

This wasn't his thing. She wasn't his type. Yet here he stood, shutting the door behind them while she disappeared into what he suspected was her kitchen. For several moments, he stood in cool silence and the pale glow of lamplight, one of which she'd evidently left on for the cat.

Daniel walked over to the window seat. Golden eyes set in a placid, furry face tracked his every move.

"Nice kitty?"

The cat set its tail in motion in quick, impatient snaps and gathered itself on the balls of its feet.

"Maybe not," Daniel concluded having seen that same tail flick on a cheetah just before it attacked.

He decided to leave well enough alone and check out his little owl's nest instead.

His little owl?

He shook off the absurd notion and looked around him. Her living room was small but carefully decorated in sea greens and silver grays and a sort of pinkish color he thought he'd heard his sister refer to as mauve. The fabrics were— Hell, he didn't know. Something soft and shiny. Chintz, maybe. Definitely not brocade. He shrugged, out of his element, although he recognized brocade when he saw it because every piece of furniture in his mother's sitting room at the brownstone was upholstered in it. He'd been warned from the time he'd been old enough to reach it that he was not to put his sticky fingers on the brocade.

The walls were painted a rich, frothy cream; the floor was polished hard wood partially covered by a plush area rug with roses or cabbages or something that mirrored the colors in the furniture and the drapes that she'd tied back from the windows.

From the glass-globed lamps to the white tapers and delicate pieces of pottery set in artful clusters around the room, the effect was all very feminine, and yet, the room felt very comfortable. A little fussy for his tastes, but still warm and inviting. It surprised him to realize that he sort of liked it.

It was also very romantic. Like her? he wondered. Did Phoebe Richards hide a romantic side behind her utilitarian clothes and no-nonsense haircut? It would explain the dreamy look he'd seen on her face as the

streetlights flashed across her features on the drive
across town.

To the castle.

Her words had made him grin. They made sense
now. Made more sense when he crossed the room to
inspect the contents of her overflowing bookcase. He
lifted a book out of a stack and smiled again.

Definitely a romance if the covers were to be believed. This one appeared to be a sweeping saga of a
manly man and a virginal woman, with a royal crest
and towering turrets in the background. He put the
book back and discovered more of the same, along
with a large collection of contemporary romantic suspense and several classics. *Wuthering Heights. Cam-
elot. Romeo and Juliet.*

He felt another tug of tenderness for the woman
who ate plain vanilla ice cream by herself on a Friday
night, a traditional date night in Boston culture. At
least it had been before he'd thrown a few things in
his duffel and set out to see the world almost eight
years ago.

A swift surge of anger boiled up when he thought
of Jason Collins. The man was a predator. He was
also slime. He was having a problem piecing together
any scenario in which Phoebe Richards would be
linked to him, and yet they had a history.

Daniel worked his scowl into a smile when Phoebe
appeared in the doorway, a tall glass of iced tea in
each hand.

"Hey, thanks." He drained half the glass. "That
hits the spot. And this is nice." He lifted his glass to
encompass the room. "Very nice."

She attempted to hide her pleasure and pride over
his statement behind a dismissive smile. "Only

twenty-five more years of monthly payments and it's mine, all mine—corroded pipes, peeling paint and all.''

He realized then what it was about her that captivated him so, besides the fact that she was pretty and refreshing and as tempting as the promise of the ice cream that was responsible for their chance meeting. Phoebe Richards was a real person. She didn't have it in her to be anything else. Her earlier admissions of nervousness and now her smiles were as honest as her heart. It was a rarity in his world, where most women either jockeyed for a favorable position or wanted something from him. Phoebe hadn't even wanted a ride home.

She crossed the room to the bay window where the cat waited with watchful eyes. She greeted him with a gentle scratch to the top of his head then stroked a slender hand lovingly down the length of his back. When the cat arched into her touch, Daniel damn near groaned, picturing himself the benefactor of that silky caress that was not only adoring but unconsciously sensual.

Well, there was a new wrinkle. He was jealous of a damn cat. Jealous. Of a cat. If he thought about it, it was probably as degrading as hell. He decided not to think about it.

''Guard cat?'' he asked, shaking himself away from the concept and the picture of her hand stroking the tabby.

''Keeper of the kingdom,'' she said with a small smile.

The smiles were coming easier for her now, and kind of like potato chips, he was afraid that he wasn't going to be satisfied with just one.

"He's also ruler of the roost. Arthur has made the rules and I've played by them since the day I brought him home from the pound three years ago."

"Lucky cat," he said, then looked up to find her watching him watch her hand continue to pet the purring feline.

He cleared his throat.

She dropped her hand self-consciously, her cheeks pinking prettily.

"Um, please, sit down," she offered and perched tentatively on the edge of a side chair. "I'm not usually so lax in the manners department."

And he wasn't usually so easily distracted by beguiling eyes and a pretty face that got prettier by the moment. It was time to exercise the better part of wisdom.

"Actually, I need to take off," he said, then immediately felt like a skunk when her face fell in disappointment.

Phoebe, Phoebe, Phoebe, he thought, helpless against another swell of tenderness. You are too open, too vulnerable. No wonder she made such an easy target for a creep like Jason Collins.

"Do something for me, would you?" he asked after hiding his unsettling reaction by finishing his tea in a long swallow. "Find someplace other than a frog to hide your house key. And get some decent locks on your doors, okay? You need a dead bolt," he added and with grim determination walked to the front door. "Better yet, get a professional to come in here and set you up with a complete security system."

She set her untouched tea on a glass-covered end table and rose, wiping her palms on her shorts. "I'm fine. Really. But thanks for your concern."

So formal. So much denial.

He frowned down at her as she joined him by the door. "The guy is a problem, Phoebe. He's not going away. I know his type. You've hurt his pride, banged the hell out of his ego. Level with me. This isn't the first time he's hassled you, is it?"

He could see her struggle to deny it, but just as he figured, her basic honesty wouldn't let her.

"He's called during the night a couple of times. Harassed me at work. But he's never approached me like—well, like he did tonight."

"Which only shows that he's building up a head of steam." He expelled a troubled breath. "I don't suppose you've ever taken any self-defense classes?"

She seemed to find his question amusing.

He tilted his head. "And that's funny because…?"

"It's funny because in my world and my line of work, self-defense is rarely an issue. I'm a librarian," she clarified. "We tend to level fines not karate chops."

Of course. Pretty, shy little Phoebe was a librarian. This was too good.

"A librarian," he said, smiling into a face that was trying to decide if he was going to tease her about her profession. He sincerely hoped she didn't have a family farm to lose, because if it came down to a poker game, she was a goner.

"Boston Public," she added, sounding a little defensive. She relaxed and expanded when she realized that he liked the idea. "The children's library."

"Why is it that they never had librarians who looked like you when I was checking out *National Geographic* in the eighth grade?"

Her eyes softened, warming to his smile. "*National Geographic,* huh? For the articles, I suppose?"

"Oh, absolutely." He was barely aware that he'd moved toward her.

She was *very* aware. Her gaze was watchful, her eyes overbright.

"It never occurred to me," he said, shrinking the distance between them to little more than an inch, "that there might be pictures of bare-breasted women between those scholarly pages. Imagine my shock when I found them in magazine after magazine after magazine."

"Imagine," she echoed with a tentative smile.

He was making her nervous again. Not an uncomfortable kind of nervous. An aware kind of nervous that painted her cheeks with a rosy blush. He liked her reaction—maybe a little too much.

"And did those very same magazines prompt you to—" she paused, sounding as breathless as a marathon runner at the finish line "—to embark on all the adventures that have made you so famous?"

His hands were on her shoulders now. They were small and fragile and yielding beneath his palms. It hadn't been a conscious decision on his part to place them there. Just as it hadn't been a conscious decision to draw her toward him. Yet he was very conscious of her eyes that had softened to a melted caramel and were watching his face with an intriguing mix of apprehension and desire.

"Absolutely. I've been searching for wisdom and—" His gaze dropped to her mouth, then lower, to the soft mounds of her breasts that rose and fell beneath her cotton top. The tight little beads of her nipples pressed enticingly against the fabric, mere inches away from his chest.

"And insight?" she suggested on a whisper. "Inspiration?"

"Inspiration, yeah. That'll work." He lifted a hand, trailed the back of his fingers along the rise of her cheek. "I've got to tell you. At the moment, I'm feeling truly inspired."

"Oh." Behind her glasses, the heavy sweep of her lashes lowered to brush her cheeks. Lush. Seductive. Inviting.

This was a mistake.

It didn't feel like a mistake, though, as he lowered his head, even though the word banged around in the left side of his brain like a pinball. What it felt like was a little bit of heaven to be this close to her, to claim the kiss he'd been fantasizing about since she'd turned around with her ice cream and blinded him with her smile.

He touched his mouth to first one corner of hers and then the other, telegraphing his intentions, offering his little bird the opportunity to fly away.

She didn't fly. She didn't even fluff a wing. She didn't go anywhere. Before she had a change of heart, he aligned his mouth with hers and took his need all the way home.

Honest, he thought again as he sank into the luxurious warmth and the dewy fresh taste of her. She was so honest with her response. Everything that she was flowed into her kiss. Innocence, guilelessness, openness. And wonder.

The lingering taste of vanilla flavored her mouth, richer than the sweetest cream. Her lips were petal soft, like summer roses. The sigh that soughed out when he slid his hands down her arms then wrapped them around her, married hesitation with restlessness. And when he asked her to open for him with a gentle nip of his teeth to her lower lip then the questing glance of his tongue, she hesitated for only a heartbeat before inviting him inside.

The tenderness he felt for her shifted, like a hot wind, to something more intense, more demanding. Heat. Hunger. Need. A desire so much stronger than anything he'd ever experienced tightened in his chest then crept, by inches, toward his groin.

Too much, the rational half of his brain warned.

Not enough, the other half insisted when her small hands clutched lightly at his waist then rose in a slow, sensual sweep up the length of his back.

Good Lord, he thought, forcing himself to lift his head and break the contact, only to dive back for more when her dreamy amber eyes and kiss-swollen lips asked for his return.

Trouble.

He was in it. Deep. And sinking deeper.

It was way past time to walk away. And in about a hundred years, he was going to. But right now, right now, he was simply going to kiss her.

With a will he'd rarely, if ever, had to call on, he finally ended the kiss. Cupping her shoulders to steady them both, he tipped his head toward the ceiling and gulped in a bracing breath. A long moment spun out, tempting him back toward the minefield before he found his bearings and with it his voice.

"Well," he said, hearing a gruffness that he had to ignore if he was going to get out of this before he took more than a kiss.

More than a kiss was out of the question. For him,

absolutely. For her, without a doubt. Phoebe Richards needed and deserved ten times more than he had it in him to give.

"Well," he said again and fabricated a smile that could have been directed at his maiden aunt. "So much for inspiration."

"Um." Her eyes were closed. She had a shell-shocked look about her as she stood there, swaying a little on her feet.

"Yeah." He couldn't have agreed more. "Look, Phoebe—"

"Wait." She opened her eyes with a little shake of her head. "I—I think I know this part. It's late. You've got to go, right? And I've got to work tomorrow, so it's time to call it a night. It's okay. Really. No harm, no foul."

Well. She certainly made *that* easy. So why did he feel so low?

Because her mouth was as tempting as Original Sin. Because her eyes were whisper soft and searching. A hundred emotions played behind them, one of them was regret.

"You're going to be okay now, right?"

She nodded once, then again.

"And you'll—"

"—see about new locks." She forced a thin smile. "Yeah. I'll check it out."

Now was not the time to question his good fortune. He wrapped his fingers around the doorknob. "Okay. Well. It's been nice meeting you."

Her head bobbed again in jerky agreement. "Sure. Me, too. I mean, *you,* too. It was nice meeting *you,* too."

He watched her face for a long moment before he

tugged open the door and walked outside. At the end of her sidewalk, he turned back, studied the incredible face that he'd never see again and swallowed back an empty feeling in the pit of his stomach. "Goodbye, Phoebe."

She pressed her cheek against the edge of the door, smiled. "Bye."

"Take care of yourself, okay?"

She nodded. "Thank you again for helping me out."

And then she closed the door.

Well, that was the end of that, he told himself as he walked to his car. Yet he sat behind the wheel for a full minute before turning the key. And when he finally shifted into reverse and backed out of her driveway, he experienced an unsettling notion that he was making a huge mistake by driving out of her life.

"Mistake for whom, Barone?" he wondered aloud as he sat at a stoplight and waited for it to turn green.

That was the issue, wasn't it? He had no question that it was the right thing to do for her. With the exception of Collins, she had a nice, orderly life going for her. She didn't need him blowing holes in it. And he would. When he left—and he always left—he'd leave her less than when he'd found her. So he didn't want to start something he couldn't end without hurting her.

He wasn't conceited but he wasn't blind. He'd seen—hell, he'd *felt* the way she'd reacted to him. It would have been so easy to talk her into bed. But Phoebe was too sweet, too real and too good to love and then leave in the morning.

So yeah. It was the right thing for her.

For the first time in his life, though, he wondered if leaving a woman—leaving *this* woman—was the right thing for him.

Four

—

"It couldn't have been that bad, sweetie." Leslie Griffin, stylish at sixty with her chic auburn hair and trim figure, grinned sympathetically the next morning as Phoebe pounded her forehead softly on her desktop at the library.

"It was worse than bad," Phoebe moaned, flattening her cheek on the infamous back issue of the *Boston Globe* that lay open in the center of her desk. She expelled a heavy sigh. "If I managed to string more than three words together in any semblance of a coherent thought it would have to have been 'I' and 'um' and 'sorry.' I am such a putz."

Wearily lifting her head, she snagged her glasses, slipped them on and slumped back in her desk chair. "I have this chance magical meeting with the most gorgeous man in Boston—strike that—the most gorgeous man in the *world*—and I make a run at Moron of the Century. What's wrong with me?''

"Nothing's wrong with you. Good grief, that scene with Jason would be enough to knock anyone for a loop. The creep. I can't believe he's still hassling you."

Phoebe propped her elbows on her desk with another huge sigh and stared morosely at the *Globe*'s spread on Daniel Barone. "Oh, well. I'll never see him again, so I guess it doesn't matter. Not that it would anyway. He is so out of my league."

"Do you know how angry it makes me when you put yourself down like that?"

"I'm not putting myself down. A fact is simply a fact. Women like me don't get the princes or the white knights," she assured her friend levelly. She could admit things like this to Leslie and not feel as if she was wallowing in self-pity. "Women like me— plain, boring and on skittish terms with their own shadow—get the leftovers in life, not the desserts, which Daniel Barone definitely is.

"Go ahead and shake your head," she said without heat, "but it's the truth and you know it. He is everything this magazine article says and more. He's unbelievably good-looking. He's charismatic and charming. He's also a globe-trotting millionaire adventurer who's probably had scores of sophisticated and exotic lovers."

She smoothed her thumb over a photo of Daniel, wind-whipped and smiling in anticipation at the base of Kangshung Face during his second triumphant but harrowing ascent of Mount Everest. "Stack all that up against a cat-coddling librarian, who according to this article is three years his senior and who is also being dogged by an ex-boyfriend turned stalker, and it's pretty much a forgone conclusion that his world and mine are not going to collide in some universe-altering cosmic explosion."

Unfazed by her little diatribe, Leslie pointed out the obvious. "He kissed you good-night, didn't he?"

Phoebe closed her eyes to enjoy the memory and ride out the delicious little shudder that rippled through her body. "Oh, yeah."

Leslie chuckled. "That's got to say something."

"It was a mercy kiss," Phoebe assured her, snapping out of her little trip into sensory overload.

"Didn't sound like it to me. Of course, I'd have to hear the details to make sure."

"I already gave you the details," Phoebe groused.

Leslie scooted a hip on the corner of Phoebe's desk. "Yeah, but having been married for almost forty years now—to a wonderful man, mind you—I live vicariously through you young 'uns to get my cheap thrills. Indulge me. Again."

Phoebe finally smiled at Leslie who was not only a co-worker but also a real friend. With her own children grown and scattered across the United States, Leslie looked upon her as a surrogate daughter. For that matter, Phoebe looked upon Leslie as sort of a mother figure. She provided a nurturing comfort that Phoebe had never received from her own mother. In fact, from the time Phoebe could remember, if there had been a mother in her life when she was growing up a lonesome and insecure only child of a single parent, she had played the role herself.

It wasn't an unusual situation for children of alcoholic parents. She'd learned this through a lot of reading and the Al-Anon meetings that had helped her deal with her mother's illness. No, it wasn't unusual, but it didn't make her feel the loss any less.

Just as she was still having trouble dealing with Jason's alcoholism. When she'd met him four months ago he'd seemed like a dream come true. Then he'd morphed into a living nightmare. To this day Phoebe couldn't figure out how she'd missed the signs. She'd lived with the disease. Possibly, as she had with her mother, she'd been too busy denying the truth to muster enough self-esteem to admit that Jason was the problem, not her, even after he'd started showing his true colors.

And quite possibly, she'd been blinded by the hope that Jason had represented the possibility of marriage and family. It wasn't that she felt she needed a man to define her, or that she needed marriage to complete her life. She was making it just fine on her own. But children. Oh, how she dreamed of having children. To love. To nurture. To give what she'd never received as a child. To watch them grow strong and secure and loved as she'd never been.

"Helloooo," Leslie crooned, making Phoebe realize that she'd lapsed into one of her little funks that thoughts of Jason and her mother always brought on. "Where'd you go?"

"Sorry. Short trip down nightmare lane. Look. I'd better get to work. I've got a dozen things to do this morning and then I need to get ready for children's hour in—" She checked her watch. "Yikes. In twenty minutes. You need to change, too."

"I know what I need to do because it's my day to work. Now, the reason *you're* working on your day off is…?" Leslie left the question dangling like an accusation as she edged toward the door.

Phoebe lifted her chin. "Because Allison asked me to fill in for her."

"You always end up picking up the slack for her. You're too easy, Phoebe. You need to think about *you* for a change."

Phoebe shrugged off her friend's words. "It's no big deal. Besides, I can use the money. According to Mr. Barone, I need to have the locks on my house updated."

"Really?" Leslie said, sounding intrigued. "So the man's concerned about you."

"More like alarmed. And that doesn't add up to interest," she clarified quickly. "If I'd acted around you the way I acted around him last night, you'd be worried that I couldn't handle brushing my teeth without supervision."

She shook her head again, mortified all over by her inability to get it together around him. "He'd show the same consideration to any dim bulb who crossed his path. He's just a nice guy."

"Nice guys don't kiss dim bulbs and up their wattage enough to light up the neighborhood just because they're being considerate. Now, how did that kiss go again?"

With a snort and a reluctant grin, Phoebe opened her desk drawer and pulled out the latest release by her favorite romance author. She thumbed through the book until she found the page she was looking for. With a flourish, she held it out to Leslie and tapped the page with her finger.

"Right there," she said. "That's how that kiss went. Read it and weep, for both of us, 'cause we'll probably never experience another one like it in either of our lifetimes."

For a fact, she'd never experienced anything like Daniel Barone's kiss. And it hadn't felt like a mercy kiss at the time. It had been all energy and heat, seduction and promise. She'd never been kissed like that before. Like she'd been special to him, like she'd been amazing to him. Like he couldn't get enough of her.

In the end, he'd had more than enough, though, she concluded as she closed the magazine and rose to dig her costume out of the storage closet. He'd left, hadn't he?

Yeah. He'd left. And sorry sap that she was, she was afraid she'd let him take a little piece of her heart with him.

On all fours and perspiring delicately beneath the lightweight but cumbersome tortoise costume, Phoebe slowed her voice to the lumbering cadence of Tommy Turtle. Twenty-plus preschool boys and girls sat on the floor in a circle around her, caught up in rapt fascination while she and Leslie, as Robert Rabbit, played out the storybook tale.

"But it's my home," Phoebe, as Tommy Turtle, said, dragging each word out and blinking in sloe-eyed shock at Robert Rabbit's absurd proposition. "I couldn't sell you my shell. Why, where would I sleep? What would I wear?"

Tommy Turtle, no doubt, had been part of the reason Allison had begged Phoebe to take her shift today. Unlike Allison, Phoebe didn't mind dressing in this ridiculous turtle getup and bumbling about on her hands and knees for half an hour. She loved this part of her job. The children's bright, excited eyes, uncensored laughter and shouts of encouragement always elevated her mood.

"I couldn't sell my shell, could I, boys and girls?" she appealed to her pint-size audience.

"No!" they all shouted in unison. "Don't sell it! Don't sell it!"

"There, see?" Tommy Turtle said to Robert Rabbit. "They agree. You'll just have to find somewhere else to live. I wish I could help you. I really do."

Phoebe smiled warmly as a little brunette with a tentative expression and big brown eyes stood back from the cluster of children, shy over her late arrival.

"Hi," Phoebe said, as Tommy Turtle. "What's your name, little girl?"

"Kayla," she said with a timid grin.

"Hi, Kayla. I'm Tommy. Say hi to Kayla, boys and girls."

A musical chorus of, "Hi, Kayla," resounded through the story room of the children's library.

"Aren't you going to say hi to *me?*"

Phoebe froze. That deep, amused voice could only belong to one man. She closed her eyes, let out a breath that would have made Darth Vader proud.

It wasn't bad enough that I played the part of a mouse last night in front of him? she appealed to a twisted fate that apparently had it in for her. *This morning he gets to see me as a turtle? How...fortunate.*

Slowly, she lifted her head. If she hadn't already been on her knees, the look of him would have put her there.

He was dressed in a black, body-hugging T-shirt and snug, faded jeans that molded lovingly over every hard angle and intriguing plane of his body. He stood with one shoulder propped lazily against the stacks, his tanned arms crossed over his broad chest. A grin the size of Texas spread across his sinfully attractive face.

What was he doing here? And why did he have to look like a hero on the cover of a hard-edged romantic suspense novel while she looked like something that ate dead flies and had recently crawled out of a sandbox?

Life was not fair.

"Say hi to Mr. Barone, boys and girls," she said, forcing herself to meet his eyes as the children rewarded him with another rousing greeting.

His smile shifted from her face to the children as he waved hello.

In spite of Leslie's sly smiles and Daniel's amused grin, Phoebe muddled through the rest of the story. As soon as the children dispersed to various corners of the room to find their favorite books to check out, she planned on making a speedy exit. She may be wondering why he was here but she didn't have any intention of finding out.

He, however, had other plans.

His hand appeared before her, offering her assistance to her feet.

When she simply sat back on her heels and ignored him, he squatted down in front of her.

"Did you hear about the snail that got mugged by two turtles?" he asked without preamble, and she had a feeling it was just to see her cheeks flood with color.

"No," she said with a weary sigh, then obliged him by biting on his joke. "What about the snail that got mugged by two turtles?"

"Well, when the police asked the snail to describe

his attackers, he said, 'I can't. It all happened so fast.'"

She waited a beat, got it, then groaned. "That's awful."

"I know. Couldn't resist." Just as he evidently couldn't resist teasing her. "Besides, you really think it's funny."

Yeah. She did, but she wasn't going to admit it. She did not want to prolong this encounter. He, quite obviously, did.

"This is a good look for you," he said, a smile in his voice. "Good color, too."

She sighed again, resigned to the fact that he wasn't going away. "Yes, well, moss green and mud brown have always been the staples of my wardrobe."

She risked a look into his eyes then and began a slow and steady meltdown at the warmth and humor she saw there.

"I was talking about pink." He brushed the back of a curled finger to her flaming cheek. "Very becoming."

Oh, boy.

Powerless against his smile, disoriented by his proximity, she resorted to her only line of defense. She lifted her shoulders and, tucking in her chin, withdrew inside Tommy Turtle's shell.

His soft chuckle enveloped her. "You really get into character, don't you? I like that in a turtle." When she didn't respond, he gave the shell three light taps. "Hello? Hello? Are you in there?"

Why didn't he just go away and let her suffer her embarrassment in martyred silence? Or, here was a thought, why didn't she just suck it up and face the music?

With grim determination, she poked her head back out of the shell. "You have an uncanny knack for finding me at my very best," she said, trying not to sound grumpy. "Let's make it a clean sweep, shall we? I have a mud pack planned for seven o'clock. You're welcome to attend."

Oh, those eyes. Oh, that smile.

He stood, commandeered her hands and helped her to her feet. "Actually, I was thinking more in terms of dinner."

"Dinner?" He was asking her to dinner?

"Even turtles have to eat, right? What time do you get off work?"

"Five. She gets off at five," volunteered Leslie, who'd been watching the exchange in absorbed silence. She doffed her bunny ears and extended her hand, the grin between her own ears stretching wide. "Leslie Griffin."

"Daniel Barone." He returned Leslie's handshake and smile before turning back to Phoebe. "So, seven-thirty will work for you? Unless you had other plans?"

"Just the mud pack," Phoebe mumbled as she cast the beaming Leslie a warning glare.

"Great. I'll pick you up."

"What should she wear?" Leslie asked when Phoebe just stood there, too flustered to think that far ahead.

"Something casual." He stopped at the door, turned. "It's too hot to dress for dinner." He tossed her another knee-melting smile and the temperature in the room heated up about fifty degrees. "See you then."

"Oh, it's hot all right." Leslie used her bunny ears

to fan her face theatrically after Daniel disappeared out of earshot. "Good Lord, Phoebe. He's incredible."

"I'm not prepared to talk about this with you right now," Phoebe muttered with a troubled scowl.

"I can wait," Leslie said with a knowing grin. "But I'll expect details on Monday," she added, her voice full of laughter as it trailed Phoebe into her office, where she shut the door soundly behind her.

Once there, she unstrapped herself from the bulky turtle shell then slumped against the wall. She forked her hair away from her face with splayed fingers, stared at the ceiling and wondered if her heart had ever before beaten this hard or this fast.

She pressed a hand over her breast, drew a bracing breath. Daniel Barone had sought her out. On a Saturday, when he probably had a hundred other things he could have been doing. A hundred other women he could have been seeing. But he'd come to see her.

He'd flirted and smiled. With her. And he wanted to take her to dinner. *Her.*

"Maybe there's something wrong with him," she mused aloud when she met Leslie in the story room, as a new and wary panic kicked in. "Maybe he's socially maladjusted, or has athlete's foot or bad breath or maybe he has a small—"

"Uh, uh, uh." Leslie cut her off with a waggling finger.

"I was going to say *ego.*"

"There is nothing wrong with that man's ego—or anything else for that matter.

"Phoebe, did you ever think that maybe he just *likes* you?" Leslie suggested, her tone and her look both supportive and censuring. "Did you ever think that maybe he's simply intuitive and intelligent and knows a good thing when he sees it? Did you ever think of that?''

No, she never had, Phoebe realized, then allowed herself a brief, delicious moment to consider the possibility.

So much for his plans to stay away from her, Daniel thought as he pulled out of the library parking lot and headed for his parents' brownstone.

It was fast turning into a day of should-have and shouldn't-haves. He shouldn't have slept so late. He should have realized that his aimless driving wasn't aimless at all when he found himself on Boylston Street and then cruising by the McKim Building, with its sloping red tile roof and green copper cresting that housed the Boston Public Library.

He should have just checked on Phoebe. That had been his excuse, after all, for stopping at the library in the first place. He'd just wanted to make sure she was okay and he'd ended up asking her to dinner. He hadn't planned it. It had just happened, and it shouldn't have. Just as he shouldn't have kissed her last night. Or thought about it as much as he had.

He should have made his first stop at his mother's, he realized with a sense of guilt when he opened the front door to the brownstone and her face lit up at the sight of him.

''Daniel, darling, it's so good to have you home!''

He returned her embrace as he shut the door behind him.

''It's good to be home, Mom. You look fantastic,'' he said, holding her at arm's length. Sandra Barone was a very young fifty-nine. Her tall frame was fit and trim, her blond hair was stylishly short and her gray eyes were lively and intuitive.

She waved a hand. "And you are a charmer, as usual. Your father is going to be so sorry that he missed you. He ran into the office for a bit."

"It's okay. I'll catch him later," he promised.

"So tell me. When did you get in? And more important, how long are you going to be home?"

For eight years, those had been her standard opening lines. For eight years, he'd given his standard reply. "Just last night and for a little while."

"Oh, Daniel." Arm linked with his, she walked him into the sitting room. "I know you get tired of hearing this but your father and I so wish that you'd settle down, return to Boston for good and finish your law degree. Baronessa Gelati could use your brilliant mind on the legal team. Besides, I worry about you. We both do."

She stopped abruptly, shook her head in self-reproach. "Here I am, nagging already when I promised myself I would stop doing that. It's just that we see so little of you."

"I know. And it's okay." And then he did the other thing he always did. He sidestepped her concerns. "So what's been happening around here since I was home last month? Anybody get married or have a baby?" It was a legitimate question. Many of his cousins and even his little sister, Emily, now engaged, had been dropping into the happily-ever-after pool at an alarming rate over the past several months.

"Oh, darling boy, how funny you should ask. Best sit down for this, I've got news that's going to shock you."

* * *

Shock had been the right word, Daniel thought later that morning when he caught up with his sister Claudia right where his mother said she'd be, at the Ritz-Carlton, schmoozing money for one of her favorite causes.

He momentarily tabled his mother's startling news as he nursed a soda and watched Claudia covertly from the bar while she charmed—or, depending on your viewpoint, steamrollered—a couple of movers and shakers out of a substantial contribution for an inner-city day-care center. Animated as ever, her blue eyes danced as she tossed her fine blond hair over her shoulder and dimpled prettily for her marks. No one could work a room like Claudia, he thought with pride.

He didn't approach her until the men had left, considerably lighter in the wallet. She was stuffing facts and figures into her briefcase when she spotted him.

"Daniel," she squealed and flew into his arms. "Where did you come from? How long have you been here? My God! It's great to see you. Sit. Sit and talk to me."

"Well," he said after they'd caught up on the basics, "now that I know *what* you're working on, care to tell me whom you've targeted for your latest personal fix-up project?"

Claudia threw him a haughty look. "I have no idea what you're talking about."

Okay. So she didn't want to talk about whom she was dating or even *if* she was dating, which told him he'd hit the nail on the head. Claudia had a tendency lately to become involved with men who needed something fixed in their lives. It worried him that maybe she'd been seriously damaged by her breakup with Jonathan Norman two years ago and that she'd rather deal with anyone's problems but her own.

"So have you been to see the folks?" she asked, making it clear that her love life was off-limits.

Fine, he thought, and they launched into a discussion of the bombshell his mother had dropped.

"I want to make sure I've got this straight," he said, then restated what his mother had told him. "We have a long-lost and recently discovered cousin."

"Karen Rawlins," Claudia said with a confirming nod. "At least that's her birth name. But the fact is that her father, who went by the name of Timothy Rawlins, was actually Dad's twin brother."

"And our uncle Luke," he mused aloud, still struggling with the news. "You know, he was lost so long ago that I rarely think about him." Their father's twin brother had been kidnapped from the hospital shortly after the twins' birth. He'd never been seen or heard from since. Until now. "Since we never knew him, he was more like this storybook character that Dad mentions when he's feeling melancholy."

"Well, he was real," Claudia supplied. "Evidently, the people who abducted him raised him by the name Timothy Rawlins. Uncle Luke—sorry, Tim Rawlins—married at some point and Karen was born. It wasn't until both Karen's parents were killed in a car accident a year ago that she started questioning the truth about her father's identity."

Daniel leaned back, slinging his arm over the chair back. "Mom said Karen had found her grandmother's diary and that had raised her questions."

Claudia pushed her hair back from her face. "That's what got her going, but since Karen's grandparents are also deceased she had no one to ask about her past. She let it go for a while but then, well, remember the family picture we had taken at the reunion last month? Right before the skirts walloped the shirts in volleyball?'' she reminded him with a needling grin. ''Well, some wire service picked up the picture, Karen saw it and did a double take when she saw Dad because he was a dead ringer for her father.''

''I'd forgotten that Dad and Uncle Luke were identical twins,'' Daniel mused aloud, thinking of his own fraternal twin, Derrick, who was as different from him as night from day.

Claudia nodded. ''Karen started digging again. Between the diary and researching old newspaper accounts of Uncle Luke's kidnapping, she pieced it all together that she was related to this bunch of gelato Barones.''

''This is too wild.''

''It's kind of cool, actually. When you meet her, you'll see that she's a Barone. The genes show. She's also very nice. And a little lost right now, I think. She's searching for something to hold on to. Dad's been pretty emotional about the whole thing, as well.''

''So Mom said. While he's sad because now he knows for a fact that Luke is dead, he's also very happy to have some small piece of his twin back.''

''Mom told you about the big welcome-to-the-family party planned for Karen?''

''Oh yeah. She was very clear that my presence is required. Don't worry. I'll stick around.'' The party was a couple of weeks away. He hadn't originally planned on hanging around that long. For a lot of reasons. One reason he hadn't counted on was a silly little turtle with beguiling pink cheeks.

"Speaking of twins, have you seen Derrick yet?"

No. Daniel hadn't seen his brother yet and that was why, after he left Claudia, he drove straight to the Baronessa Gelati manufacturing plant in Brookline. He always made the rounds when he came home, and since his other sister Emily and Derrick both worked in Quality Management—Derrick as VP and Emily as Derrick's secretary—he'd kill two birds with one stone.

"I can't believe Derrick's got you working on a Saturday." Daniel grinned as Emily looked up from her desk and spotted him. It was like an instant replay of the scene with Claudia. She flew up and into his arms with a squeal. "What does your fireman have to say about that?"

"Shane pulled the weekend shift so it's okay."

Daniel searched her sparkling brown eyes and liked what he saw. "And life with the fireman? That's okay, too?"

"More than okay." Emily beamed, then blushed. "In five more months I'll be Mrs. Shane Cummings and then it will be even better than okay."

Daniel touched a finger to her cheek, happy to see her so in love. "I'll be there," he answered her unspoken question. "Nothing could make me miss it."

He hugged her against him, touching his lips to the top of her head. "Derrick around?"

"Derrick is always around," his twin said gruffly from behind him. "Unlike you."

Daniel turned. His brother was standing in his open office doorway, wearing his usual designer suit and dour expression. It was hard sometimes for Daniel to believe they were from the same gene pool, let alone that they were fraternal twins. Sometimes it seemed that the only thing they shared in common was the Barone name and their brown hair. Derrick's eyes were brown to Daniel's blue, his manner harsh and grim compared to Daniel's easygoing nature.

"Well," Daniel said with an amiable smile, "someone has to be the slacker in the family."

"You said it, I didn't," Derrick said with a sour smile.

"It's always so good to see you, too, Derrick." Daniel tucked Emily under his shoulder. "It's leveling, you know?"

"You guys," Emily interrupted, squeezing Daniel's waist and scowling at Derrick. "If anyone walked in on this little exchange and didn't know you, they'd think you hated each other."

Yeah, Daniel thought later as he pulled out of the parking lot and replayed his strained conversation with Derrick. Anyone would think that they hated each other, even though they'd both sucked it up and made an effort to be civil for Emily's benefit.

Things had always been that way between them. Tense—bordering on hostile. Lately it had even been worse, with Derrick's actions defensive, bitter and on edge. Their strained relationship was one of the reasons Daniel didn't stick around for long when he came home. It crossed his mind then that Derrick might be one of the reasons he'd left in the first place. And his own frustration with his twin was one of the reasons he found himself looking forward to dinner with a certain librarian.

The honest truth was that he hadn't been able to stop thinking about her, though he still didn't have a firm handle on why. Maybe, he thought, heading west on Storrow along the Boston side of the Charles River, it had something to do with the way she managed to make him smile for no apparent reason other than the simple fact that she existed.

Five

It was later afternoon, heading toward evening, by the time Daniel had checked in with his dad and a couple of his married buddies. He made a quick pit stop at his apartment to shower, shave and pull on a clean black T-shirt and a pair of tan chinos. Shoving his bare feet into comfortably worn loafers, he snagged his keys and headed for Phoebe's, still trying to pin down his preoccupation with her.

On the way over, he had a breakthrough.

''Bingo,'' he said aloud, slapping the flat of his palm on the steering wheel.

During the past few years, he had wined, dined and bedded some of the most glamorous and sought-after women in the world. Among them were a Swedish model, an American actress and an Austrian princess. All were sophisticated and self-assured, witty and willowy. They'd been big thrills, wild nights and high maintenance. What they hadn't been was comfortable.

That was what Phoebe gave him. Comfort. She was like comfort food for his soul, he decided, grinning over his analogy. Well, maybe that was going a little overboard, but basically, that was it.

He'd spent, what? A total of an hour, hour and a half with her during two brief encounters? He hardly knew her, yet she made him feel a sort of peace, a pleasant fullness, an ease like he'd never felt before, even with his own family.

His mother was deeply embroiled in her civic projects and bridge marathons. His father was married to his work. Both wanted him to be something he wasn't, to do something he couldn't. Claudia, God love her, was single-handedly championing every worthy cause known to man. Emily was so wrapped up in her fireman that she saw nothing but him, which was exactly the way it should be. Then there was Derrick.

That hollow, empty feeling he often felt around his twin only seemed to intensify as the years and the distance between them widened. It frustrated him that they couldn't find some common ground other than blood to bind them, saddened him that he missed what they should have had together.

And then along came Phoebe. Out of the blue, she popped into his life, made him forget about what was lacking in it and simply made him smile.

"Comfort food," he mused aloud, warming to the idea as he pulled into her driveway. It would explain a lot of things, like maybe that comfort level she induced was what had drawn him to her in the first place.

He was feeling smug over his conclusion and congratulating himself for recovering his perspective when Phoebe answered his knock at seven-thirty sharp. He took one look at her and any misaligned notion of associating her with chicken soup and apple pie cut and ran like a tight-end sprinting toward the goal line.

So did the power of speech.

She looked incredible.

She looked edible—and he wasn't talking PBJ's.

She looked like a long night of self-restraint.

"Hi," she said when he just stood there, captivated by the sight of her.

Unaware of the slow smile playing at the corners of his mouth, he let his gaze linger over her gauzy, lemon-yellow sundress. It was soft and feminine and so whimsically sheer it was almost as transparent as the uncertainty in her eyes.

She had no idea how sexy she looked. No idea that even though the sleeveless dress was cut modestly low above her breasts and draped over slim hips to fall to midcalf, there was something inordinately seductive about it. Something essentially romantic.

A row of delicate shell buttons started at her knees, nipped in at her waist then ascended to that warm, mysterious place between her breasts. Though the possibilities those buttons brought to mind were implied not overt, they brought a very erotic image to his mind. One flick of his finger and those lush breasts that she'd successfully hidden behind a blousy tank top and a cartoon tortoiseshell would spill warm and heavy into his hands. More than fill them.

The surprises didn't end there. She'd gone to special pains for him, he realized, and along with the pleasure, he experienced a twinge of guilt over her efforts.

She'd curled her hair. Soft, silky wisps lay about her face like glossy, butterscotch taffy. Subtly applied makeup heightened the natural peaches-and-cream color of her cheeks and enhanced the softness of those wide, full lips that he couldn't look at without associating with rose petals and hot, wet kisses.

"No glasses," he said as it occurred to him what else was different about her.

"Contacts." She gave a little shrug and met his gaze with huge, round eyes of the palest, most soulful caramel that were framed by lashes as thick and lush as sable.

She's so shy, he thought as she averted her gaze and turned back toward the living room.

"I'll, um, just get my purse."

He shoved his hands in his pants pockets and was busy catching his breath, regrouping his thoughts and studying the stupid plaster frog sitting on her stoop when she breezed out of the house and closed the door behind her. Her toes caught his attention then. The same hot-red toenails that he'd noticed the first time he'd seen her peeked out from flat, white espadrilles and brought his runaway hormones to heel.

Go figure that it was the siren-red toenail polish that settled him down. It was the toenail polish that reminded him that this was a woman who guarded herself closely. She would never intentionally flaunt her sexuality. Instead, she indulged in little ways. Secret ways.

Like let's-get-naked red toenail polish that hardly anyone would ever see or even notice.

It made him wonder what else she indulged in. A

hundred illicit pictures of what lay beneath that simple yet seductive dress played through his mind like flash cards as he walked her to the car. White lace? Silky and sheer? A teddy or a thong? Or nothing at all.

"All set?" he asked, finding his voice as he settled her into the passenger seat.

She nodded.

"Lookin' good, Phoebe," he said belatedly, because she was and because it was suddenly important that she knew it. And because, he realized as his heart thumped him hard in the chest, if he hadn't said something, he might have hauled her across the console and onto his lap and discovered just how fast he could get those buttons undone.

"Must have been the mud pack," she said with a little quirk of her lips that sent an arc of arousal shooting through his blood that he tried to cover with a chuckle.

Comfort food? What a joke. A man in his present state of simmering arousal was far from comfortable—especially when he knew there wasn't going to be any relief from that quarter. Not with her.

So now what, Barone? He'd railroaded her into spending time with him for purely selfish reasons. His reasons were still selfish, but they'd shifted from a simple quest for companionship to something else entirely. And that just couldn't happen.

It was going to take everything in him to keep his hands off her. And it wasn't because he'd been out in the Kalahari too long. It was because he wanted her.

Because he could hurt her, though, he wasn't going to act on that wanting.

He pulled out into traffic, then realized the silence had become awkward. He had to end it if they were going to make it through this night with any semblance of normalcy. "So, what are you hungry for?"

She stared out the window. "Your call."

As he zipped through the streets, Daniel tapped his thumbs on the steering wheel, aware that she was still uncomfortable around him. Her face, when she'd discovered him at the library had asked, Why? Why are you here?

Well, he'd thought he had it figured out. Until now. Now he knew only one thing: She wore red toenail polish. Convoluted as that leap of logic seemed, it served to remind him that he absolutely could not get involved with her romantically.

Everything about Phoebe added up to long-term commitment, hearth, home, family. You name it, she should have it. Everything about him subtracted from that package. But damn it, he liked being with her. He *wanted* to be with her.

No harm, no foul, she'd said last night when he'd left her. Okay. She'd made it clear that she knew there was no romance on the horizon between them. With that kind of sanction, why not just stay the course? Just keep it loose and friendly between them? He knew how to do that. He was a master of no strings, no complications. He could say the right words and make the right noises that would guarantee they kept it casual.

And this libido of his that had stepped front and center and volunteered to take things to a different level didn't call the shots. It hadn't in the past, and he wasn't going to let it now. He wasn't going to hurt her. And if he took their relationship past platonic, he would.

What he was going to do was simply enjoy her friendship for the little bit of time he was in Boston. In the process, maybe he could figure out a way to help her deal with Jason Collins.

He felt himself level out again. That would work. He was worried about her, after all. He could help her cope with that creep and not feel as if he was being entirely self-serving.

He cut a glance her way, then back to traffic as his jaw clenched. All he had to do to evade complications was avoid thinking about the way she looked in that dress, avoid imagining what she looked like out of it. All he had to do was forget about that kiss, the one that shouldn't have happened. The one that shouldn't have been so sweet and so wild and so incredible that he was starting to wonder if it had been a hallucination brought on by jet lag and sleep deprivation.

If only...

"So how do you feel about pizza?" Phoebe heard Daniel ask through a haze of thick, face-flushing embarrassment.

How did she feel about pizza? At the moment? Well, she felt the same way about pizza that she felt about raw liver and an old maid librarian who tried to be something she wasn't. The thought turned her stomach.

"Pizza's fine," she said and fought back the humiliating recollection of Daniel's blank reaction when he'd opened the door and gotten a gander at her all decked out in her finest, like this was a real date or something. Like she'd thought he was going to take one look at her feeble attempts to look pretty for him and sweep her into another toe-curling kiss. Like he really cared that she'd shaved her legs and opted to slip into one of two sets of truly sexy underwear that she owned.

"In addition to ice cream, one of the things I miss most when I'm out of the States is pizza," he said, checking his rearview mirror and changing lanes. "Ever been to Bella Luna?"

She clutched her purse on her lap, felt her cheeks flame with another surge of humiliation over her misconception of his intentions. She was thirty-three years old, for heaven's sake, not sixteen and starry-eyed over her first real crush. She forced herself to respond. "Bella Luna. Isn't that over in Jamaica Plain?"

He nodded. "On Centre Street."

"Heard of it," she managed to say between concentrated breaths. "Never been."

"Then you're in for a treat."

Of course she was. Everything about this day was turning into a treat.

She physically suppressed a groan. What had she been thinking? And what must he be thinking? How to let her down easy, if his lengthy silences offered any clues. She'd experienced enough of them in her life, both letdowns and lengthy silences, to know where this night was headed.

She stared out the window, blinked furiously to get her emotions back in check. Well, sorry. It was too late to be let down easy. Too late to deny what had been happening since the moment he'd charged in to save the day then kissed her until her bones had liquefied.

It was also too late to fool the fool into believing that she wasn't already half in love with him. Maybe more than half, she conceded miserably and accepted that she would have to deal with that bit of late-breaking news later. When she was alone. In the dark. Between cool sheets. In her big empty bed. And her lacy panties and bra were tossed in the clothes hamper instead of strewn recklessly across her bedroom floor because he just couldn't get her out of them fast enough.

Mercifully, they arrived at Bella Luna a few minutes later. The place was packed, and the crush and buzz of the crowd momentarily curtailed any desperate attempts at more strained small talk. The yellow-and-blue decor, the large open kitchen and the hand-painted plastic plates gave the place a homey feel. Phoebe might have even enjoyed it if she hadn't been so miserable.

When they were seated at a small table complete with a red-checkered tablecloth and a lit candle in a bottle, Daniel nodded toward the eclectic paintings covering the pizzeria walls. ''They rotate the art exhibits weekly. And on Sunday nights they bring in a psychic.''

''That would probably be to help you figure out what to order,'' she said, digging for some composure as she scanned a menu that included about a billion pizza combinations and a slew of toppings that ranged from asparagus to zucchini.

''How about I order for us?''

She folded the menu, grateful to be relieved of that decision. ''How about you do that.''

As the waiter appeared, she let her gaze drift

around the room while Daniel ordered their pizza and a beer for himself.

"Just water," she said, responding to his inquiring look.

"So, how are you?" he asked, commanding her attention when the waiter left. "No ill effects from last night?"

Ah. So that was what tonight was about. Lesson number two in Heroes 101: It's considered good form for the rescuer to follow up with the rescuee to make sure his heroic efforts weren't made in vain.

"I'm fine. Fine," she repeated, folding her hands on top of the table, then lowering them to her lap, then raising them to the table again, all the time juggling her gaze between the artwork, the tabletop and the wall behind Daniel's head.

"Get your car home okay?"

Chitchat. Wasn't this special?

"Leslie picked me up for work this morning and drove me over to get it." She didn't bother to mention that the word BITCH had been deeply scratched in the driver's-side door. Of course, she couldn't prove who'd done it, but it went without saying that Jason had probably used her own keys to do the deed.

Daniel's beer and her water arrived, snapping her away from the ugly picture and back to the moment. She played with the condensation on the glass while he scanned the room. It gave her small solace to realize that he, too, was a little uncomfortable. Well, why wouldn't he be? He'd counted on a mercy dinner to follow up on his mercy kiss and she'd curled her hair and put in contacts, for Pete's sake.

He may not be interested but he wasn't stupid. One

look at her and he'd known that she'd thought—
Well, he'd known what she'd thought.

Lookin' good, Phoebe. He could just as well have
said: Combed your hair, Phoebe, or, Lost the turtle
shell, Phoebe, or the increasingly obvious and ever
popular, Don't mistake this for something it's not,
Phoebe.

"My grandma Barone had a saying."

The warmth of his voice brought her out of the
little cocoon of misery she'd been spinning around
herself. She chanced meeting his eyes. Blue. Lord,
they were so blue.

"Quello che ci mette, ci trova."

The lyrical words rolled off his tongue as if he'd
been born speaking the language. The warmth in his
smile could have melted the candle flickering between
them. For sure, it melted any number of things inside
her.

"Great ear that I have for linguistics, I recognize
that as Italian, right?" she somehow managed to say.
"What does it mean?"

"Loosely translated, the expression goes, 'What
one puts into a dish, one finds.'"

She leaned forward, then back, her eyebrows knit.
"At the risk of repeating myself, what does it mean?"

"I don't really know," he said with staged con-
fusion. "But she said it a lot and it's one of two
Italian phrases that I can repeat without stumbling
over the words."

Well, heck. What could she do but smile. It wasn't
his fault that she'd gotten the wrong idea. It wasn't
his fault that her heart had decided to do some stumbling of its own. It wasn't his fault that he was so
gorgeous and that she was so needy.

Letting go of the last little remnant of the dream, she dug deep and put on her game face. "And the other phrase would be?"

He lifted his beer, held it aloft. Slowly, she raised her water until glass met glass over the table with a soft, celebratory clink. *"Questa festa è solamente per te."*

Just when she'd thought she was in control, the look on his face stole her breath. "Meaning?" she asked on a whisper.

"Meaning, 'This party is just for you.'"

She stared into that beautiful, smiling face and avoided sliding bonelessly to the floor at his feet only by dredging up a mandatory reality check. What she thought she saw—interest, intensity, heat—was just Daniel being Daniel. Charming, kind, unconsciously sensual.

It meant nothing.

She sighed. Just her luck he was so gorgeous. Just her luck that he was such a nice man. He was so many things. The key thing that he wasn't was interested.

Deal with it, Phoebe. Just suck it up and deal with it.

She dragged out a smile and the will to make the best of the night. The only way to do that was to cut her losses and once and for all accept that there was no romance on the horizon with Daniel Barone.

She lifted her glass again then forced a perky smile when he followed suit. "To that I say, Obbe, doobe, wah."

One corner of his mouth kicked up in another one of his dangerously seductive grins. "Which is…?"

"Gibberish for 'Then let's party on, dude.'"

His eyes danced with mirth. "And she's bilingual, too."

"She's also bipolar under certain conditions," she said in a confidential whisper, "but we won't talk about that now, okay? It might ruin our dinner."

He sat back and chuckled, then shaking his head murmured something to the tune of, "What am I going to do with you?"

She had several suggestions, but she kept them to herself. Just as she was going to keep her feelings to herself and her emotions on a tight leash. She was not going to write herself deeper into a fantasy that coupled her and this man as the hero and heroine of a romantic adventure.

What she was going to do was get through this night. And helping her was knowing that every set of estrogen-fueled eyes in the place were sizing him up and shooting envious glances her way.

These women didn't have to know that this wasn't a date.

They didn't have to know that she was dying a little inside because this wonderful man would never be more than a friend.

And they didn't have to know that she was "lookin' good," when what she'd wanted to look was loved.

They left Bella Luna around nine-thirty. Daniel was a little perplexed by his actions when he walked her to her door and had more or less given her no choice but to ask him in. She'd excused herself with a "Be right back" the moment they'd stepped inside. When she joined him again in the living room, she was wearing her glasses and carrying two tall iced teas.

"Dry eyes," she'd said, explaining the glasses as she set his tea on the table beside the sofa where he'd sat. Then she settled herself in a wing chair across from him.

Daniel knew that if she'd had her way, this little scene wouldn't be playing out. She hadn't planned to ask him in. But, since he hadn't wanted to leave just yet, he'd merely smiled, walked through her door and gotten comfy.

That had been ten or fifteen minutes ago. Now he was slumped back, drifting on a pleasant haze to the dreamy strains of a moody, bluesy sax that played softly on the CD system. The cool hum of her air conditioner and the vanilla scent of a burning candle soothed him. The sight of her curled up in the wing chair across from him, the cat purring on her lap, made him smile.

He'd done that a lot tonight, he realized, closing his eyes and sinking into a contentment he hadn't felt in quite some time. Shy, timid little Phoebe Richards had a wicked sense of humor when she finally dropped her guard and let it come out to play. Somewhere during the course of the evening—right around her "party on, dude" line, he calculated, one corner of his mouth twitching into a crooked grin at the memory—something had definitely loosened up between them.

He hadn't yet defined it, but something had altered in the way she regarded him. It almost felt as if she'd decided, The heck with it. What you see is what you get. Like it or lump it. It matters not to me.

He'd liked it. A lot. He liked that she gave back as good as he gave her. He liked that she laughed and asked him questions and had enjoyed the heck out of her pizza.

Yeah. He'd liked it. Well, except, maybe for the dawning realization that from that defining point on, she had also started looking at him differently.

Her cheeks had no longer pinkened with that pretty, delicate blush when their gazes had connected over the table. Her eyes had lost that tentative, almost dreamy spark of sexual awareness. It was almost as if she'd made a conscious decision to stay clear of those dicey sensual waters and take the low road.

Actually, there was no almost about it, he realized the further he thought about it. It was exactly what she'd decided to do. She was attracted to him—that had been apparent from the get-go—but she'd purposefully pulled away.

He let that thought snag then finally settle. This was good, right? This is what he wanted.

Right.

No spark, no sizzle. Just friendship. Just comfort. He hadn't even had to outline the ground rules for her. With her subtle but concise temperature shift, she'd done it for him.

"Are you asleep?" he heard her whisper, as if she was afraid to wake him if he was.

"I hope you don't take offense," he said, never opening his eyes, his head lolling against the sofa cushions, "but I could easily get there."

"So much for my sparkling and witty conversation."

A lazy grin curved his mouth. "Your conversation *is* sparkling and witty. But the pizza, the music and a delayed case of jet lag seem to have the upper hand at the moment.

"Man…" He forced himself to sit up then shook his head to clear a few cobwebs. "Sorry. It doesn't seem to matter how many times I cross time zones, jet lag is still a bitch."

"Having never traveled any farther than upstate New York, I guess I'll have to take your word for it."

She was stingy with information about herself, Daniel had learned during the course of the night, but very skillful in extracting information about him. She'd had him singing like a canary. Her warm smiles and interested questions had prompted him to share stories of the places he'd been and the things he'd done.

In fact, he'd talked so much that he was a little hoarse. He hadn't spilled this much information since— Well, he couldn't remember ever sharing so much of himself with anyone.

"Why is it," he wondered aloud, "that you have a detailed account of damn near every month of my last eight years and I still don't know anything about you?"

She stroked her hand across Arthur's back. "Possibly because you live a fascinating, amazing life and I don't?" she suggested with a lift of her eyebrows.

He met her eyes then, not at all surprised when she shifted her gaze back to the cat. She didn't want the attention focused on her. She felt uncomfortable when it was, and had capably transferred it back to him all evening.

Not this time. He'd had a question burning for about twenty-four hours now and he was determined to get an answer.

"Phoebe, tell me something. You and this Collins

character. How did you..." He paused, searching for a delicate way to phrase it.

She did it for him. "How did a nice girl like me get involved with a loser like him?"

He reached for his tea. "Yeah. I guess that's what I was going for."

She let out a breath, ruffling the soft tumble of hair from her forehead. "A friend of a friend introduced us. He seemed nice. Thoughtful. Attentive." She paused then shrugged, relaying how uncomfortable she was talking about the subject. "I don't know. Something changed. Thoughtful turned to needy. Attentive changed to possessive. Possessive— Well, you saw what it changed to."

"Yeah," he said, swallowing back the knot of anger provoked by the memory of Jason Collins's hands on her. "I saw."

He sat forward, propped his elbows on his widespread knees and, wedging his glass between his palms, stared at the tea. His heart was suddenly beating hard and fast. He looked up from his glass.

"Did he hit you, Phoebe?"

She stiffened, swallowed, then visibly dealt with the tension. Her hand came up to tug on her hair. "Once."

Daniel closed his eyes as a red-hot haze of fury burned behind them. "The bastard."

"He's ill," she said, more by way of explanation than defense.

"And that makes it all right?"

"No, but it makes it easier for me to accept."

He saw in her eyes how truly hurt she was by what Collins had done to her.

"Jason's an alcoholic," she continued. She shook

her head, her look as thoughtful as it was regretful. "I should have seen it. I should have known. I should have gotten him help."

"Seems to me that getting help is up to him not you."

"In the end, yes," she agreed. "It's all up to him."

He studied her lowered head, sensed that she wanted him to back off, but couldn't make himself. "Was he important to you?"

Her hand paused then resumed her repetitive strokes along Arthur's back. "I guess that's irrelevant now, isn't it?"

It didn't feel irrelevant. Not to him. But she clearly wasn't going to talk about it. And he wasn't going to think about the tight knot of tension that grabbed his shoulder when he thought about her and Collins together.

"You know, I was serious about the locks."

She nodded. "I know."

"And the self-defense class. It's just good sense that a woman knows how to protect herself."

She fidgeted, finally lifted Arthur off her lap and, rising, settled the cat in the chair. She walked past Daniel to the CD player and busied herself changing tracks. "I tried a class once. I didn't make it past the first hour." She glanced at him over her shoulder then turned back to the CD player with a self-conscious shrug. "I'm not good at violence."

"Self-defense is all about avoiding violence," he said reasonably.

"Well, yes. I know. But you still have to use violence to defend yourself. I—I couldn't do it. The thought of it makes me physically ill."

She turned to face him, her arms crossed beneath

her breasts, hugging herself as if she was warding off a chill. "We could sugarcoat it and say I'm nonconfrontational, but the honest truth is that I'm pretty much a coward."

"An abhorrence to violence doesn't make you a coward. It makes you human. The flip side, however, is that avoidance of reality makes you vulnerable. The way you were last night. I don't like to think about what would have happened if I hadn't been there."

She gave him a tight smile that didn't quite conceal the fear she tried to hide. "I don't like thinking about it either."

But they both knew that she had to think about it. She had to think about it a lot because Daniel had a very strong feeling that Jason Collins wasn't going away anytime soon. Because of that feeling, Daniel had pretty much convinced himself that he had a viable reason for not going away anytime soon either.

He stared into his glass for a moment, realizing that what he was about to propose probably wasn't wise.

After spending the evening with Phoebe, he understood that what he really wanted from her was something he couldn't take. He wasn't sure he entirely trusted himself, either, to do the right thing by her and keep their relationship platonic. Because he cared about her, though, he was going to give it his best shot, even though he knew he was pushing his luck.

"Phoebe, sit down. I've got a proposition for you."

Six

"A proposition?" There was enough skepticism in her eyes to launch a congressional inquiry. But when he reached for her hand, she let him pull her down on the sofa beside him.

"What do you say we do something about this non-confrontational aspect of your personality?"

She snorted rather indelicately and managed to detach her hand from his. "Short of a lobotomy, I'm not sure there's a whole heck of a lot to be done for it at this late date."

"We can use the lobotomy as a backup plan, but in the meantime, I had something a little less Dr. Frankensteinish in mind."

"Like?" She tucked her feet, which were now bare, beside her hips on the sofa, effectively creating a wall of resistance between them. He wasn't sure if she was doing it intentionally or if it was just natural.

Either way, he decided it was a good thing that one of them was throwing up barriers.

"Like how about *I* teach you?"

"To perform a lobotomy?"

He gave her a hard look. "To defend yourself, woman."

She eyed him with caution. "But that would mean—"

"Confrontation. I know. Scary as hell, right? But think about it. It will be *me* teaching you, not some stranger."

She scrunched up her face, tilted her head and, to his way of thinking, looked adorable. "This might be a good time to remind you that until last night, we *were* strangers."

"I know," he agreed and, hiking a knee up on the sofa, faced her. He met her eyes in earnest. "But, Phoebe, do I really seem like a stranger to you? I mean, haven't you felt it, too?"

"Heartburn? Yeah. I thought it was the pizza."

He let out a long-suffering sigh. "I'm talking about a connection. We click."

"We do?"

"We do. At least we have since you got past the Barone syndrome." When her frown deepened, he drove his point home. "Do you know how refreshing it is to be able to sit and talk—just talk—with a woman who doesn't have some ulterior motive for spending time with me?"

She bit her lower lip, considering. "Is this the part when I'm supposed to say, 'Oh, you poor maligned little sex object you'?"

"Now, see? That's what I'm talking about. I can't

think of a single other woman I could have this conversation with.''

''Because of that maligned-sex-object thing?''

He grinned. ''Because you're a real person who doesn't necessarily want anything from me. I feel comfortable with you.''

She looked down, plucked at the gauzy fabric of her dress. ''Like you feel comfortable with a pair of old shoes, huh?''

His gaze snagged on all those buttons. He let out a breath, shook his head and tried to think about shoes, old shoes, not perfect breasts with tight little nipples that pressed provocatively against gauzy yellow fabric.

''Kind of like a friend,'' he said, grounded again, after he zeroed in on the pretty red toenails that peeked out from the folds of her skirt and reminded him how much he could hurt her.

Her head came up. ''A friend?''

He tilted his head. ''Don't say we don't know each other well enough. Time isn't necessarily the qualifying factor in friendships.''

''So…'' She plucked at the skirt again. ''You want to like…hang out with me?''

''Yeah. I want to like…hang out with you,'' he mimicked. ''Maybe go to a movie sometime. Take in a ball game. And like tonight, go out for pizza and then sit on your sofa and listen to jazz and just be…''

''You?'' she suggested softly.

''Yeah. Just be me. Am I so far off base here?''

''No. No, you're not off base,'' she said after a while.

Their eyes held for a long moment before she

pasted on that prickly smile he'd come to recognize as a precursor to one of her wiseass remarks.

She didn't disappoint him.

"So, buddy, you wanna pop the top on a brewski and watch some porn?"

He wiped a hand over his face, shook his head. "You're a funny lady, you know that?"

"That's me. Barrel of laughs."

"You are. You make me remember why I like my life, why I like what I do. My family—God love them—they want me to come back to the fold, join the Barone law team and settle down. They start on me the moment I walk in the door and pretty much keep it up, with apologies and love, until I blow out of town again.

"I don't have to worry about that with you," he continued when the frown that had been threatening to crease her wide, intelligent forehead finally furrowed. "You don't have any expectations of me. You don't have any designs on me. You don't want me to change or to settle down. And I like that. I really, really like that.

"What I don't like," he added, sobering, "is the thought of you being vulnerable to Jason Collins."

She had nothing to say to that, but that was okay because he had plenty to say on the subject.

"So, what do you say? Let me, as your friend, give you something back. Let me teach you how to take care of yourself. Just a few lessons. Simple stuff. And I promise I won't let you hurt me."

That finally got a crooked smile out of her. "Well, gee, if you're going to take all the fun out of it…"

He laughed again, then against his better judgment

reached for her hand and folded it in his. "Please, Phoebe. Please let me do this for you."

"'Please, Phoebe. Please let me do this for you,'" Phoebe mimicked Daniel's words as she straddled the potter's wheel in her basement studio the next afternoon.

"'Let me, as your friend, teach you how to take care of yourself.' Not 'Let me lay you out on the table and make wild monkey love to you.'"

"You could have said no," she grumbled, bracing her elbow into her hip as she leaned into a five-pound lump of clay and tried to focus all her concentration on centering it on the wheel.

That was the key in throwing pots. You had to center the clay before you continued the process of opening, drilling and forming it into what she'd decided, in this case, was going to be a vase for Leslie.

"You could have said, 'Look, Daniel, you're really a nice guy and I understand that you don't want any place—let alone any woman—tying you down, but what I want from you involves lip locks and the horizontal tango, not karate chops and pepper spray.'"

She slumped back on her stool, let out a deep breath. Lord, she had it bad. She'd never considered herself a sexual person, certainly not a sexually aggressive one, and yet she didn't have a single thought about Mr. You're-a-funny-lady Barone that didn't involve him naked and stretched out over her, or under her or inside her.

An electric rush of arousal shot from her breasts to her belly and lower as the erotic picture played out in her mind. Hopeless. From the first moment she'd laid eyes on that incredible face, looked into his sky-blue eyes, heard his gravel-and-honey voice, she'd wanted him.

Now it was worse. Now she knew him. Knew his kindness, his sense of humor, his white-knight tendencies. And now she wanted him more—for the beautiful person he was inside as well as out.

And he wanted to be her buddy.

Yippie-Skippie.

She should have sent him on his merry way last night with a firm no thank you.

"But no," she muttered aloud, "you had to develop latent masochistic tendencies."

Yep. She definitely had them because she'd finally heard herself say, "Okay. Teach me to break shins and how to bloody noses. Teach me to be bad, Barone. I'm ready to knock some heads."

He'd laughed, of course, and said he'd see her today at three o'clock for their first lesson.

Well, she thought, leaning back over the clay, she hoped that he'd gotten more sleep last night than she had or they could huff and puff and simply blow each other over. She'd pretty much spent her night sifting through a hundred scenarios that involved Daniel Barone and how she was going to survive being his friend.

"Like this ball of clay, Grasshopper," she said, à la an old but, thanks to cable reruns, never-forgotten TV series, "life must first be centered before moving on to the more defined and refined aspects of substance and form."

So much for centering. Thanks to Daniel, she was about as far from dead center as a cross-eyed archer.

"I don't want to be his friend," she whined aloud as she let up on the foot pedal to stop the wheel. After dipping her hands in a bucket of cool water, she leaned back over the clay. She sent the wheel in motion again, set the bottom and then the top of the vase. Then she began to count through her slow, gradual upward pull.

One—one thousand.

He was coming over in less than an hour.

Two—one thousand.

After Sunday mass and dinner with his family.

Three—one thousand.

He was going to show her how to defend herself.

Four—one thousand.

"Fudge," she muttered when she torqued her pull. The wall thinned due to her uneven pressure and the top collapsed into the bottom of the vase. Staring at the disaster, she let up on the wheel and slumped back in her chair, defeated.

Lord help her, he wanted to teach her self-defense and she just didn't think that she had any defenses left.

Phoebe answered the doorbell wiping her hands on a grimy towel and wearing a white butcher's apron covered in what looked like mud. Whatever it was, Daniel realized that it was also smudged on her chin and her cheek and on the shoulder of a white T-shirt that had definitely seen better days. She'd even managed to smear some of it on the frame of her glasses.

"You're early," she accused with a flustered scowl made all the more endearing by the flush that spread from her forehead downward to disappear beneath the round neck of her shirt.

"Sorry. I guess I am." He checked his watch. "A little. Did I catch you— Just what the hell *did* I catch you doing?'' he asked on a laugh then couldn't resist teasing her. ''Wait, I get it. It's mud-pack time. Right?''

She looked a little self-conscious then shrugged. ''Come on. I'll show you.''

''You're a potter,'' he said, incredulous, as she led him down her basement steps and into a room lined with metal shelves and cluttered with equipment. Pottery in various stages, from recently thrown, to drying, to bisque fired, to an array of beautifully finished pieces glazed in a rainbow of stunning colors, filled the basement studio.

In the center of the room was her potter's wheel; off to one side, an electric kiln. On the other side of the room, an old stereo system took up an upper shelf, while a hodgepodge of tools and sponges, boxes of clay and things he didn't recognize and couldn't define filled the rest of the spaces.

''Those pieces in your living room—you did them?''

''Guilty.''

''You're good.'' He walked over to a display shelf and admired a pitcher molded of elegant lines and fluid grace. ''Really good.''

''It's just a hobby and, trust me, I'm strictly an amateur,'' she insisted without a speck of false modesty. ''But I'm getting better.''

He turned around and grinned at her. ''A woman of hidden talents.''

She avoided his eyes by fumbling around behind her to untie her apron then slip it over her head. ''A woman with mud under her fingernails,'' she said, giving them a passing glance.

''And on your face.'' Before he stopped to think

about it, he touched his thumb to her cheek, brushed lightly at the smear of dried clay.

Her skin was very soft—and suddenly very hot beneath his touch. His gaze dropped to her mouth and he remembered another kind of heat. Another kind of softness that involved that mouth, wet and willing and sexy as hell.

"Well," she said, stepping away, an effective reminder of the lines that he, himself, had drawn and of the places that were off-limits. "Look all you want. Just, um, let me jump in the shower quick and I'll be ready to learn some bloodcurdling yell or something equally self-defensive or offensive or…something.

"Oh, wait—" She stopped and turned back toward him, her eyebrows pinched together. "Is this going to involve sweating? Because if there's sweating involved, maybe—"

"No sweating," he promised. "Go ahead and take your shower."

She opened her mouth, shut it, then without another word turned and headed up the stairs. He stood there a long time, looking at her pottery and thinking about the shape of her tidy little butt packed into a pair of old, faded jeans as she'd walked away from him.

It was, without question, a very fine butt. But it was attached to his very fine friend and he had no business thinking about it the way he'd been thinking about it—bare and filling his palms. Just as he had no business thinking about *anything* involving him and her and sweating.

He dragged a hand over his face.

Look all you want, she'd said. To that, he added the qualifier, *but don't touch.*

So he touched her pottery instead. He could see

something of her in every piece. Delicate yet enduring. Whimsical and elegant. Romantic.

He let out a long breath, raked his hands through his hair and wondered just why the hell he was here messing with her life. And then he thought of Jason Collins and he knew exactly why.

"Okay, let's do this," Daniel said as they faced off in a small room off her studio that was partially finished into what Phoebe liked to think of as her future den. So far, all she'd been able to afford was a cheap, tight-napped tweed carpet and drywall. The ceiling still wasn't finished. An old desk that housed her aging computer and a couple of folding chairs were the only pieces of furniture.

"I want you to think about a few things before we get started on the actual physical techniques."

Oh, Phoebe was thinking, all right—and some physical techniques came to mind that had nothing to do with self-defense. He stood before her in another one of his seemingly endless supply of black T-shirts that hugged his chest and broad shoulders, and a pair of those windbreaker-type jogging pants, and she thought about a lot of things. Not enough of them involved getting out of this lesson with her sanity intact.

"First off, you need to be aware."

Got that covered, she thought dismally, way too aware of the way his biceps strained at the cotton of his shirtsleeves.

"Awareness of where you are," he continued, thankfully not aware of her wayward thoughts, "and of what could happen is one of the most important self-defense mechanisms anyone, man or woman, can have in place. And never, ever, act or look like an easy target.''

''But I am an easy target,'' she pointed out.

''Not anymore, you're not.''

''You mean I've already passed some test and didn't even know it?'' She batted her lashes with staged brightness.

''I mean that starting today, things are going to be different. Phoebe, a woman can prepare against any number of threats by simply thinking about normal everyday items as potential weapons. If you're inside, for instance, chairs, ashtrays, bottles, even ordinary kitchen utensils can all be used as weapons.

''Okay, what?'' he asked with narrowed eyes as she battled a grin.

''Oh, I was just picturing a scenario that involved taking someone out with a wire whisk. Okay, okay,'' she said hastily when he planted his hands on his hips and glared. ''It was just a thought.''

''Outdoors,'' he continued, his voice and face stern, ''look for bricks, sand, sticks. Your car keys can gouge, your cell phone can be used as a club. Think about what's in your purse. A pen or a long-tailed comb can cause a lot of pain and give you that window you need to run away. Hair spray can temporarily blind.

''And then there's this.'' He dug into his pocket and pulled out a small canister about twice the size of a tube of lipstick. ''Pepper spray.''

''Oh, you shouldn't have,'' she said demurely, accepting it like a cherished gift.

He angled her another hard look. ''Are we going to get serious anytime soon?''

She rolled her eyes, wobbled her head. "Okay, fine. We're serious."

"Look, I know what you're doing. You're trying to joke your way through this because it scares you. You can get past the fear, Phoebe, if you build a little confidence in the belief that you can take care of yourself."

Properly chastised, effectively sobered, she nodded. "Okay. I'm sorry. No more fooling around."

It was hard, but she managed to make it through the next hour or so listening to him talk, watching him show her things that she wouldn't in a million years have equated to self-defense tactics. Most of them were basic and so painfully simple that she felt foolish for not having had a better awareness.

"All right," he said after they'd reviewed and discussed to his satisfaction. "How are you feeling about all this now?"

"Better. Really," she said with a thoughtful nod and realized that she meant it. "Thanks."

She *did* feel better—right up until the time he said, "We'll save the next lesson for another time."

"What? Wait." Panic in the form of a herd of butterflies winged its way from her tummy to her throat in .005 seconds flat. "What next lesson?"

As it turned out, there were several "next" lessons over the coming week. Daniel stopped by after she got home from work on Monday, Wednesday and again on Friday. Multiply his visits by eighty-seven, subtract twenty-three and add five thousand four hundred and fifty, and that's how many times Phoebe's heart had stopped on each one of those momentous occasions. Mainly because there *was* sweating involved in these sessions, and there was contact.

"How do you know all this stuff?" she asked, afraid there was no end.

"I listen, I learn. I took classes," he said, somehow managing to "kindly" imply that everyone should.

"Okay, we're going to work on a kung fu move," Daniel said on Friday night as he stood before her in black gym shorts and, of course, another one of his black T-shirts. He was also barefoot.

She'd never thought of a man's feet as sexy. But then, she'd never seen Daniel Barone's feet. She'd seen them a lot this week. And they were attached to such spectacular legs, tanned and toned. The way the muscles rippled beneath his skin and the way his baby-fine, silky-soft hair lightly dusted that skin—

"Phoebe?"

"Huh?" She looked up and realized she'd spaced out on him again. Drawing a bracing breath, she tried to look interested in his lesson. "I'm listening."

If he noticed her little side trips into lust-land or any of the other mini vacations she'd taken this week—he didn't let on. All business, that was Daniel Barone. He showed up looking like eye candy that shot off the calorie charts and ran through his bulging repertoire of self-defense moves with the single-minded determination of a drill sergeant training a raw recruit.

It was as hard on her ego as it was on her heart, this buddy business.

"This is a great technique against an attack from behind," he began.

It was all she could do to keep from glaring at him. Did he feel nothing? Sense none of the heat that threatened to spike her temperature into the melt-down zone?

"Let's say you're waiting at a bus stop—"

"Why would I be at a bus stop?" she asked a little testily and used the opportunity to back a step away. Anything to put a little distance between her and the way he smelled, the heat of his body, the way he was going to touch her.

Already there had been a lot of touching this past week. Just thinking about lesson number one put her poor little heart out of commission again.

"It's a for instance, okay? For the sake of illustration, just go with me here.

"Now, you're at a bus stop," he restated, setting up his scenario, "maybe reading the newspaper while you wait. It's dark, you're alone and someone approaches you from behind. Okay, you play the attacker and we'll walk through this."

He turned his back to her. "Move in fast and grab my shoulder. Yeah. Like that."

Phoebe closed her eyes and endured.

"My reaction is to drop the paper, turn and deliver a right palm strike directly into your face."

He turned in slow motion, walking through the technique. "See how I keep my arm straight? The idea is to hit him like a bullet."

Again he demonstrated, shoving his hand toward her face at striking speed but pulling up short so he didn't make contact and hurt her.

"What happens next is that he'll double forward. Double forward, Phoebe," he instructed, "and then I follow up with a knee strike to the chest."

Again he demonstrated in slow motion. As she

doubled over at the waist, he lifted his knee toward her chest, stopping just short of contact.

"See, that's going to throw him off balance, and when that happens, you move right on in and push him away."

With steadying hands, he showed how her body would react. "Then you finish him off with a front kick right in his breadbasket.

"Okay," he said, looking down at her. "Do you think you've got it?"

"Yes." Actually, it was kind of a blur. She'd say just about anything at this point to get all of this touching and looking and concentrating over with. "I've got it."

"Okay. Now you try."

She'd already known this was coming. There was a lot of rehearsing, she'd learned, in practicing self-defense moves. Which was why they called it practicing, Daniel had said with a tolerant grin after their Wednesday-night session.

It was with no small amount of frustration that she let out a bothered breath, turned her back and waited for his attack.

He touched a hand to her shoulder. With a speed fueled by three days of frustration and the nervous dispatch of a gun with a hair trigger, she whirled around. She slammed the flat of her hand into his face, hiked her knee into his chest when he doubled over, shoved, then drove her foot into his diaphragm.

He landed spread eagle on his back with an "Umph."

Then he just lay there.

For the longest moment Phoebe stood looking down, waiting for him to get up.

He didn't so much as move a pinkie.

"Um, Daniel?" she asked carefully as she gave the bottom of his bare foot a cautious nudge with her toe.

His chest started to heave.

"Oh my God." She dropped to her knees by his side. "I hurt you!"

"No," he said just as she realized he wasn't fighting for breath. He was laughing. "Damn, Phoebe." His blue eyes danced as they met hers. "When you finally decide to put your heart into it, you really make a statement."

"You mean I really laid you out? You weren't just acting?"

"You got me good, girl." He sat up, propped his elbows on his knees and grinned at her. "Congratulations. I think you just passed the course."

She felt the blood drain from her head, felt her stomach roil at the knowledge that she, passive Phoebe Richards, had committed a violent act on another human being.

"Phoebe?" His voice tightened in alarm. He grabbed her arms to steady her when her knees folded and she plopped down on the floor with a thud.

"I think I'm going to be sick."

"You okay now?" Daniel asked a few minutes later.

Embarrassed, Phoebe stood and, to make sure he understood that she really was okay, she brushed off her sweatpants and forced a smile. "Fine. Thanks. I told you I was a weenie when it came to physical violence."

"You aren't a weenie. You just had a strong reaction when you realized that you actually have the ability to put a man on his back.''

I've put plenty of men on their backs, mister, she thought, suppressing the urge to glare. Well, not plenty. A few, though. Okay, two. Counting him. And he didn't really count since she hadn't ended up on top of him. Where was the satisfaction in that? she wanted to know.

At least she hadn't completely embarrassed herself and gotten sick, even though it had been touch-and-go for a while there. Daniel had shoved her head down between her knees, ordered her to breathe and hadn't let her stop until she'd turned from green back to pink again.

''You know what?'' he asked once he was satisfied that she really was okay. ''I think this calls for a celebration.'' He checked his watch. ''If we get moving, we can catch a movie. We could even grab a bite to eat and make it before the coming attractions if you're up for it.''

Phoebe was up for a lot of things. One of them *wasn't* torturing herself by sitting across from Daniel for another chat-and-chew session that could only end with her feeling frustrated and edgy and sexually supercharged by all the pheromones he emitted to the tune of about a bazillion per second. Another thing she wasn't up to facing was the prospect of sitting beside him in the dark intimacy of a movie theater, their arms accidentally brushing and their fingers tangling in a tub of buttered popcorn.

A thousand excuses winged through her mind. She had to do laundry. Scrub her bathroom tile with a toothbrush. Clean her refrigerator and send the mold she found there to the lab for analysis. Any one of them would ensure that she avoided both the dinner and the movie. Most of them were viable; all of them were wise.

She opened her mouth to spout one, and to her utter amazement what came out instead was, "Okay."

"Great. I brought a change of clothes. Mind if I use your shower?"

She couldn't manage a verbal response to that one. He was already on his feet and heading toward the basement stairs anyway.

She was still sitting on the floor when she heard the shower go on upstairs. He was naked. And wet. And tonight, she was going to sleep wrapped in the towel he used to dry himself off.

With a groan, she lowered her head to her knees again. And breathed.

Seven

Phoebe made it through dinner, but only because the restaurant had been packed and she'd taken the opportunity to avoid a potentially difficult one-on-one with Daniel by enthusiastically volunteering to share their table with a middle-aged couple from some obscure little town in Idaho. She now knew more about potatoes than she'd ever dreamed possible.

She even made it through the movie, but only because she'd insisted they see a macho action-adventure flick with lots of sweating, grunting, flying bullets and random acts of violence. And blood. There had been lots of fake blood.

Of course, Daniel had laughed a lot because she'd watched most of it between the index and middle finger of the hand that she'd slapped over her face. That was fine. She'd rather be squeamish over fake blood than steamy love scenes any day.

And there'd been no popcorn. Not for her. Not even when he'd offered several times. She wasn't going to take a chance on any tangled, buttery fingers.

It was with a huge relief that the ending credits rolled, the lights came up and it was time to leave. Now all she had to do was make it home, cuff him on the shoulder like a good ol' boy—would a belch be taking it too far—and escape inside her house. Alone.

"So, you really enjoyed that, huh?" Daniel asked as they walked out of the theater lobby and into the sultry August night.

"You bet."

He laughed. "Do all librarians make lousy liars or is it just you who's particularly inept?"

She looked up into his warm blue eyes and fessed up. "I think maybe it's just me."

He draped a companionable arm over her shoulders and gave her a little squeeze, pressing his body against hers from shoulder to thigh. He lowered his mouth to her ear. "Well, here's a tip," he whispered confidentially. "Don't ever cheat on your taxes. You'd never be able to lie your way out of an audit."

She didn't hear anything past the word *tip*. A soft, low buzzing sounded in her head, drowned out the rest of his words as his breath stirred the fine hair above her ear and the long, hard length of his body jolted every erogenous zone to high-alert status.

"Um, uh, what?" she heard herself mumble when she realized he'd stopped just outside the theater doors and had asked her a question.

He grinned at her. "I said, do you want to go for ice cream?"

"Ice cream?"

"You know? Cold. Sweet. Sometimes comes with hot fudge and—" He stopped midsentence as his eyes cut across the street. His expression turned hard as stone. "Son of a bitch," he swore and pulled her protectively to his side.

Startled out of her mini-stupor by his drastic shift of mood, Phoebe gathered her wits enough to follow his gaze. Her heart rate kicked up several beats when she saw what had drawn his attention.

Jason Collins was parked across the street from the theater. He'd rolled down his window, making sure that he was seen and recognized.

"The bastard is stalking you."

In a slow motion that was frightening for its staged and precise casualness, Daniel's gaze shifted from his combative stare-down with Jason to Phoebe's face. His features softened as he looked down at her then touched his hand to her cheek.

"Let's see if we can funnel some of his anger in another direction," he said, nudging her backward.

Before she could assimilate what was happening, her back connected with the outer wall of the theater and Daniel connected with her front.

"He wants to be ticked off at someone, let's get him ticked off at me. Hold on," he whispered as his mouth descended. "We're going to make this look good."

Look good? she thought. Make what look good?

Eyes wide and round, Phoebe opened her mouth to ask but the words stalled in her throat. In the end, it didn't matter anyway. Just as it didn't matter that she'd lifted her hands and pressed them to his chest to...to do exactly what, she didn't know.

Maybe she'd been about to suggest that he rethink

this. Maybe she'd been going to tell him that this was a really, really bad idea. Maybe she'd been going to push him away.

But then his mouth touched hers, covered hers, opened over hers. With the press of his body, he demanded that she do the same.

Then nothing but his mouth mattered anymore.

He kissed her, deeply, sweetly, and wrapped her so tightly against him it was hard to breathe, let alone think. Let alone protest. Let alone remember why she'd thought this was a bad idea in the first place.

She blinked and watched his face, watched those thick dark lashes lower to brush his cheeks, and on a groan that married surrender to desire, she let her eyes drift shut and let him take control.

His kiss. Oh, his kiss. It was everything she'd ever dreamed a kiss should be. Everything that Jason's kisses had never been. It was rough yet tender. It was intense and demanding. It was filled with passion and need. She lost herself in it and in him and totally forgot that it was all for show.

She lifted her arms, wrapped them around his neck, and with a sigh that was part shock and all swift, instant arousal, let him nudge her legs apart with his knee. When his big hands skated down her back and settled over her bottom then pressed her up and into his hips, she lifted up on tiptoe to encourage the contact, enhance the fit.

He was so…so much as he slanted his mouth over hers, changed the angle and dived back for another long, lingering mating of their mouths that involved tangled tongues and sultry sighs.

Someone whimpered—probably her—when he lifted his head. He heaved a deep breath and touched his forehead to hers. She swallowed, then dared to meet his eyes, slumberous and dark, full of wanting and wonder and desire.

"Maybe," he said, his voice gruff, as he pressed her deeper into the brick wall at her back, "we ought to give him another demonstration. Just to make sure he gets the message."

"What...what exactly is the message?" Phoebe murmured, breathless and afraid to hope she'd read more into his kiss than a staged strategy to redirect Jason's anger toward Daniel and away from her.

He answered her with a searching look, then lowered his mouth again. Kissed her again. It was a study in sensuality, all warm breath and thrusting tongue that set a rhythm to mirror the act of making love and turned her legs to jelly. Her heart hammered so hard she could hear every beat in her ears, feel every pulse point in those places where their bodies met and meshed and made promises of the things they could do and the way they would fit in the dark.

The loud squeal of tires had Daniel lifting his head. She peeked over his shoulder. Together, they watched Jason's taillights disappear down the street in a screaming blur.

"I think," Daniel said, his voice as rough as sandpaper, his breath as labored as hers, "that might have done the trick."

Well, it had certainly done it for her.

"You okay?" He slowly pulled away.

She met his eyes, gauged the latent heat there and gave a jerky nod.

Liar, liar, pants on fire.

If he noticed the lie in her eyes, he decided to ignore it. "Come on. Let's get you home."

On a shaky breath, Phoebe took the hand he offered and walked silently beside him to his car.

So they'd just delivered a message. And she was still wondering exactly what that message was. Wondering—no hoping—that Daniel Barone had just gotten a message, too.

Maybe there was more here. Maybe he could actually care about her a little. Maybe even care a lot.

By the time they'd reached her house after a long, silent ride that did not include a stop for ice cream, reality had crashed her little party with a vengeance.

Daniel Barone, male extraordinaire, was not going to fall for a dowdy, unsophisticated librarian, who, her saner side reminded her, was not only three years older than he was, but was light-years away from the kind of woman who could really turn him on, reel him in and embark on the road leading to happily-ever-after.

But, oh, she thought as she lay alone in her bed that night, could that man fake a kiss.

Daniel stared at himself in the bathroom mirror the next morning. He looked like hell. He dragged a hand over his face. A sleepless night would do that to a man. Several sleepless nights, in fact.

So would an ice cream–eating, tortoiseshell-toting, pottery-making, mud-packing, red-toenail-polish-wearing liar of a librarian.

He'd always thought of Phoebe as honest. But she'd been lying to him all week. With her eyes. With her tight little smiles. She'd been telling him that all the togetherness, all the touching that resulted from working through the self-defense moves hadn't affected her. That she wasn't as hot for him as he was for her.

The little liar.

He splashed cold water over his face then braced both hands on the edge of the sink. He hung his head and finally admitted that he'd been lying, too. To himself and to her.

This could not continue. He could not continue to mosey over to her house, pretend he wanted to be her buddy and then fabricate reasons to touch her, excuses to kiss her. Not when she felt like liquid fire in his arms. Not when her mouth opened so sweetly, so greedily beneath his. Not when she looked at him with those baby-owl eyes that begged him to take her to bed.

Which was exactly where he wanted her.

"So, hotshot, now what?" he asked his reflection.

The phone rang. He considered letting his machine pick up but in the end he walked into his bedroom and answered.

"Barone," he said on a gruff bark.

"Daniel?"

"Ash? Is that you?"

"Not if your mood is as foul as it sounds."

"Hell. I'm sorry. You caught me…preoccupied," he said, amazed at the magnitude of his understatement. "Where are you?"

"In Boston."

"No joke?"

"I would not joke about something like that, Daniel."

Daniel smiled. No. Sheikh Ashraf Saalem, the prince of Zhamyr, would not joke about something like that.

They'd met several years ago at the Soldeu ski resort in Andorra in the Pyrenees. Ash had been on vacation. Daniel had just dropped by on the way to somewhere else and Andorra had been a convenient stopover. He'd hit it off with the independent financial consultant immediately. He and Ash had not only forged a friendship over snifters of cognac in the lounge, it had been the beginning of a successful business relationship.

After running a check to make sure that Ash was who he'd said he was and that he was damn successful at what he did, Daniel had turned over a small portion of the inheritance he'd received from his grandfather. Ash had parlayed it into a tidy profit. Over the past five years, Daniel had gradually turned his entire portfolio over to Ash to handle.

"So what brings you to the States?"

"A little of this. A little of that. Business for the most part. And it's been some time since we've met, my friend."

"Too damn long," Daniel agreed.

"Are you free anytime this week?"

"Name the time and the place and I'll be there."

"Tomorrow, then. Lunch?"

After they decided on specifics, Ash rung off. Daniel thought about his friend on and off all day. At least he did when he wasn't thinking about Phoebe.

How had he let things get out of hand with her? How had he convinced himself that she hadn't been looking at him with hunger in her eyes and a need that matched his growing need for her? And why hadn't he recognized that every time he saw her, he was doing the equivalent of crawling into the engine of a freight train called Danger and heading straight toward a cliff?

Would it be so terrible, he rationalized under the shower spray the next morning as he got ready to meet Ash. Would it really be so terrible to indulge in a physical relationship with Phoebe? It wasn't as if she wasn't an adult. It wasn't as if she wouldn't understand going in that while what they could have together would be very special, it couldn't be a relationship in the traditional sense of the word. Not a lasting relationship at any rate.

Couldn't they both just enjoy it while it lasted?

He knew he could and would enjoy it to the fullest. Until it was time to walk away.

He twisted off the faucets. It was at the walking-away part that things got sticky. He could do it. No problem. Would he miss her? Absolutely. She was sweet and funny and sexy and kind. And gentle. And there were times when he looked into her eyes that he found himself wanting to look into them forever.

Snagging a towel, he dragged it over his hair then rubbed himself down. Forever. Now *there* was a word.

He tossed the towel on the bed and strode to the bureau. He pulled out clean boxers and stepped into them, then sat on the edge of the bed to drag on his socks.

Forever. It all boiled down to that word. She deserved it and he couldn't give it to her. If he started something, something they both wanted, it would hurt her when he walked away.

And that led him back to square one. He could not have an affair with her, no matter how hot, how steamy, how off-the-charts incredible it would be. But how could he just walk away from her? How could he leave her at the mercy of Jason Collins?

He was still turning the thought over in his mind when he met Ash at the Ritz. As he watched the sheikh walk toward their table, turning every female head in the place, an idea started taking shape.

The last time he'd spoken with Ash, his friend had confided that he was in a settling-down mood. He wanted everything that Daniel didn't. He wanted to get married. He wanted a family. He wanted a woman to look at him as if he was the most important thing in her world.

Phoebe looked at Daniel that way. It made his heart hurt to see that look in her eyes. Mainly because it was directed at the wrong man.

All through lunch as he and Ash caught up, talked a little business, slung a little bull, an idea floated around in the back of his mind. He couldn't turn it off and by the time lunch was over, he'd decided what he had to do. He wasn't the right man for Phoebe, but maybe Ash was. He was darkly handsome, charismatic, loaded, and he wanted a wife. Plus, Ash would meet every one of Phoebe's romantic fantasies.

"So," he said, crossing an ankle over his knee, "there's this party Wednesday night at my parents' brownstone."

He filled Ash in on the sudden appearance of his long-lost cousin, Karen Rawlins, and the fact that it was a welcome-to-the-family party in her honor. "Why don't you come? You know my parents and brother and sisters, but I'd really like for you to meet the rest of the family. And I have this friend I'd like you to meet."

Ash lifted an eyebrow. "Friend?"

Daniel found that he had a bit of difficulty forcing a smile. "Phoebe," he said, and now that the die was cast, he felt a hollow ache spread through his chest. "Phoebe Richards. She'll be there." He'd make sure she'd be there. "You'll like her. You'll like her a lot."

And then he proceeded to tell him about Phoebe. About her smile and her quirky sense of humor. About her inability to recognize and accept how beautiful she was. How she was the perfect match for a man with marriage on his mind.

How her eyes shined when something tickled her. How she had the ability to listen, really listen and not make a man feel like a fool for unloading like a dump truck.

Ash's contemplative silence seemed to tell the tale. He was interested. And that was great.

That was just great, Daniel thought with a dark scowl as he dialed Phoebe's number the next day.

After their little "play date" on Friday night, Phoebe had spent a miserable weekend waiting by the phone for Daniel to call. She'd known it was foolish, hopeless even, but she'd done it just the same. Some lessons took a long time to learn.

She'd moped and moaned and taken out her frustration on a lot of hapless lumps of clay. There weren't enough flowers in Boston to fill the vases she'd thrown. She knew that Leslie had noticed her dark mood at work on Monday, but she hadn't asked, recognizing that if Phoebe wanted to talk about it, she would.

By the time her phone rang Monday night, she'd

given up on the possibility of Daniel Barone being on the other end.

"Goes to show how much I know," she murmured, pleased yet puzzled and a little bit panicked after Daniel said goodbye.

After she snapped out of her shock-induced ministroke, she dialed her friend Carol.

"Help," she squeaked when Carol picked up.

"Phoebe?"

"Cinderella, actually," Phoebe said a little breathlessly. "And I just got invited to the ball."

"Gee," Carol said after Phoebe filled her in on the fact that Daniel had just invited her to attend a family party in honor of his new cousin. "And me without my pumpkin."

"I don't need a pumpkin. I need something to wear."

Somebody pinch me, Phoebe thought as she stood at Daniel's side Wednesday night in the large, crowded living room of his parents' home. She was drifting on a haze of disbelief that she was here as Daniel's date, meeting his family. How had the fat, shy, ugly duckling twelve-year-old girl who'd grown up in the seedy side of Boston ended up rubbing elbows with Boston royalty?

She wasn't exactly fat anymore, but she still battled her weight, and even if she dropped the ten pounds she was always struggling to lose, *thin* was not a word that would ever be used to describe her. She was still painfully shy when she was out of her element, as she was tonight. And she was as far from a princess as she'd been at twelve—in looks or bearing. Princesses generally wore white and diamonds and diaphanous smiles. Still, she was more than glad she'd listened to Carol's advice and opted for the basic black sheath.

She'd found the dress in a frantic search through the racks at Elegant Repeats, a dress shop where the upscale Boston elite sent their once-worn clothing to die with dignity so they could make room in their closets for more designer originals that they would wear once and then start the cycle all over again. New, the sleeveless crepe that hit her just above the knee would have cost the better part of her weekly paycheck. Even "delicately worn" as the tag had indicated, it had made a major dent in her budget.

It had been worth every penny. At least on the surface, she appeared to fit in, as all around her the room was full to bursting with the famous and elegantly dressed Barone clan. All of them were beautiful and completely comfortable in their element. All, perhaps, except Karen Rawlins, the guest of honor. Oh, she was definitely beautiful. But comfortable? Phoebe didn't think so.

Daniel had introduced her to Karen shortly after they'd arrived. Phoebe had felt a tug of empathy for the pretty woman with the wide hazel eyes and wavy brown hair. She looked a little overwhelmed. She was glad to see that Karen and Daniel's cousin Maria had hit it off so well. She'd even overheard Maria offer Karen the use of her old apartment and a job at the Baronessa gelateria.

Yes, the Barones were a boisterous lot, but Maria had proven that they were also warm and friendly, if unintentionally intimidating for their confidence and close camaraderie. At least they all seemed close, with the exception of Daniel's twin brother, Derrick, who, to Daniel's mother's disappointment, hadn't made an appearance.

At one time or another, Daniel had mentioned with affection both his sister Emily, whom she'd met a few minutes ago, and his sister Claudia, whom she hadn't yet met. When his brother's name came up, however, she'd sensed a lot of tension. Derrick was a topic that Daniel steered clear of.

Tonight, however, Derrick seemed to be at the top of everyone else's list of topics. Phoebe hadn't intended to eavesdrop, but in such close quarters it was impossible not to hear snippets of conversation. There was a lot of speculation on why Derrick hadn't shown up and about his behavior lately. It seemed he'd become more and more withdrawn and aloof.

She looked at the man at her side while a knot of Barones clustered around them, talking about children and business and fun. She'd been trying to ignore it, but Daniel seemed a little withdrawn and aloof tonight himself. He just wasn't quite Daniel. He was quieter than usual, almost as if he was trying to erect a bit of distance between them.

"Did you say curse?" she asked abruptly, tuning in to something Daniel's cousin Nicholas had said.

Even though they were cousins, not brothers, Daniel was a younger, mirror image of Nicholas.

"You mean Daniel hasn't told you about the dreaded Valentine's curse?" Gail Barone, Nicholas's wife, asked with grin and a staged shiver of dread.

Phoebe had liked Gail Barone instantly when they'd been introduced. She was down-to-earth and friendly, her hazel eyes full of fun as she smiled from her husband to Phoebe.

"Now, Gail. You know it's not nice to joke about

the curse," Nicholas said with a playful frown as he wrapped an arm around her shoulders.

"What curse?" Phoebe asked, really curious now.

"It's nothing. Just an old family legend," Daniel said, shaking his head at his cousin who was urging him to flesh out the story.

"That goes something like…" Gail prompted Daniel as she wrapped her arm around Nicholas's waist and snuggled closer.

Dutifully picking up his cue, Daniel explained, "When our grandfather Marco was a young man, he waited tables at Antonio Conti's restaurant down on Prince Street. Apparently Antonio had always hoped that Marco would marry their daughter, Lucia."

"But it didn't quite work out that way," Nicholas supplied.

Gail picked up the story from there. "Instead of marrying Lucia, Marco fell in love with Angelica Salvo, who was the ice cream maker at the restaurant and who just happened to be the girlfriend of the Contis' son, Vincent."

"Uh-oh," Phoebe said. "I think I see where this is going."

"Long story short," Daniel put in, "Marco and Angelica eloped."

"On Valentine's Day," Gail prompted.

"On Valentine's Day," Daniel restated with a nod to Gail. "It broke Lucia's heart, and Vincent, who had looked upon Marco as a brother, felt betrayed."

"The entire Conti family felt betrayed," added Nicholas. "And Lucia, in her anger, placed a curse on Marco and Angelica. Gail, you want to take it from here?"

"Let's see if I remember it right. 'You got married

on Valentine's Day and may your anniversary day be cursed. A miserable Valentine's Day to both of you from this day forward.' Did I get it right?''

''Perfect, darling.'' Nicholas kissed her when she lifted her face to his.

''And so, did anything bad happen to your grandfather and grandmother?'' Phoebe asked, both unsettled and charmed by the story.

The two cousins exchanged a look. Daniel shrugged. ''Well, they established Baronessa Gelati. I wouldn't exactly call that bad.''

''But Angelina miscarried her first child on their first anniversary, and for that reason, they began to take the curse seriously,'' Nicholas explained. ''A number of minor things happened after that, nothing disastrous, until Daniel's father was born.''

''Oh dear.'' Phoebe said, suspecting she already knew the answer to her question. ''Your father's twin brother, Luke. Was he…''

''Abducted on Valentine's Day? Yes.''

''How sad.''

''What's even sadder is that there's been a rift between the Contis and the Barones ever since. All because of that silly curse.''

''What happened to Lucia and to Vincent?''

Nicholas filled in that blank. ''Vincent eventually married and took over the Conti restaurant. Lucia never married. I can't remember who told me this, but they said that the last time they saw her, she looked like a bitter old crone.''

''I'm so sorry to interrupt this,'' Gail said, smiling apologetically, ''but I just spotted someone I must say hello to. Excuse us, will you, Daniel? Phoebe, it was so nice meeting you. Daniel will have to bring you for dinner sometime so we can get to know each other better.''

"I—I'd like that," Phoebe said with a smile that faded when an unsmiling Daniel stiffened beside her.

"You're out of champagne," he said. "Let me see if I can find another glass for you."

Well, Phoebe thought as she watched him go. Okay. So he was uncomfortable with the idea of thinking past tonight. Maybe he was having second thoughts about bringing her home to meet his family. And maybe she had been a little quick on the trigger when she'd thought she was here as anything other than Daniel's buddy.

But surely being here meant something, didn't it? Surely it said something? Like maybe he wasn't content for them to just be friends any longer?

She wanted so much to believe that as she watched him work his way back to her, carrying two flutes of champagne. He looked incredibly handsome in black tie and tux.

"Sorry I took so long." He relieved her of her empty glass, set it on the mantel behind her and placed the fresh glass in her hand.

"There's someone I want you to meet. Phoebe, this is Sheikh Ashraf Saalem, prince of Zhamyr. Ash, this is the friend I told you about, Phoebe Richards."

Phoebe looked up and into a face right out of the *Arabian Nights*. Sheikh Ashraf Saalem was one of the most exotically handsome men she'd ever seen.

His eyes were so brown they were almost as black as his hair; his smile was warm and interested. He was taller than Daniel's five-eleven frame, but not by much, and even in his formal attire, it was apparent that every inch of his body was sleekly muscled and sinfully elegant.

"Ms. Richards," the prince said, and taking her hand in his, brought her fingers to his mouth. "It is my extreme pleasure to meet you."

"The pleasure is mine," she assured him, proud as heck that she'd managed the response without a single um, ah or duh. Her speech impairment seemed to be limited to her response to Daniel.

"Well. I'll just let you two get to know each other," Daniel said with a tight smile. Then he turned and walked away.

Phoebe blinked, opened her mouth to stop him, and realized she didn't know what to say. With a sickening roll of her stomach, she did, however, realize what had just happened.

Daniel had arranged for her to be alone with the sheikh. The implication was obvious. He was setting them up.

Her face flamed red. Embarrassed, she lowered her gaze to the floor and held it there. Anything to keep from watching Daniel leave. Anything to keep the sheikh from seeing the bewilderment and hurt that must be painted across her face like a banner.

Oh, how rich. Daniel hadn't brought her here to meet his family. He'd never intended that she think she was his date. He'd brought her here to set her up with his friend. Because, after all, she thought bitterly as hurt transitioned to humiliation, she was nothing more to Daniel than a *buddy*.

The sudden pain of that undeniable truth clenched tightly in her chest and twisted.

She had to get out of here.

She had to get out of here now.

Eight

"**P**hoebe? Ms. Richards?"

Phoebe heard Ashraf's voice through a haze of painful longing that quickly transitioned to anger—at herself as much as at Daniel. The anger finally drew out her pride.

"Are you all right?" the sheikh asked, touching a hand to her arm.

Drawing a bracing breath, she lifted her head, smiled her brightest smile. "I'm fine. I'm simply overwhelmed by the idea that I'm actually standing here talking to a real live prince. How do I address you?"

"Just Ash, please," he insisted. "And I assure you, it is I who am overwhelmed. Daniel told me you were beautiful, but his description did not do you justice."

She was not beautiful. She had never been beautiful. And she didn't need a psychology degree to know that Ashraf Saalem knew how to spread honey as thick as the asphalt in a parking lot. Or that she had just been dumped on a date that was never really a date.

"You're very kind," she said with a forced smile.

"And you are very much in love with my friend Daniel."

If he'd whipped out a magic carpet then sailed it across the room, he couldn't have shocked her more.

So it showed that much. Phoebe sighed, too defeated to deny it—even though she was still fighting it for all she was worth.

"And he is very much in love with you as well, I think."

Phoebe pushed out a humorless laugh. "I'm afraid you're mistaken. Daniel couldn't have made it any clearer. We're friends, he and I. That's the way he wants it."

Ash smiled kindly. "That may be the way he wants it, but I know my friend. That is not the way it is. He is very taken with you, Phoebe. He simply hasn't figured out yet that he's fighting a losing battle as he tries to deny his feelings."

She was still digesting that unlikely bit of wisdom when a tall, lovely blonde sidled up beside them and looped her arm through his.

"Ash, you handsome devil. What are you doing to this woman that's making my poor brother clench his jaw and glare as if he'd like to cheerfully choke the life out of you?"

She kissed him on the cheek before he could respond, then turned a brilliant smile on Phoebe. "I'm Claudia, Daniel's sister. And you would be the first woman he's ever brought home and the only woman

I've ever seen him look at like he wants to drag you away by your hair and have his way with you. How absolutely fascinating.''

"Claudia," Ash addressed Daniel's sister with an amused smile, "this is Phoebe Richards. Daniel just tried to set the two of us up.''

Claudia's smile widened, her eyes dancing with speculation. "Better and better," she said, clearly intrigued by her brother's behavior. "This could be serious. Ash, darling, be a dear and go away. Ms. Richards and I have to have a serious talk.''

Phoebe watched, speechless, as the sheikh smiled. "I'm going, but not before I give Daniel a little something to think about.''

To her utter amazement, he leaned forward and kissed her, lingeringly, on the mouth.

"Oh, now you've done it," Claudia said, her voice bubbling with mirth. "I don't believe I've ever seen Daniel's face that shade of red.''

"And, present company excluded, I don't believe I've ever seen such a beautiful woman.'' The sheikh's gaze was locked on someone behind Phoebe's field of vision. "Who is she?''

Claudia followed his gaze. "That's Karen. Our guest of honor.''

Still reeling over Ashraf's kiss and his conclusions about Daniel, Phoebe listened with half an ear as Claudia related Karen's story.

"We're so glad to have her as part of the family,'' Claudia added. "And yes, she is beautiful.''

The sheikh had evidently tuned out, too. He was already cutting a path across the room where an impromptu receiving line had formed. Barones were lined up to give and receive hugs and kiss their new-found family member on the cheek.

Ash however, didn't believe in such casual expressions of welcome. Claudia and Phoebe laughed when he cut the line and grasped Karen's shoulders in his broad hands and drew her toward him. No buss on the cheek or air kisses for this man. He whispered something that surprised a shocked smile out of Karen, then he covered her mouth with his.

"I love a man who knows what he wants and goes after it," Claudia said before turning her attention back to Phoebe. "Which brings us back to the subject of my brother, a supposedly smart man who obviously doesn't know what he wants or, for that matter, how to get it."

Phoebe sat in the passenger seat of Daniel's Porsche as he drove her home from the party an hour or so later. He didn't have much to say. Neither did she. That was understandable to her way of thinking since she'd gone from glowing to grief-stricken to amazed all in one brief night.

First she was Daniel's date, then she wasn't. Then she was the sheikh's date, then she wasn't. And finally, she was the answer to a sister's prayer that her brother—who has an old soul, Claudia had confided with a sad shake of her head—had finally found the woman.

Not *a* woman. *The* woman.

Phoebe glanced across the dark interior at Daniel's perfect profile as he steered the sleek car across town. Could it be possible? Could she really be *the* woman for Daniel Barone?

And if so, did she have what it took to, as Claudia

had suggested, "Bring him to his senses, girl. And the best way to do that is to bring him to his knees."

"Um," had been her articulate response as yet another Barone had reduced her to monosyllabic mumblings.

"To his knees," Claudia had repeated then smiled and spelled it out for her. "Seduce him, Phoebe. He's got too much honor to seduce you. If I know Daniel, he's got it in his head that he can't love you and leave you. He just doesn't know yet that he's not leaving. Not this time. Do you see what I'm telling you here?"

Well, no, she didn't see. It was all so out there, way on the other side of the realm of possibility. She couldn't wrap her mind around the idea, let alone process it.

"Daniel has always been the golden boy," Claudia had continued, reacting to Phoebe's puzzled frown. "He was the smart twin. The handsome twin, the athletic twin. Men admire him and want to emulate him, women and dogs adore him. Life for Daniel has always been easy. Do you know what kind of pressure that puts on a man? To always be expected to be the best, do the best? And to know that his brother has lived all of his life in Daniel's shadow?"

Fascinated, Phoebe had simply listened to Claudia talk with love and concern about Daniel.

"He once confided in me that he wished it had been Derrick who'd gotten the looks and the easy intelligence that had allowed him to breeze through everything. He feels guilty over the fact that everything has been a stroll for him and a struggle for Derrick.

"I think that's why he cut out of here after college. He'd never admit it, but I think he has this misaligned notion that if he disappointed Mom and Dad, maybe Derrick would have his moment. And then maybe he and Derrick would grow closer. It's always hurt him, the animosity Derrick feels for him.''

Phoebe had been stunned, heartsick, at Claudia's revelations. And she felt selfish and immature suddenly for not seeing that Daniel of the quick smile and kind eyes had his own ghosts that haunted him.

Her ghosts may be a bit more visible—Jason for one, her abusive, alcoholic mother for another—but Daniel's were every bit as intrusive on his life.

"I know my brother. And I know that he's crazy about you,'' Claudia had insisted then added with a laugh, "Help him. For heaven's sake, help that poor bumbling fool.''

Phoebe was honestly starting to believe there might be something to what Claudia said.

But was she woman enough? she asked herself as they turned onto her street. Did she have it in her to seduce him, as Claudia suggested. Or was she too much of a coward to go after the man of her dreams for his sake, not hers?

If it was just for her, she didn't think she could do it. But for Daniel, she decided she could do anything.

She could be strong for him. She could be brave for him. He didn't need a coward in his life. He needed strength. He needed *her* strength, and if ever there was a time for her to test it, it was now.

She drew a deep breath, let it out. Then she made him a solemn promise. You're going down, buddy. To your knees. And I'm just the woman to get the job done.

"What the hell?" Daniel leaned forward, squinting through the windshield as he approached her house.

Phoebe followed his gaze then gasped.

A police cruiser sat in her driveway. Another was parked at the curb. Lights flashed everywhere.

"Arthur," she cried when Daniel pulled up behind the cruiser and she realized her front door was wide open. "Please let Arthur be all right."

"Stay here." Daniel opened his door.

Phoebe was already out of the car and running up her sidewalk. With a muttered oath, Daniel caught up with her, wrapped his arm around her waist and pulled her back against him.

"You folks have business here?" A uniformed officer blocked them from entering the house.

"I live here," Phoebe wailed. "Arthur. I have to find Arthur!"

"Her cat," Daniel explained.

"Big tabby?"

"Oh, God. Is he all right?"

"He's fine. Last I saw him, he was scooting under a bed."

Phoebe almost collapsed with relief.

"What's going on?" Daniel asked, keeping Phoebe snug against his side.

"We're not sure yet. Got a call from a neighbor. Said she saw someone sneaking around, looking suspicious. We just did a walk-through. There's no one here now. Ma'am, do you suppose you could come in, take a look for us and tell us if anything's missing?"

"There won't be anything missing," Daniel said in a hard voice. "The son of a bitch just wanted to scare her."

The officer lifted an eyebrow. "You know who did this?"

"Oh, yeah." Daniel's voice was as tight as the lines bracketing his mouth. "His name is Jason Collins and she wants to file a restraining order against him."

It was over an hour and a half later that the police finally left—without the restraining order. Hugging Arthur to her breast, Phoebe closed the door behind them then leaned her forehead against it.

"Do you think they'll turn up anything?" she asked, looking and sounding exhausted.

"Honestly? No. He covered his tracks on that count. There weren't any prints. And you won't find anything missing. He did his damage by letting you know he could get to you anytime he wanted to."

Daniel stood with his tie undone, his hands shoved deep in his pockets. He didn't trust himself to touch her right now. He had so much rage inside him for Collins and so much frustration over the limitations of the law that he was afraid some of it would spill over and he would bruise her by simply holding her.

He understood why she couldn't file a restraining order against Collins. There was no proof that it was he who had broken in. Add that to the fact that Phoebe hadn't filed police reports the other times he'd harassed her or the time he'd hit her, and there was no legal basis for the order.

So yeah, intellectually, he understood. It didn't, however, do much to assuage his anger.

"Come on," he said. "You're staying at my place tonight."

She looked up, seemed to consider complying, then something came over her that he'd never seen before. Anger. Defiance. And she slowly shook her head.

"No," she said, a determination made strong by conviction. "I'm done. I'm not letting him call the shots for me anymore. He's not going to run me out of my own home. I'm not going to let him do it."

Daniel looked at the face that so fascinated him. Her lush lips were unyielding. Though the smudges of violet beneath her eyes showed her fatigue and her stress, her eyes were clear and dry. Her shoulders were back, her head erect.

Before his eyes, his little owl transformed into an eagle. He felt more than pride at her warrior stance. He was so turned on by it, it hurt to draw breath.

"Then I'll sleep on your sofa," he said, battling to keep a rein on his libido, "because there's no way in hell I'm going to let you stay here alone."

All business, he tossed his tuxedo jacket aside, sat down on the couch and toed off his shoes. "If you've got an extra blanket, I'm good to go." He'd just removed his socks when her continued silence brought his head up.

He narrowed his eyes as she set Arthur on a side chair then advanced toward him, one steady step at a time. "You are not sleeping on the sofa. But you are sleeping here. With me."

There was no mistaking her intentions. The huskiness of her voice and the invitation in her eyes made it very clear. He forced himself to stand, gathered himself to be the voice of reason.

But then she moved directly in front of him, filling his field of vision with amber eyes flecked in gold. Filling his senses with an awareness of her woman's scent, of every breath she drew, of the pale skin visible above the scooped neckline of her dress. Of the gentle round of her breasts that pressed against the black crepe.

He swallowed, shook his head and strove for restraint while his heart damn near hammered out of his chest at the thought of her naked and warm and willing beneath him.

"No." The word came out on a strangled croak. "This can't happen."

It *shouldn't* happen. And he was the one who needed to make sure it didn't.

"Look, Phoebe, you're running on adrenaline. It's doing your talking and your thinking at the moment."

She moved so close that the warmth of her breath fluttered against his jaw, so close that the giving softness of her breasts pressed against his chest and made him groan.

"My adrenaline's talking, huh?"

He swallowed thickly. He nodded, when the power of speech took a hike to Brazil—where he ought to be.

"Tell me," she whispered, placing her hands on his chest, fingers splayed wide. The heat of her palms burned through his shirt. "What, exactly, is it saying?"

"Phoebe." Rock hard and trying his damnedest to resist her, he shackled her wrists with his hands. "Don't—"

"Shh," she whispered against his throat then slid her nose in a sensual caress along his jaw. The butterfly kiss of her lashes fluttered against the corner of his mouth. "Listen. Listen to what it's saying."

Oh, he was listening. He couldn't hear, of course. The teaspoon of blood that wasn't pooled in his groin had shot to his ears where it pounded like a battalion of kettledrums. He didn't have to hear what she said, though, to get her message loud and clear. She wanted what he wanted. And he wanted it bad.

He'd never considered himself a weak man. But with her pressed up against him that way, her lips parted, her warm breath feathering his jaw, he felt about as strong as Samson after Delilah had gone crazy with her shears.

So much for steely resolve. He didn't even bother to fake another argument.

"Tell me you're not going to regret this," he demanded, releasing her wrists and wrapping her in his arms.

"Just a sec." The little tease had the nerve to gloat over her victory. "I'll need to consult with my adrenaline."

Sliding her hands up his chest then along his throat, she cupped his jaw and brought his mouth to within a breath of hers. "Good news. Me and my glands are up for it."

He exhaled on a serrated breath. "Glad to hear someone's glands are in good working order."

She smiled then. And so did he.

"You are turning me inside out here," he growled against her mouth.

"I don't want you inside out." One slim, questing hand journeyed down his chest, past his belt and lower, to cup and caress the length of the ridged flesh pressing against his zipper. "I just want you inside. Of me."

"Well," he muttered, scooping her up in his arms. "Now you're in trouble."

She linked her arms behind his neck and ran the

tip of her tongue along the outer edge of his ear. "About time."

"Keep it up—just keep it up and this is not going to happen with the benefit of a bed."

Tiny teeth latched on to his earlobe, tugged. "And that's bad because?"

"That's bad," he managed to say on an involuntary shudder, "because once I get you naked, I'm going to keep you that way for a very long time. And you're going to want a mattress, not a wall against your back."

The implication of that threat finally stopped her busy mouth and wandering hands.

"Oh," she said, a sudden bout of uncertainty arresting her.

"Yeah. Oh."

It was too late for second thoughts. He was so hot for her, nothing short of an unqualified "I changed my mind" was going to stop him now.

He'd never seen her bedroom before. He didn't see much of it now. All he saw was her. All he wanted was her. It seemed as if he'd wanted her forever.

He set her on her feet by the bed and reached for the switch on the bedside lamp.

"You, um, want the light on?"

"I want the light on." Easing down on the edge of the bed, he took her hand, recognizing that she was suddenly feeling shy again. He tugged until she stood between his splayed legs. "I want to see you. I've been going crazy wanting to see you."

"Even when you tried to pass me off to Ash?"

He slid his hands in a slow, exploring caress from her hips past her waist and then up the length of her back. His fingers found the zipper tab and tugged it slowly down. "Especially when I tried to pass you off to Ash. I wanted to drop-kick him across the room when he kissed you."

The zipper slid almost soundlessly past the small of her back then stopped where the sweet cheeks of her bottom met. He pressed his face against her stomach, felt her heat through the black crepe, felt the slight tremble of her muscles against his lips. He lifted his hands to her shoulders.

"What...what if you're disappointed in...what you see?"

He tipped his head back, looked up at her. "Do you have a long furry tail?"

One corner of her mouth tipped up. "No."

"Do you have fish scales on your bottom?"

A generous smile this time. "Not the last time I looked."

"Then I won't be disappointed."

Another beautifully sensual shiver eddied through her body as he hooked his fingers over the neckline of her dress and pulled it slowly down.

Soft crepe rustled against satin skin and pooled on the floor at her feet. A softer sigh soughed through her parted lips. He looked up, past the generous swell of her breasts that practically spilled over the top of black lace cups. She closed her eyes when his blunt-tipped fingers found the clasp between them, flicked it open.

Her breasts sprang free. Warm, giving, much fuller than he'd imagined, heavy with arousal. Her nipples puckered into tight little beads as he cupped her, lifted, then scraped the edge of his thumbnails across dusty-pink areolas that were so delicate and so utterly female he could have wept.

"Beautiful."

Another shiver. Another breathy sigh.

And he was lost.

He tumbled her to her back on the bed and propped up on an elbow, to look and touch his fill.

"So pretty," he whispered and lowered his head to taste one pale, quivering mound. He flicked his tongue over the crown of her nipple. She arched up to meet him, whimpered when he withdrew, making him smile into her slumberous eyes as he went back for more. Taking more this time than a glancing thrust of his tongue, he cupped her breast with his hand, drew her inside his mouth and feasted.

She seemed to be having trouble breathing. And figuring out what to do with her hands. Her stiff fingers plucked at the spread beside her hips, then rose to tangle in his hair and press his mouth closer against her. She said his name on a desperate moan when he skimmed a hand down her tummy and cupped the heat still covered in damp black silk.

"Tell me what you want." He lifted his head, then dipped to nuzzle her other breast.

"You. Inside me. Now."

He managed a strangled laugh. "You're really going to have to learn to express yourself."

"And you're really going to have to learn not to tease a desperate woman."

Surprising him, she reared up. Pushing him to his back, she swung a leg over his hips and straddled him all in one fast, fierce and amazingly coordinated motion.

Triumphant in her conquest, she smiled down at him. "Not so funny now, huh?"

Well, yeah, it was. Funny and wonderful and sexy

as hell. He couldn't help it. He laughed again when she went to work on the buttons of his shirt then wrenched it off his shoulders and dragged it down his arms.

She was a wild, erotic dream bent over him. Her lips were swollen from his kisses, her breasts wet and free and pink where the stubble on his jaw had abraded her tender flesh. And she was all woman as she rose to stand on her knees, her fingers flying to unbuckle his belt, unfasten his pants and—

''Whoa.'' He stilled her hands before she did some real damage. ''Easy. We'll both be happier if you take it easy.''

Her gaze locked on his, she drew a shaky breath, steadied herself. ''You do it.'' Her hands turned in his, covered them then guided them to his zipper. ''Hurry.''

The urgency of her whispered command damn near sent him over the edge. So did the way she looked, her knees pressed into the mattress on either side of his thighs, her bare breasts rising and falling with each fractured breath, her lower lip caught, in anticipation, between her teeth.

He watched her face as he slowly lowered the zipper, lifted his hips and shoved his slacks and boxers to his knees.

Her eyes grew dark with desire as her gaze rose to his, then back to the rock-hard length of his erection.

And suddenly he didn't feel like playing anymore. ''Touch me.''

Nine

It felt as if she was having an out-of-body experience, Phoebe thought dreamily. Only she didn't want to be out of her body. For one of the few times in her life, she wanted to be in it. She wanted *him* to be in it. The look on his face told her he wanted that, too, that he didn't care if she was far from perfect. He didn't care if her hips were a little too wide, if her breasts were a little too heavy and had never been described as perky. He thought she was beautiful.

What she was looking at was beautiful, too.

She sank back on her heels so she could see him better. The hard muscle of his thighs pressed against her bottom, the heat in his eyes sent liquid fire pooling in that part of her that so wanted to be part of him.

That such a man, such an intelligent, interesting

and incredibly sexy man, could be this aroused by her seemed like a miracle.

He was the miracle. He was so…so…everything. Everything that a bookish, thirty-something librarian with the backbone of a snail had never thought, never dreamed, could be hers. Even if it was just for a night.

He talked about her adrenaline, but it was really his that had brought them to this point. Tomorrow, it would be important to remember that he was reacting to his anger at Jason and his concern for her. Tonight, she didn't care what had landed him in her bed. What she cared about was his need. It made her strong, made her brave. It made her want him in ways that would embarrass her in the morning.

But not tonight. Tonight, she was a siren, wanton and uninhibited. Tonight, she was a temptress. Tonight, she was in his arms—and she was driving him crazy.

She slid her hands in a slow glide along his upper thighs, past his hip points, lingered over the concave of his belly, the delicious indentation of his navel. Oh, she knew where he wanted her to touch him, but she played it out, glancing her fingers over his taut nipples until he groaned, teasing her fingers through a mat of dark curls that so beautifully covered his chest.

Power. It was a heady thing this *power* she wielded. She could feel the stunning effects of it in the beat of his heart, fast and unsteady in his chest, see the heavy pulse of it thrumming through the thick artery at the base of his throat.

She lifted her gaze to his. He was watching her. His blue eyes were as dark as cobalt, dangerous even, as his broad chest rose and fell in shallow breaths that appeared to take all of his control to keep level.

He wet his lips, closed his eyes. "Please."

It shouldn't have been love that washed through her in a wave so strong it made her tremble. It shouldn't have been love that was born of his one tortured and desperate whisper. But it was. It most definitely was.

Please.

Tears burned then blurred her vision. She'd been half in love with him since the first night she'd seen him. Her knight in shining armor. Her slayer of dragons. That this strong man would let himself be weak for her, that he would let himself beg for her broke down her last defense and sent her tumbling. Headlong. Happily. Into a love she'd been fighting since the first time she'd seen him.

Tomorrow, she would see the foolishness of it all. But tonight, oh, how she loved him tonight.

Eyes locked on his, she trailed her hands downward, splayed her fingers through the soft nest of curling hair that framed his sex, and then she touched him.

He jerked once, caught his breath.

She took him in her hand, reveled in his low groan of pleasure. He was forged heat and pulsing need, thick and heavy with arousal.

For her.

Beneath her, his muscles tensed, then gathered, and the next thing she knew she was flat on her back again and he was looming over her. The full measure of his weight stretched out over her, chest to breast; his erection nestled in the vee between her thighs as he kicked his pants and boxers to the floor.

His elbows dug into the mattress on either side of her shoulders, his forearms caged her head as his hands tangled in her hair and he crushed his mouth to hers.

She'd never felt so wanted. She'd never felt so much.

She opened her legs for him, wrapped them around his hips and locked her ankles. Heat, hunger, need. She felt them in every pore of her body as his tongue mated with hers and his hips pumped into hers in a hard, rocking rhythm.

He tore his mouth away, sucked in a ragged breath and swore. "Protection. Please." He pressed his forehead to hers, his breath coming in hard, heavy gasps. "*Please* tell me you've got something."

She was too far gone to think about whether this was a good thing or a bad thing that he didn't carry condoms on the off chance he'd get lucky. And she was too needy to worry over what he would think about the fact that she had a full box of them in her nightstand drawer.

"Top drawer. Left. Hurry."

He rolled off her and dragged open the drawer while she shimmied out of her panties. He was suited up and clench-jawed when he turned back to her. She held out her arms, opened her legs, and he found a place for himself between them.

"You deserve finesse," he apologized as he reached between them. "I promise next time, I'll make it up to you, but right now..."

She drew his mouth close to hers "Right now. I need you to shut up and—" She gasped as he hooked an arm behind her knee and pushed into her.

Gasped again when he withdrew, then drove into her again and again in a hard, fast, earth-moving, heart-pounding rhythm.

She'd barely caught her breath, hadn't cataloged the unbelievable depth of the pleasure when a climax so electric, so sustained, so off-the-charts powerful screamed through her body. She flew over the top on a gasping sob, swept up in a flood of sensations so fierce they were almost frightening, so consuming she was lost to anything but the feel of him moving inside her.

Somewhere in the midst of this current of mindless bliss, she heard him call her name, heard him swear her name, then groan her name as he thrust one final time and found his own shattering release.

When he could breathe again, when he could assimilate words into a cognitive stream of thought, when he could convince his muscles and his mind that he needed to roll off of her and give her some breathing room, Daniel still couldn't make himself move.

He wanted to stay right where he was—buried inside of Phoebe Richards—for another millennium or two. By then maybe he'd have had enough of her.

He waited another several heartbeats, then reluctantly levered his weight up on his elbows. "Are you still with me in there?"

A small, dreamy smile tilted her lips. "Mmm."

He pressed a kiss to one closed eyelid then the other. "I could move—"

"Shh." One very limp hand lifted and with effort pressed an index finger against his lips. "No talking. Not yet." She stretched sinuously beneath him, exhaled on a deep, satisfied sigh. "Just let me ride the wave until I'm sure it's played out."

He snagged her finger between his teeth. "And that

was only the first wave. The seventh is the big one. Just think how long we can ride that one.''

Her eyes popped open. ''Seventh?''

He grinned. ''Hi.''

She caressed his jaw then raised her arms over her head and stretched again, long and lazy and catlike. ''Hi back.''

He lowered his head, kissed her sweet, swollen mouth. ''You okay?''

She pushed out a smug little laugh. ''I'm perfect.''

''Yeah,'' he agreed softly. ''You are.''

When she smiled up at him another kind of wave—tenderness—washed over him. He thought, in that moment, that he could look at her face for hours. Listen to her sounds of pleasure for days. The thought of the sounds she would make when he loved her the way she deserved to be loved made him want to rectify that oversight as soon as humanly possible.

''Me, on the other hand,'' he said, pulling out of her and easing up on an elbow so he could watch her face, ''I get demerits for fast-forwarding to the end of the movie and missing all the good parts.''

''Good parts?'' She let out another deep sigh. ''Let's see. Technicolor, fireworks, surroundsound, special effects. What other good parts could there possibly be?''

''Well.'' He cupped her breast in his palm, loving the weight of her in his hand, the resiliency, the instant response as her nipple pearled. ''Here's a good part.''

He lowered his head, tasted. ''A very good part.''

''Um. Oh.''

He slipped lower, pressing kisses to the underside of her breast, lingering over the adorable indentation of her navel that he couldn't resist exploring with his tongue. "And yet another good part."

She struggled to hike herself up on her elbows, her expression stunned and electric with anticipation as he slid to his knees on the floor at the foot of the bed. When he bracketed her hips in his palms and dragged her to the edge of the mattress, she stopped breathing.

"And here's the best part of all." He ran his tongue along the inside of her thigh, a slow glide from knee to just shy of that place he had yet to taste. Eyes locked on hers, he draped her legs over his shoulders. Then he lowered his head, nuzzled her damp curls, breathed in the scent of her and of him and of arousal.

"The very best part," he murmured as his fingers opened her feminine folds and he finally tasted that wondrous place that defined her as a woman. It was sensual, swollen and so sensitive she came apart for him at that first intimate stroke.

"Daniel," she gasped his name on a trembling sigh.

"Shh." He gently bit the inside of a thigh, soothed her with a light brush of his fingertips over her belly.

And when the tremors had ebbed and her breathing had leveled, he loved her all over again. Slowly now, taking his time, drawing out her pleasure, heightening her need until she begged him for release then cried out in his arms when he gave it.

Silk, he thought after he'd turned off the light, maneuvered them under the covers and drawn her snug against his side. Her skin was like silk.

He lay in the dark, her slight weight pressed against him, her head on his shoulder, her bent knee nestled against his sleeping sex. And he wondered what he'd gotten himself into and how, when it was time, he was going to find it in him to get himself out.

"It's not like you haven't had a guy sleep over before," Phoebe muttered to herself the next morning as she inventoried her refrigerator for the makings of omelettes.

Granted, it had been Leslie's grandson and he'd been six years old at the time and he'd slept on her sofa in his Power Rangers pj's.

Her cheeks flamed with heat. Daniel didn't sleep in pj's, although he could definitely fall into the Power Rangers category.

A nervous laugh burst out. The things they had done in her bed.

She flashed on a memory of his dark head at her breast, between her legs and almost had a meltdown over the vegetable crisper.

"Snap out of it," she sputtered and started cracking eggs.

She was a big girl. And now she had a lover.

"A lover." A goofy smile stretched her mouth.

She hadn't been a virgin but neither had she experienced anything like the pleasure Daniel had brought her last night.

Several times.

She covered her heated cheeks with her hands.

Who knew that those red-hot love scenes she read in her romance novels weren't necessarily figments of the authors' imaginations. And who knew that Daniel Barone could hold his own—and then some—with those fictional lovers who knew exactly where and how to touch a woman until he reduced her to a mindless, whimpering lump.

Many, many times.

Another river of heat sluiced through her blood. She honestly hadn't known she'd been capable of so many— Well, to sum it up concisely: until Daniel Barone landed in her bed the only time "multi" had preceded a word describing her, it had been attached to "tasking."

She set a skillet on the burner, turned on the heat and wondered if a person could become a nymphomaniac overnight. Then she wondered if nymphomaniac was a hyphenated word. If so, she would have two new hyphenated terms—nympho and multi—to add to her growing list of 'Things she'd never been'.

And then she wondered if she was just plain nuts when she realized she'd thrown the eggshells in the bowl and the eggs in the garbage.

She closed her eyes, drew a deep breath.

"Get a grip."

She glanced at the clock. It was a little past eight-thirty. She'd been up long enough to take a quick shower, check to make sure Daniel was still sleeping, slip in a fresh set of contacts, check on Daniel again, fluff her hair, check on Daniel yet again, decide what to wear and then change her mind seven times, check on Daniel one final time, and have a nervous breakdown in her kitchen.

By anyone's standards, it had been a pretty full morning. But nervous-breakdown time was now officially over. She glanced down at her pink shorts and her pink tank top, under which she wore no bra because earlier she'd had another moment of insanity and now she was afraid to go back in the bedroom and have him wake up and catch her in the act of changing.

She looked fine. Except possibly for the condition of her nipples, which poked against her top like new erasers on number-two lead pencils and more or less gave away what she'd been thinking about since she'd awakened with a beautiful naked man sprawled in her bed this morning.

"Help," she pleaded skyward and started over on the omelettes. When both the yokes and the whites landed in the bowl this time, she took it as a good sign. When she heard the bathroom door open then close down the hall, she considered running out the back door.

The dreaded morning-after scene was only moments away.

She'd thought it all out in the shower. She would play it casual. He was bound to have second thoughts. She wasn't going to cling; she wasn't going to come undone when he walked out the door. She was going to feed him, thank him for a lovely night and wave goodbye with a smile.

She could do this. She could.

What she couldn't do when she heard his footsteps coming down the hall toward the kitchen was turn around.

So she didn't. With unsteady hands, she poured her egg mix in the skillet.

"Smells good." His morning voice behind her was as gruff and smoky as she'd imagined.

Ordering herself not to hyperventilate, she tossed her best Martha Stewart imitation over her shoulder. "Hope you like omelettes."

"Omelettes sound great. I'm just not sure I'm dressed well enough for this obviously fine eating establishment."

Keep it perky, she told herself. "Well, we *do* have standards. No shirt, no shoes—" She couldn't stand it anymore. She turned around...to see him standing there in nothing but his boxers. Her heart flat out stopped.

"No service?" His lips quirked.

She swallowed. "No problem."

He was so gorgeous. Sleekly tanned muscles, long, sinewy limbs, broad chest. His hair was so artlessly mussed, so melt-your-bones sexy, it made her want to cry. Coupled with the dark stubble of his morning beard, the penetrating blue of his eyes, he was a walking, talking erotic fantasy.

And at the moment, he was *her* walking, talking erotic fantasy.

She couldn't move. Couldn't speak. Could only watch as he moved around her table like a sleek, prowling cat and stopped directly in front of her.

"Turn it off, Phoebe."

Turn it off? she thought desperately as her gaze fastened shamelessly on his mouth. I can't turn it off. Not if the *it* you're taking about is me. Not when you look like that. Not when you look at me like that.

Dumbly, she followed the motion of his hand as he reached behind her and turned off the burner on the stove.

"Oh," she said. "Um," she added, articulate as ever.

He relieved her of her spatula. "Do you have to go to work today?"

She had an answer for that. And as soon as the sludge cleared out of her brain, she'd do her darnedest to give it.

He was grinning as he took her hand and, walking

backward, led her out of the kitchen and down the hall toward the bedroom. "One nod for yes, two for no," he instructed as if he was dealing with the village idiot. Which, of course, he was. "Can you do that for me?"

She could. She did.

"Yes? You have to work?"

Another nod as they cleared the bedroom door.

"What time do you have to be there?"

She needed to blink but she didn't want to miss even a nanosecond of the view. His smile was playful, his blue eyes teasing but telling what he had on his mind. So was the tenting action going on below the waistband of his boxers.

Oh, joy!

"Ten." She wet her lips and swallowed. "Thirty."

When the back of his knees hit the bed, so did the rest of him. He tugged her backward with him until she was sprawled on top of him.

"So what do you say?" She wasn't the only one who shuddered when his hand tunneled up under her top and found her bare breast. "You think I've got time to tip the cook?"

"Ve haf vays of making you talk." Leslie loomed over Phoebe's desk at noon that same day, a dark scowl in place, one eyebrow cocked in her best maniacal interrogator impersonation. "Now you vill tell me zee truth if you ever vant to zee your homeland again. Did you or did you not get zome last night?"

"Yes!" Phoebe shouted in a dramatically staged confession, giving up and joining in on the silly game Leslie had been playing since Phoebe had stumbled into the library, loopy with love and muzzy-brained from amazing, knee-weakening sex. "I admit it! Is that what you wanted to hear? We did the big nasty! Satisfied?"

Leslie broke into a broad grin. "The question is, are you?" She laughed then and so did Phoebe. "Okay. Asked and answered. So give. I need details."

Phoebe slumped back in her chair, a happy, boneless lump, and hugged herself. "Not a chance. It's way too good to share."

"Uh-oh." Suddenly serious, Leslie eased a hip on the corner of the desk. "You know what you're getting into here, don't you, sweetie?" she asked softly.

Recognizing her tone for concern, Phoebe sobered, drew a deep breath. "I do. I'll be fine."

And she would be.

"You've fallen in love with him," Leslie concluded gently.

It wouldn't do any good to deny it. "Yeah. I've fallen in love. And I'm going to enjoy every single moment of it for as long as it lasts."

She rose, walked around her desk and tugged a resource book from the top of the bookshelf. "If it's just for today, or for a week or however long Daniel wants it to last, I'm going to enjoy it."

Leslie's silence relayed more apprehension.

"Look, Les, I'm not foolish enough to think that he loves me. He likes me. A lot. He *likes* making love to me," she added and felt her toes curl inside her shoes. "But I don't have any illusions about where this is heading."

No matter what Claudia and Ash had said last night—maybe even because of what they'd said—she'd taken a long look at things on her way to work and finally understood that Daniel did not want to fall in love with her.

She rounded her desk, sat back down and hugged the book to her breast. "He likes his life the way it is. He likes me because, unlike his family, I don't put any pressure on him to change. He can be himself with me, which means that he can leave when the wanderlust hits him or when he needs an adrenaline fix that can only be satisfied by climbing to the top of a mountain or diving off a cliff."

She sniffed, ran her thumb along the book's binding. "And I'm okay with that. I'm going to take whatever time he'll give me.

"Does that make me pathetic?" she asked with a shrug, then answered her own question. "I don't think so. I think that for the first time in my life it makes me brave."

She met her friend's eyes. "I'm tired of living *on* the world, Les. I want to live *in* it. I want to experience it. And I want every experience with Daniel Barone that I can get."

Leslie let out a deep breath. "He's a fool if he leaves you."

"No. He's a kind, funny, sexy, honest man. It wouldn't be honest for him to compromise who he is. And it wouldn't be fair for me to ask him to."

Leslie forced a smile. "Well. At least make sure that when he walks—*if* he walks—he knows he's walking away from the best thing that ever happened to him."

"Oh, I intend to," she said, her mind already wrapping around a scenario that would ensure she'd be on Daniel Barone's mind for a long, long time to come.

* * *

Daniel lay in the dark, aware that Phoebe was awake beside him. It was after midnight on a Friday night. They were in his bed tonight. The super king had added dimensions to their lovemaking that wouldn't have been possible in her standard double. So had their choice of reading material. Earlier, while she'd read an article in one of his *National Geographic Explorers* he'd read a love scene from one of the romance novels she always carried with her in her purse. Well, what choice had he had? He'd had to take her back to bed and put his own spin on that hot little scene.

Now she was soft, naked and as spent as he was. They'd just thoroughly exhausted each other again, so he didn't know what was keeping her awake. He had a pretty good handle, however, on the reason he was wide-eyed and restless.

It was time he was moving on. Time to be moving out. He didn't have a single obligation that required his presence here in Boston. So why was it so hard to leave her?

At first, he'd used the excuse that he was worried about her. But he'd hired a locksmith and her whole house was now as secure as Fort Knox. He'd spent some time at the police station and they'd promised him they'd have a little "off the record" chat with Jason Collins. He'd taught her everything he could think of to make sure she could defend herself against the creep.

Then, he'd been sticking around for Karen's party. Well, that had passed over a week ago, just before he'd lost his mind completely and ended up in Phoebe's bed.

Now he couldn't seem to get enough of her. And

that was the part that worried him. He kept finding other reasons to stay. There was a new movie playing, one she actually wanted to see. Then he'd found out that she'd never been to a baseball game. Well, come on, it had been his *duty* to take her to Fenway. And then Claudia had called with extra tickets to a concert in the park. Phoebe loved concerts in the park. So, of course, he'd taken her.

Yeah. He'd found a lot of things to do with her, but mostly they talked. God, he loved to talk to her. And they made love. She was so incredible. So open and responsive *in* bed, so undemanding *out* of it. She hadn't asked him about the future. But then, he hadn't expected her to. Not Phoebe. She'd never ask him for what he couldn't give. And he just couldn't be what she needed.

There was really nothing else he could do, short of throwing a few things in his flight bag, hitting the road and picking up where he'd left off on a life he liked just fine, instead of lying here trying to fabricate some reason to stay a little longer.

Yet when she sighed heavily beside him, his heart picked up a beat at the possibility that she might be about to say something, anything, that would make him change his mind. Something to give him a reason to stay a little longer.

Just a little longer.

Ten

"**Y**ou're thinking awfully hard. What's on your mind?"

She turned her head on the pillow and with sleepy, sated eyes smiled up at him. "I've just made a decision."

Play it cool, Daniel told himself as he spread his fingers across her bare tummy and kneaded gently. "You've decided that you like sex?"

"Oh." She wrinkled her nose. "It's okay, I guess. Ouch," she yelped then laughed when he tweaked her hip. "If you're going to get all broody about it, I *love* sex. With you."

"Ditto."

"Such a way you have with words," she teased, turning on her side and smiling at him.

He traced a finger around the shell of her ear. "So, what's this big decision?"

"Well, I've decided that life was not meant to be a spectator sport."

She averted her gaze to his throat, as if she was debating what to say to clarify that statement. On a bracing breath, she met his eyes again. "My mom is an alcoholic. Sometimes, when I was little, she was a mean one." She paused, looked away again. "Sometimes she could be very generous and loving, but mostly, she was verbally abusive and cruel.

"No." She touched a hand to his jaw, then withdrew it and tucked it under her chin. "Don't look like that."

He knew how he looked. Angry and sorry and as though he wished he would have been around for her when she'd been going through that hell.

"I'm not telling you this to elicit sympathy. I just want you to understand that I learned real fast to sort of blend into the woodwork. It was great as a self-preservation technique, but the residual effects slopped over into the rest of my life. It's why I tend to watch from the shadows, too much of a coward to come out and play.

"Let me finish." She flattened three fingers against his lips this time when he started to interrupt her again. "I *have* been a spectator. You, on the other hand— Oh, how I wish I could be more like you."

He kissed her fingertips, wrapped them in his hand. "I can think of a number of reasons why I'm glad you're not. For instance, I like how you're so soft here." His hand found her breast under the sheet, then moved to cup and caress her saucy bottom. "And here."

"Yeah, well, I like that you like that, but I was referring to the way you submerge yourself in life, the way you mix it up and dive right into the thick of things. You're so brave, Daniel. You aren't afraid to face down your greatest fears and then conquer them.''

He didn't even know what to say. He didn't think of himself as brave. Mostly he thought of himself as selfish. He did what he did because it was fun and because he had nothing—no commitment, no ties— keeping him from it.

''Now me, on the other hand… Well, watching the popcorn bag explode in my microwave is about as exciting as my life ever gets.''

She levered herself up on an elbow. ''I want to break the mold,'' she said decisively. ''I'm tired of me. I'm tired of my life. It's been nothing but an endless string of *Seinfeld* reruns.''

He couldn't help it. He laughed. *''Seinfeld?''*

''You know. That old sitcom about nothing? That's my life. Nothing. I want to do something to change it. Something wild, something scary. Something—''

''—that convinces you about something I already know about you? That there's more to you than you've ever let yourself be,'' he concluded gently.

''Yeah. Exactly that.''

She lay down again, crossed her arms over her breasts and stared at the ceiling.

She looked so cute in her determination, but he didn't want to make light of it. This was a huge decision for her. ''Anything particular come to mind? Anything that—''

She turned her head to look at him. ''—that just the thought of doing scares me to death?''

Her eyes were so wide, so bright with thoughts of staring down her greatest fears that he had to smile.

"That'd be a start. So what are you thinking? There's a great roller coaster over at—"

"Skydiving," she whispered, sounding as if she was afraid if she said it too loud, he might actually think she meant to do it.

The funny thing was, he did. "Skydiving? You're sure?" he asked with a lift of his eyebrow.

"Are you kidding? I'm definitely *not* sure. But it's what I need to do. I can't think of anything that terrifies me more."

He regarded her with new interest, understood the resolve she had mustered to even suggest the idea. He was going to do this for her, he decided right there and then. He was going to make sure she proved to herself just how brave she really was.

"Okay," he said and promised himself he wouldn't let her back out of it. "I've got a friend just outside of Cambridge. He runs a skydiving school there. It's where I got certified. I'll set it up. How about this weekend?"

"This weekend?" she squeaked as he lifted her then shifted her until she was straddling him in all of her soft, naked glory.

"We'll jump tandem the first time. I'll be with you every inch of the way."

"The first time?"

He took her mind off her fear then. And took his mind off leaving. She'd just given him his reason to stay a little longer. Just a little longer, he promised himself as she settled over him, onto him, and took him deep.

As the four-passenger Cessna bumped down the runway, Phoebe sat on the floor where the seats used to be and tried to think about how blue the sky was overhead. She didn't look at the big hole in the side of the plane that was covered only by a roll of canvas with plastic windows and held in place by Velcro. Soon that canvas was going to be rolled up and she was going to— Oh, God. She couldn't think about it.

So she stared at the sign on the back of the pilot's seat: Sit down, shut up and hang on!

Well, that wasn't a problem. She had to sit; her legs wouldn't support her. She couldn't talk; she was scared speechless. And hang on? Like she would even consider letting go?

"Relax." Beside her, in his black jumpsuit, helmet and goggles, Daniel squeezed her knee then double-checked the harness that would soon bind them together. "You're going to love this."

She reached deep for a smile. When he laughed, she knew how unconvincing she'd been. She did not love this. She did not love knowing that they were going to jump into space at eleven thousand feet and that the pilot would slow the plane to around ninety miles an hour, then cut the engine just before they jumped, which, in effect, gave them two chances to die on this little quest to rub out her yellow streak.

Another sign, this one above the canvas that was loosely referred to as a door, caught her terrified attention as they lifted off the runway: If riding in an airplane is flying, then riding in a boat is swimming. If you want to experience the element, get out of the vehicle.

She so did not want to get out of the vehicle. Not now that it was about to leave the ground. She closed her eyes and tried not to watch as the earth fell away and her stomach went into a marathon pitch and roll.

Yes, she'd sat through the instructional video, and yes, it made her feel a little better to know that Daniel was a veteran of over two hundred jumps and was a certified instructor. It was the actual diving-to-the-ground part that was giving her trouble.

"Okay, Phoebe, it's time."

Already? Oh, God.

Funny thing about absolute terror. It affected everyone differently. In Phoebe's case, it made her as malleable as a lump of clay. She sat like a slug as Daniel rolled up the canvas, then physically turned her toward the jump door before he sat down behind her, straddling her hips with his legs.

Everything registered in a blur then as he hooked them together and the pilot yelled over his shoulder, "Are you ready to skydive?" to which Daniel yelled back, "Yes!"

And the next thing she knew, her heart was in her throat and they were free falling through space. The following sixty seconds were a terrifying, exhilarating, breath-stealing blur. And then they were at four thousand feet and Daniel had pulled the rip cord on the parachute.

Suddenly, everything was silent and peaceful. She felt as if she was in suspended animation as they floated slowly toward the ground. And there was no more fear. Just a glorious, spectacular descent made sweeter by the notion that quite possibly she wasn't going to die after all.

She heard a voice, possibly hers, say, "This is incredible!" And then, in a landing so soft a baby would have slept through it, they were on the ground.

She was crying softly when Daniel unhooked their harness and started reeling in the chute. When he turned her to face him, she threw herself into his arms. "Thank you! Oh, thank you, thank you, thank you!"

He was grinning from ear to ear when she pulled away, wiping tears from her eyes. "When can we do it again?" she asked. "Do you think I could go solo next time?"

Phoebe was still pumped on an adrenaline high the next morning. She left Daniel in bed and jumped in the shower. After setting the coffee on to brew, she threw on an old tank top and cutoffs and headed for her studio in the basement.

Yesterday had been one wild day; the night had been even wilder. Once she'd made that first jump, she'd had to do another and then another. Never, ever, in her entire life had she experienced such unqualified exhilaration and such a sense of accomplishment. She couldn't begin to put it into words. She'd been bouncing off the walls when they returned to Boston and her bed last night. And then, well, the thrills had started all over again.

Her life, suddenly, was the stuff that romance novels were made of and she was living every glorious moment to the fullest.

She'd just centered her clay on the potter's wheel and her hands were gunky with slurry when she heard the stairs creak under the weight of Daniel's footsteps.

A shiver of anticipation eddied through her. How could she want him again, after the way they'd spent the night tangled and sweaty in each other's arms? Maybe because she was a different person now than she'd been before Daniel had charged into her life and saved her not only from Jason, but from spending the rest of her days in a dull and colorless void.

"Good morning," he said softly as he came up behind her. His voice was husky. From those two little words, she understood that she wasn't the only one with raging hormones this morning.

"Ever see that old Demi Moore movie *Ghost*?" he asked, sitting down behind her. The inside of his thighs were warm and hard against the outside of hers. His bare arms were encompassing and strong as he wrapped them around her midriff, pulled her back and against him and lowered his head to nuzzle her neck.

Oh, yeah. She'd seen it. In fact, she'd bought her potter's wheel shortly after seeing the film.

"No," she lied and leaned back against him, loving the feel of his warm, naked chest against her back, the cocooning warmth of his arms around her. "Any particular reason that I should have?"

She felt his smile against the curve where her neck met her shoulder and knew that he knew she was lying. "Oh, there's this one scene…I've always had this fantasy about playing it out."

"Well, far be it from me to kill a man's fantasies."

There wasn't much talking after that. But there was a lot of soaping and rinsing and soaping again after they'd made randy love and stumbled to the shower to wash away the mess they'd made of each other.

When he left her at her door early Monday morning with a lingering kiss, Phoebe couldn't imagine what her life had been like before Daniel. Just as she could no longer imagine it without him.

* * *

Daniel was shaving when his doorbell rang. Snagging his jeans and quickly tugging them on, he slung a towel over his shoulder.

"Hey, come on in," he said, grinning as he swung open the door to his sister Emily and her fiancé, Shane Cummings, whom he had finally met at Karen's welcome party. "Want some coffee?" he asked after he'd excused himself to pull on a shirt.

"No thanks, we've only got a minute," Emily said. "But we want to ask you something. It was so crowded at Karen's party we didn't get a chance to corner you then."

"Or catch up with you since," Shane, whom Daniel had liked immediately, added with a grin. "You're one busy man."

Busy? No. Wrapped up in Phoebe? Yes. And he had to do some serious thinking about that.

"So what's up?" he asked as the thought niggled away in the back of his mind.

"Well," Emily began with a smiling glance at Shane, "we want to ask you if you'll stand up with us at the wedding."

"I'd be honored," he said, pleased for both of them. "As a matter of fact, I'd have been disappointed if you hadn't asked."

Shane extended his hand. "That's great. Thanks."

"Maybe Shane will be able to return the favor soon?"

Emily's expectant grin froze Daniel's smile. "Return the favor?"

"You and Phoebe. You looked so great together at the party. I liked her, Daniel. I liked her a lot. Everyone did."

"Whoa." He held up a hand as an almost suffocating pressure expanded in his chest. "You know me better than that. Phoebe— Well, she's very special, but marriage? No."

His sister took his hands in hers. "Why not marriage? Why not with Phoebe?"

Because he didn't do commitment, that was why. Because there wasn't a woman in the world—even Phoebe—who could put up with his lifestyle. And because there wasn't a woman in the world he'd give it up for.

Even Phoebe.

Panic raced through his blood.

Is that what everyone thought? That he was ready to settle down? Ready to commit to someone who would depend on him to be there? Someone who would want to make babies with him, to tuck those babies in at night and be there when they woke up in the morning?

More important, was that what Phoebe thought? Yes, he realized with a horrible sinking sensation in his chest. That was exactly what she thought.

"Um, I think maybe we'd better be going, Em," Shane said and Daniel realized he must have zoned out on them completely. He was still only half there as he walked them to the door, smiled the requisite smile and exchanged goodbyes.

He leaned back against the door, stared hard at the floor. Wasn't that always the way it was? It took someone on the outside looking in to draw the picture, flesh it out and jar things into perspective.

Things had gotten out of hand. Things that he'd known better than to start in the first place because he didn't have it in him to finish them. And yet he'd done it anyway.

He wiped a hand over his jaw. It was going to be

hard. Really hard. But he knew what he had to do. And he knew he had to do it today. The longer he stayed, the more he would hurt her. And hurting Phoebe was the last thing he'd ever wanted to do.

"Nice job, hotshot," he muttered as he pushed away from the door.

Phoebe looked up from her desk at the library when a soft rap sounded at her door. "It's open.

"Daniel." She broke into a smile when he poked his head inside. "Hi."

"Hi," he said and stepped all the way into the room.

That was when she saw the flight bag slung over his shoulder.

Later she would remember exactly how her body reacted to the conclusion her mind had so quickly and accurately drawn. The dizzying rush. The sense of absolute sorrow. It was like being swept away by a wave of loss and longing. Like the blood in her head had narrowed and drained, down her cheeks and past her throat, then sucked the warmth from her fingers as it converged to the pit of her stomach and left her heart empty.

She stood up slowly, amazed that her legs could support her. "You're…you're leaving."

He drew in a breath, let it out. And he wouldn't look at her. "Yeah. Something's come up."

She waited for him to meet her eyes. When he finally did, she understood. He wasn't just leaving, he was running away. From her. From them.

"There's this dive." He rolled a shoulder, walked to the bookshelf, fingered a leather binding. "It's off the coast of Tahiti. Something I've been wanting to get in on for a couple of years now.''

She watched him in silence, feeling vulnerable and confused and suddenly angry.

She shouldn't ask. "When will you be back?"

He was slow to turn around and face her. When he did, she understood why. He wasn't coming back. Not to her.

"Phoebe, what we've had together...I'll never forget it. You are an incredible woman. Any man would be lucky to have you. But, Phoebe, I never should have gotten involved with you. I was being selfish. I knew going into this that it was temporary. I guess I'd hoped we both did."

He stopped, swore under his breath. "God, tell me to shut up. I'm botching this. I sound like every creep who's ever—"

"—dumped someone?" she concluded and saw by the guilt clouding his eyes, that was exactly what he'd been trying not to say.

"Phoebe, I am so sorry. I never meant to hurt you. Please understand that."

"I don't think you're asking for understanding, Daniel," she said, beyond pain for the moment. It was temporary, she knew. It would be back, but right now she was numb. And she was angry. "I think you're asking for forgiveness. And the funny thing is, a week ago I would have given you both.

"A week ago I would have been willing to take whatever you gave me until you left. Well, guess what? I'm not the same woman I was a week ago. I hadn't been loved by you then. And you hadn't been loved by me."

It was surprising how calm she felt. Amazing how

sure. "Once I was afraid to experience life and you taught me how to overcome that fear. Interesting how that worked out. Now *you're* the one who's afraid."

He worked his jaw, looked away. If denial had a name, it was, in this moment, Daniel Barone. His inability to look at her told her how desperate he was to get away from the truth. There was nothing she could do, nothing she could say to make him see it. When he only repeated, "I never meant to hurt you," she knew he was as good as lost to her.

"So you said. You never meant to fall in love with me either," she added with a sadness that left her empty, "but you did." Of that she was sure. She'd never been more sure of anything in her life. "And now you're running scared." She actually managed a smile then. "It's kind of funny, really. Once, I didn't think I was woman enough for you."

It was a challenge. Prove to me that you're man enough for me. Stay.

But of course, he didn't.

She closed her eyes when he came to her, touched a hand to her hair then let it slowly fall away. "Be safe, Phoebe. Remember what I taught you."

"Oh, I'll remember." He didn't see the single tear trail down her cheek. He was already out the door. "I'll always remember."

Falling in love was awfully simple. Falling out of love was simply awful.

During the next week, Phoebe understood those words as she never had before. Her emotions ran the gamut from anger to understanding to grief. She was angry with Daniel for his sudden retreat and his inability to admit his feelings for her. But it made her realize that she wasn't the only one who was sometimes afraid. Did she forgive him for leaving her? No. But she did try her best to understand.

Claudia Barone didn't understand. She'd shown up at the library on the Friday after he'd left, just as Leslie and Carol were set on dragging her off to a bar to drown her sorrows.

That had been five hours ago and Phoebe had had enough.

"Don't go home, Phoebe, not yet. We just got started."

Above the vibrating beat of a bass guitar and the heavy metal licks slamming out of the jukebox, Claudia and Leslie echoed Carol's protest with an enthusiastic, "Yeah, don't go!"

"Do you know how long it's been since this old woman has had a girls' night out?" Leslie whined, although Phoebe knew she was fussing for her benefit.

When they continued to make noises about her staying, Phoebe held a hand in the air to quiet them down. "Come on, guys. I have to work tomorrow."

And I have to get out of here, she said to herself.

The Tycoon—or any bar, for that matter—wasn't her scene. But the three women had insisted. They meant well. She hadn't known how to put them off without hurting their feelings, but she'd made more than an appearance and now it was time to beg off.

"I've gotta go," she persisted to their round of good-natured boos.

"But it's ladies' night," Carol reminded her with a turn of her head that encompassed the bar packed with nine-to-fivers ducking in out of the heat, looking for some wind-down time or a little action at the end of long workweek. "Who knows. You might get lucky."

Phoebe snorted. "Lucky is a relative term."

"They're not all like Jason." Carol's expression was sympathetic but firm when Phoebe stood to go. "Or Daniel. No offense, Claudia, I know he's your brother but—"

"None taken," Claudia agreed.

"It's okay." Phoebe dug into her purse for some tip money for the waitress. She nodded toward the crowded bar. "They're all yours, ladies, and I use the term loosely," she added with a grin. "If you find one, kiss a prince for me, okay, 'cause lately, all I've bumped up against are frogs."

"I thought you said that guy you went out with Wednesday night was a leprechaun," Leslie said, referring to Sam Spalding who had been after Phoebe for months. In a weak and defiant moment, she'd finally agreed.

"Leprechaun. Frog. Same difference. They're both tiny, they're both green and neither qualify as princes."

"Not that he necessarily has to be a prince," Leslie and Carol chimed in, then laughed as they finished their standing joke together. "A white knight'll do."

White knight. Yeah, well, white knights weren't all they were cracked up to be either, Phoebe thought as she waved goodbye.

Smoke-stale air and the rocking sounds of Sheryl Crow followed her outside into the hot Boston night. She'd just reached her car, which she'd parked a couple blocks from the Tycoon under a streetlight that she hadn't noticed was burned out, when she realized she was no longer alone.

She turned quickly. And there was Jason, looking angry and mean and more than a little drunk. A sickening sense of déjà vu washed over her as he walked toward her.

"I've been looking for you, Mouse."

It surprised her to realize she didn't feel fear. What she felt was unmitigated, undeniable anger. And what she knew was that she was done being his victim.

"Go away, Jason." She dismissed him and started digging in her purse for her keys.

"Don't turn your back on me."

When his hand clamped on her shoulder, she didn't think. She just reacted. She whirled around, slammed the flat of her hand into his face and hiked her knee into his chest. He made a surprised "Oomph" and wobbled off balance, and when he doubled over, she went in for the kill. She drove her foot into his diaphragm and sent him sprawling on his back.

Before he'd even realized she'd knocked him flat, she had her pepper spray in her hand and her foot on his throat.

"What the hell… Hey, Mouse," he whined.

"That's *Mighty* Mouse to you." Filled with a stunning sense of pride that she'd been able to defend herself against Jason's bullying, she let him have it. "And this is the last time you're going to bother me."

"But I miss you. I need you."

"You need help, Jason." She dug into her purse again, searching for her cell phone so she could call 911. "You need help," she said more kindly, then frowned when she couldn't come up with her phone.

"Looking for this?"

The deep voice came from behind her. She didn't have to see the man to recognize the source. She'd know that voice anywhere. In the dark, in the light, at eleven thousand feet whispering encouragement in her ear.

Slowly, she looked down to the cell phone that lay in the palm of Daniel Barone's hand.

"It flew out when you put the moves on him."

For a moment, all she could do was stare at his hand. It took more courage to look up than it had taken to drop Jason to his back.

"So, guess you don't need me to save you anymore, huh?"

Her heart flipped, tripped, stumbled and fell at the caress in his voice. She met his eyes with hope and longing and just enough uncertainty to undercut it all.

"No," she said carefully, "I guess I don't."

"I might be good for other things, though." He watched her face with those intense blue eyes that she'd dreamed about every night since she'd met him.

"Such as?"

"Well, for starters, such as showing up at the right place, at the right time and dialing 911?"

Eleven

Phoebe had to drive down to the police station to press charges. Since she now had the proof she needed, she also filed a restraining order against Jason. Before she left, however, she asked to see him. She felt minimally relieved when she finally extracted a promise from him to get involved with some kind of program to help with his problem.

Daniel never left her side. She wasn't sure what to make of that. Just as she wasn't sure what to make of him following her home, or his explanation that he just happened to be driving by when he saw her.

"So how was Tahiti?" she asked when time had stretched taut and the sound of Arthur purring on her lap was the only thing interrupting the tentative silence of her living room.

"Tahiti?" He lifted a shoulder and met her eyes

from the sofa where he'd settled. "Never quite made it."

Could a heart actually survive all the thumping it had undergone tonight? she wondered. Could he see it, slamming against her breast? Could he see the nervousness in her eyes as she sat across from him and by the slimmest thread of pride kept from dropping to her knees and begging him to love her?

"About those other things…"

Through the maelstrom of emotions swirling inside her, she heard but didn't comprehend his statement. "Other things?"

"You know, those other things that I might be good for—since you don't need me to protect you anymore."

"Oh." She must have squeezed Arthur a little too hard because he jumped off her lap with an indignant snap of his tail. "Did…did you, um, want to…elaborate?"

He clasped his hands between his splayed knees and stared at the steeple he'd made of his thumbs. "Well, I might be good at being your friend."

When he looked up, she willed herself not to cry. She'd already been there. They'd already done that. She couldn't be his buddy again. It hurt that much more to think he'd shown up like this, given her hope and then expected her to—

"I've missed you, Phoebe." The gruff sincerity in his voice brought the tears she'd worked so hard to keep from forming. They misted her eyes and she tried desperately to blink them back. "I've missed my friend. I know it's been less than a week, but I've missed you every day. Every hour. I've missed the woman I could talk to, the woman I could laugh with and who never asked me to be something I didn't want to be.''

He was pouring his heart out because he needed her to be the one thing she couldn't be. And he was killing her.

"I've missed the woman I made love to. The woman I fell in love with.''

It was another one of those moments that she knew she'd remember as long as she lived.

The woman I fell in love with.

She covered her mouth with her hand and begged him on a choked whisper, "Please. Don't...don't do this. Don't say this if you don't plan to stay.''

Through a blur of tears, she watched him drop to his knees in front of her.

He gathered her hands in his, pressed his lips to her ice-cold knuckles. "I do love you, Phoebe. I've loved you from the first time I saw you.''

The sob broke then as she looked down on his dark head bending over her hands.

"I don't know how it happened. I wasn't going to let it. But I think I was a goner the first time I saw you wearing that hot-red toenail polish and grinning over a vanilla ice cream cone.''

She stopped fighting, stopped denying that she'd heard him wrong, that she would wake up and find this was just another one of her dreams. His eyes, when he lifted his head and met hers, told her how very real this was. He loved her. She threw herself into his arms, hung on for her life.

"Shh. Shush, baby,'' he said. "Don't cry. I'm so sorry I was so stupid. I tried. Lord, I tried to convince myself I was hanging around to protect you and then

I started fabricating any excuse I could come up with to stay. And that scared the hell out of me.''

''And it doesn't scare you anymore?''

He pushed out a laugh and set her gently away from him. Bracketing her face in his hands, he wiped away her tears with a sweep of his thumbs. ''It scares me to death. I don't know if I'll be any good at this commitment thing, Phoebe. But I'm going to give it everything I have. I learned something recently. This beautiful, wiser, older woman taught me that by confronting my fears, my life could be so much richer.''

He brought her hands to his mouth. ''Marry me, Phoebe. Tonight.''

She laughed through her tears. ''Tonight?''

''Okay. So that's rushing it. Tomorrow, then. But don't make me wait any longer. I have so many things I want to show you. So many places I want to take you. We'll start at the family compound in Harwichport. I want to honeymoon with you there where I can get my fill of you in a bed, in a bath, in the kitchen. Hell, I want you everywhere. I want to make love to you under the stars at the Cape.''

He stopped, laughed. ''Say yes, Phoebe, and it'll be just you and me and several days of showing you how sorry I am that I hurt you and how much I love you.''

''Yes. Yes, yes, yes.''

He drew her into a long, drugging kiss that told her as much about how he loved her as the amazing words he'd just spoken.

''You're the best adventure I've ever had, Phoebe Richards,'' he said, scooping her into his arms and carrying her toward the bedroom. ''And you're the only one I'll ever need.''

She laughed again with pure, unbridled joy. "But what if I want to see Borneo?"

He planted a knee on the bed then eased her to her back and started dragging off his shirt. "Then I'll take you to Borneo. Better yet, I'll take you to the Galápagos." He grinned as he started working on her slacks. "You'll love it. They have turtles."

"Not only didn't I make it to Tahiti," Daniel confessed later as they lay in each other's arms, "I didn't even make it out of Boston. Oh, I was going—at least I thought I was—but I just kept coming up with reasons to stay."

"What kind of reasons?" she asked as she trailed her fingers back and forth over his chest.

"Well, after I left you at the library, I went back to my place. I'd decided I'd forgotten something. I hadn't, but hey, I was in total denial and it was another excuse to postpone leaving. Anyway, Ash happened to drop by as I was on my way out for the second time. And he laid into me good."

"About me?"

"Yeah," he said, squeezing her arm. "About you."

Phoebe thought of everything the sheikh had said to her at Karen's party. She had no doubt that he could be very convincing. He'd certainly convinced Karen that he wanted to stake a claim when he'd kissed her. Bless you, Ash, she said silently. And good luck.

"Anyway, he said I couldn't leave. Made up some pretense of needing to go over my portfolio. I knew what he was doing. He was giving me time to think through the panic and I was just desperate enough for another reason to stay that I let him convince me.

"And then there was Claudia."

Phoebe lifted up on her elbow so she could see his face. "Claudia?"

"Yeah, Our Lady of the Eternal Lost Cause." He tucked a drift of hair behind her ear. "She took over where Ash left off. And as long as I'm confessing, I didn't just happen by the bar tonight. Claudia was a plant."

"A plant?"

He pulled her back down beside him. "Don't be mad, but I sent her to the library to test the waters this afternoon. When your friends were determined to take you out, she went with the flow and invited herself along. You didn't notice that she left the table several times?"

"Well, yeah, but— Oh. She was calling you, wasn't she? Giving you a play-by-play. And that's how you just happened to be there."

He nodded and tucked her head beneath his chin. "I was so proud of you when you flattened that creep."

"I was proud of me, too."

Her bedroom grew quiet again before Daniel finally spoke. "Can you ever forgive me for being such a fool?"

Could she forgive him? How could she make him understand that she already had?

"I think," she said, as it came to her, "that this story will answer your question.

"Once upon a time," she began, making up her romantic fairy tale as she went, "there was a handsome, fearless knight. He'd slain many dragons, conquered many evil foes and was known throughout the land for his brave deeds and stalwart courage. There was only one thing the white knight feared. He was afraid to trust his heart to a princess for safekeeping.''

He shifted to his side, caressed her face with his hand, with his eyes. "I think I know this guy. He was a bigger fool than I was.''

"No, no, he was very wise. One day,'' she continued, snuggling against him so that her lips brushed his throat when she spoke, "the handsome knight was struck from his horse in the heat of battle. He landed so hard that his heart spilled right out of his chest. And as he lay there, watching it beat, exposed and vulnerable, who do you think was there to pick it up and give it back to him, proving that he could trust her to keep it safe?''

He stroked his hand down the length of her back and made her shiver. "His princess?''

"No. It was a turtle. But the knight didn't care. He was so happy to have his heart back safe and sound that he kissed the turtle—''

"—who had pretty pink cheeks,'' he interrupted with a smile so tender it brought tears again, "and she was really a princess under the spell of an evil witch.''

"Wrong again,'' she said patiently and tipped her head up so she could see his face. "He was right not to trust the princess because his true love was the turtle who, as you said, was under a spell. When the prince kissed the turtle, she transformed into a librarian who had given up waiting for her white knight to come and save her from an empty and lonely life.''

His eyes were as misty as hers now. "And did he save her, Phoebe?''

She cupped his face in her hands, loving the feel of his stubbled jaw against her palms, the beauty that made him Daniel. ''She *let* him save her because it was important to his ego.''

She felt his love and his trust wrap around her as surely as the arms that held her.

''I think I know how this ends,'' he whispered, moving over her. ''And the knight and the beautiful librarian spent the rest of their lives in an enchanted kingdom, with Arthur the cat, where they all lived happily ever after.''

She smiled into his eyes, secure in his love, empowered by his trust and, as always, stunned by the depth of his need. ''Very happily ever after.''

*   *   *   *   *

DYNASTIES: THE BARONES
continues…

*Turn the page for a bonus look
at what's in store for you in
the next Barones book—
only from Silhouette Desire!*

Expecting the Sheikh's Baby

by Kristi Gold

is on sale in September 2004

Expecting the Sheikh's Baby

by

Kristi Gold

The man could be her father, but that was impossible. Her father was dead.

Karen Rawlins touched her trembling fingertips to the photograph of Paul Barone included in the Boston newspaper along with a story covering the Barone family's latest reunion. And so was the tale of the unsolved mystery from years ago surrounding the abduction of Paul's twin brother, Luke, serving as confirmation of what Karen had recently learned from the yellowed pages of her grandmother's diary.

Karen sat in the only home she had known, deep in the heart of Montana, while too many unanswered questions haunted her as keenly as her memories. Had her father known about the journal Karen had found among her grandmother's belongings? Had he learned of the deception before his untimely death? Had he known he had been born to a wealthy Massachusetts family only to be kidnapped by the woman he had always considered his mother, and that his name was not Timothy Rawlins but Luke Barone?

Karen tossed the newspaper aside knowing she would never have all the answers she craved. Everyone who could fill in the blanks was gone—her grandparents, who had died only months apart two years before in peaceful slumber, and her parents, who had died a year ago in a devastating car crash, were all dead.

Dealing with the overwhelming loss and this new insight into her family tree might have been easier if Karen hadn't ended her engagement to Carl. But that had been a blessing. She preferred to live her life alone as long as she could live her life as she wanted. That had not been Carl's intent. Carl's intent had involved control. He'd wanted a wife who would hang her life on his whims, not a woman with dreams and opinions and career goals. She refused to mourn that ending.

Karen wrapped her hands around a mug of coffee, trying to absorb some warmth though the June weather outside was warm and wonderful. Still she felt chilled to the marrow, even in the comfortable kitchen that smelled of cinnamon and radiated kindness, an ideal depiction of home and hearth. She felt utterly alone.

Needless to say, it had not been a banner year for Karen Rawlins. It then occurred to her that she had no reason to stay in Silver Valley. The single-stoplight town had nothing to offer but bittersweet recollections and the realization that much of what she'd believed about her family, her legacy, was false—except for the fact that her parents and grand-parents had loved her without reservation.

Perhaps Boston held more opportunities. Exciting opportunities. A place to regroup and grow. Karen decided then and there to seek out the Barones, to tell them what details she knew about their missing son and with the hope that they would welcome her with open arms and open minds. She would find a good job and maybe one day establish her own interior-design business. She would make a good life for her-self. A new life. And in order to fill the empty space in her soul, Karen would also attempt to have a child, someone to love her without conditions.

No, it had not been a banner year for Karen Raw-lins, but it could be—would be—from this point for-ward. She would simply have to make it happen, and she would achieve all of her goals without the inter-ference of a man.

* * * * *

DYNASTIES: THE BARONES
continues…

Turn the page for a bonus look
at what's in store for you in
the next Barones book—
only from Silhouette Desire!

Born To Be Wild

by Anne Marie Winston

is on sale in September 2004

Born To Be Wild

by

Anne Marie Winston

"**S**he said *what?*" Twenty-one-year-old Reese Barone, seated in the parlor of his family home in Boston's Beacon Hill district, stared at his father in shock.

"Eliza Mayhew says that she's pregnant and you are the father." Carlo Barone stood before the elaborate marble fireplace, hands clasped behind his back. He eyed his second-to-eldest son sternly. "Needless to say, your mother and I are very disappointed in you, Reese."

"But I never—"

"Reese." His father's voice was colder than he'd ever heard it. "There will be no discussion. You will do the right thing and marry Ms. Mayhew at the end of the month."

"I will not." Reese leaped to his feet, nearly upsetting the elegant wing chair in which he'd been sitting while he'd waited to find out what could possibly have gotten his old man's drawers in such a twist. "That baby isn't mine."

On the love seat facing them, his mother Moira bowed her head as a sob escaped.

Carlo's face darkened with anger. "Haven't you already done enough to damage our family name?" he demanded. "First you get involved with that fisherman's daughter in Harwich—"

"There's nothing wrong with Celia," Reese said hotly, "except that she doesn't come with a pedigree."

"It's not the lack of family connections," his mother said. "I would hope you know us better than that. It's just that…oh, Reese, she's so young. And she comes from a world that's very different…"

"I already told you," Reese said tightly, "I can't be the father of Eliza's baby. I—"

"Enough!" Carlo made an angry gesture. "I will not tolerate lying. Ms. Mayhew is the daughter of a family friend as well as a classmate of your sister's. How could you be so careless?"

"Has she had a paternity test done?" Reese demanded. "Maybe you'd better think about who's being careless." He could feel his temper slipping the tight leash he'd held, and the words spilled out. Even the pain in his father's eyes couldn't halt his tongue. "Taking someone else's word without giving me a chance to defend myself? Fine." His eyes narrowed. "I don't need this, Dad. I'm not marrying Lying Eliza and you can't make me." He strode toward the door to the hallway.

"Don't you dare walk away when I'm speaking to you!" Reese had come by his temper honestly. Carlo stepped forward and reached for his son's arm, but Reese shoved him away in a red haze of anger.

"You ever put your hands on me again and I swear

you'll be sorry,'' he snarled at his father. He barreled down the hall to the heavy front door, oblivious to his mother's frantic cries. As he slammed through the door and the thunderous sound of its closing echoed behind him, he swore one thing to himself: he would never set foot in the same room with his father again until he'd received an apology from the old man.

▼ SILHOUETTE®
DESIRE™ 2-IN-1
AVAILABLE FROM 16TH JULY 2004

BEAUTY AND THE BABY Marie Ferrarella

The Mum Squad

Lori O'Neill surprised herself when she kissed her late husband's brother. Maybe it was the pregnancy hormones, but Lori saw Carson in a new light. This could be her last chance to give her baby the perfect father.

SOCIAL GRACES Dixie Browning

John MacBride was determined to protect his innocent step-brother and the only person who could help was socialite Val Bonnard. But caring and beautiful Val was nothing like John expected...

TEMPTING THE TYCOON Cindy Gerard

Millionaire lawyer Nate McGrory was intent on seduction and Rachel Matthews was his target. Rachel was finding Nate's pursuit hard to resist, but once Nate had won her heart, was he in danger of losing his own?

AWAKENING BEAUTY Amy J Fetzer

Stunning heiress Lane Douglas had to escape the scandalous rumours that followed her everywhere. Moving to a new town with a new identity, she never imagined that high-powered playboy Tyler McKay could awaken her hidden desire...

PLAIN JANE & THE HOTSHOT Meagan McKinney

Matched in Montana

Camping in the wilderness seemed the perfect way for Jo Lofton to heal her broken heart. But the camp's matchmaker had other ideas and soon fireman Nick Kramer was setting off enough sparks in Jo to ignite a wildfire...

CHARMING THE PRINCE Laura Wright

Prince Maxim wasn't ready for marriage, so began a romance with veterinarian Francesca Charming—a commoner he could never marry! They both knew it could never last, but with each passionate kiss, his seduction was leading to love.

AVAILABLE FROM 16TH JULY 2004

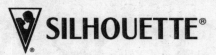

Sensation™

Passionate and thrilling romantic adventures

NIGHT WATCH Suzanne Brockmann
DEAD CERTAIN Carla Cassidy
AIM FOR THE HEART Ingrid Weaver
A DANGEROUS ENGAGEMENT Candace Irvin
DEAD CALM Lindsay Longford
NO PLACE TO HIDE Madalyn Reese

Special Edition™

Life, love and family

THE ONE AND ONLY Laurie Paige
PRINCE AND FUTURE...DAD? Christine Rimmer
THE BABY SURPRISE Victoria Pade
MARRY ME...AGAIN Cheryl St. John
MIDNIGHT, MOONLIGHT & MIRACLES Teresa Southwick
GUARDING THE HEIRESS Debra Webb

Superromance™

*Enjoy the drama, explore the emotions,
experience the relationship*

THE BABY PLAN Susan Gable
RIGHT PLACE, WRONG TIME Judith Taylor
THE NEW MAN Janice Kay Johnson
MY THREE GIRLS Susan Floyd

Intrigue™

Breathtaking romantic suspense

HIS MYSTERIOUS WAYS Amanda Stevens
INCRIMINATING PASSION Ann Voss Peterson
OPERATION CRADLE Joyce Sullivan
DR BODYGUARD Jessica Andersen

2 FREE

books and a surprise gift!

We would like to take this opportunity to thank you for reading this Silhouette® book by offering you the chance to take TWO specially selected titles from the Desire™ series absolutely FREE! We're also making this offer to introduce you to the benefits of the Reader Service™—

- ★ FREE home delivery
- ★ FREE gifts and competitions
- ★ FREE monthly Newsletter
- ★ Exclusive Reader Service offers
- ★ Books available before they're in the shops

Accepting these FREE books and gift places you under no obligation to buy, you may cancel at any time, even after receiving your free shipment. Simply complete your details below and return the entire page to the address below. *You don't even need a stamp!*

YES! Please send me 2 free Desire books and a surprise gift. I understand that unless you hear from me, I will receive 3 superb new titles every month for just £4.99 each, postage and packing free. I am under no obligation to purchase any books and may cancel my subscription at any time. The free book and gift will be mine to keep in any case.

D4ZED

Ms/Mrs/Miss/Mr ....Initials.............................
BLOCK CAPITALS PLEASE

Surname ....

Address ....

....

....Postcode..................

Send this whole page to:
UK: FREEPOST CN81, Croydon, CR9 3WZ
EIRE: PO Box 4546, Kilcock, County Kildare (stamp required)